THE MASTER
AND
HIS SLAVE

BY
KEM AUSTIN

The Master And His Slave
Copyright © 2013 by Rob Shelsky
Published by GKRS Publications at Create Space

* * * * *

DEDICATED

IN MEMORIAM

TO

GEORGE A. KEMPLAND

Author, Friend, And So Very Much More

1929 — 2013

Wherever You Are Now, George,

May You Always Be Happy, At Peace, And Enjoy Yourself.

Wherever You Are, I Hope I May Get To See you Again…
Somewhen.

* * *

Table of Contents

The Master

And

His Slave

By

Kem Austin

Chapter 1 —A Slave Of Rome

"Hold!" Marcus Darius Macro shouted at the obese slave trader, who was in the process of throttling his slave, even as he was still vigorously trying to mount him from the rear, rape him. Marcus hurried forward, intent on interceding. As a Roman magistrate, Marcus felt he should do something. After all, a crime was being committed, if not a very serious one.

To kill a slave was only a minor offense, as decreed by the former emperor, Caesar Augustus. He had tried to be a moral leader. Sadly, often he'd been frustrated in this task, even by his own daughter, the infamous nymphomaniac, Julia. Her sexual escapades were now the stuff of urban legend.

"Hold!" Marcus shouted again, this time more loudly still. He increased his pace.

The trader paid neither him nor anyone else any attention, but continued his rutting efforts. His piggish face was flushed red now, even as the young slave's face was slowly turning blue, for the fat man's hands encircled his neck, squeezing it. In his sexual heat, or perhaps on purpose, he was clutching too tightly. The youth was going to die if Marcus didn't do something and quickly.

However, what could he really do? Often, there were no charges filed in such cases. The more serious offense was the public raping. Public nudity might be all right at the baths, but not on a city street in the very heart of Rome, and in broad daylight at that.

The corpulent man had raised his tunic high now, so his hairy thighs and flabby-looking, white ass were clearly visible in profile. Even a purplish portion of his erect penis, looking like some ape's cock, was observable, that is when he withdrew it far enough from the youth for one to see it, before trying once more to ram the thing up the slave's rectum.

The young man twisted and turned, trying to avoid the onslaught of the man's prick. However, as he was slowly choking to death, Marcus knew the youth's efforts would soon fail him…one way or the other.

"I said hold!" Marcus yelled, now with all the authority he could muster, as he hurried the short distance down the street. He was almost there, but still he was ever mindful to keep the hem of his linen toga out of the dust, dirt, and offal that so liberally littered the paving stones of Roman streets.

Now Marcus saw clearly that the young man couldn't do anything to aid himself. With his hands shackled in irons behind his back, the slaver had him bent almost double over the wooden railing of the auction platform upon which the two of them stood. The boy's ragged loincloth was down around his slim ankles. He was virtually naked for all practical purposes and his exposed ass made an excellent target for his owner's continued sexual assault. The trader went at him as a horde of legionnaires with a battering ram went against the gates of some city.

"You will cease your activities or I'll have you arrested on the spot." Marcus used a tone of a voice that brooked no argument.

At last, the slaver paused in his efforts. He turned his head slightly to squint down at this intruder, Marcus, who now stood just below him, at the base of the platform. The man's bloated and red-faced expression was one of extreme annoyance at this interruption.

"What do you want?" the man snarled.

"I want you to cease what you're doing. And I want you to do it now. I command you." From where he stood, Marcus stared up at the pig of a man. He knew him by sight, although he'd never spoken to him. Still, he'd seen him in passing many times before on this street, selling his slaves like so many heads of cattle. He never treated them well, struck them often, but Marcus couldn't do anything about that for the man was within his rights under Roman law. Nevertheless, this was the first time Marcus had seen him attempt to simultaneously rape and throttle one of his slaves.

The man, still leaning his corpulent form over that of the younger man, released his hold on the youth's neck. "Who are you to command me?" he demanded to know, as he did this. "I'm within my rights. You have no right to interfere. Be about your business, or I'll call the guard."

Marcus granted the man a small, but sardonic smile. Then he said, "Please call them if you like. If you continue this business, I will. And this is my business. You see, I'm the magistrate here. And you, sir, are breaking the law."

"Magistrate or no, this is my slave. So I break no law." The man's tone was one of aggressive defiance, as was his expression.

"I think you'll find you're in violation and on several counts," Marcus smoothly said, and all the while trying to maintain a pleasant, even placid demeanor, as if nothing could ruffle him as a magistrate. "Under the law, you may not kill a slave. Even more importantly, Caesar Augustus decreed no one is to have sex in an open place in Rome where all can see. He also banned public nudity, as you full well know."

"Caesar Augustus is dead," boldly stated the trader. "Emperor Tiberius now reigns and he is of a different mind." But even as he added this, he withdrew himself from between the young man's tight buttocks, and then dropped his tunic over his erect cock, seemingly out of modesty.

The youth, with his loincloth still draped in disarray down around his ankles and still bent naked as he was over the railing, didn't attempt to move other than to continue to gasp for much-needed breath. His face slowly resumed its natural color as he did this.

"Mighty Augustus may be dead, but his laws survive him," Marcus primly reminded the man. "What's more, despite whatever personal preferences the Emperor Tiberius may have in private, in public, he upholds those laws strictly. And you're in violation of them. I could have you arrested and heavily fined if I so wished, or even flogged. Perhaps, I should have all your property confiscated, since you refuse to obey me as a lawful magistrate. It can be done, you know, and the government would welcome the extra property."

"Surely, there is no need to go so far," the merchant said, suddenly nervous, as he spread his pudgy fingers in a placating gesture. His fleshy lips quivered, as he added, "It's only a slave, and he is of no consequence, surely?"

"I'm more concerned with your lewd public behavior," Marcus said. "There are children playing about the streets, married woman, and maidens busy making their purchases. They shouldn't have to be accosted by such as you, subjected to what you're doing. The question remains only as to what penalty I should assign to you."

"Under the law, I'm entitled to a trial," the slaver said, managing to look belligerent, stubborn, and sly all at the same time.

"You may have one, sir, if you so wish. I will preside over the trial, of course, since this is my jurisdiction." Now Marcus smiled, before saying, "You would prefer this matter to be put to a public trial, then?"

The trader remained silent a long while, as if thinking. Then he said in a clearly grudging tone of voice, "No, I suppose I don't wish that. What is it you would have of me?"

"Your slave, since you're so intent on killing him anyway. He would have been of no further use to you in just a few minutes' time, being dead, I mean. So I might as well have him."

Now the slaver's face turned a bright red, as if he was suffering from a sudden bout of extreme apoplexy. "This…this is sheer extortion!" he spluttered. "You have no right whatsoever—"

"I have every right under the law," Marcus said, calmly. "You are trying to kill your slave while in the act of publicly fornicating with him. You have caused him and yourself to be in an improper state of dress and are performing vulgarities. The fines for this would certainly be equal to the cost of one slave, especially considering the condition he is now in, after you nearly choked him to death. The fact you were killing him also makes it clear to me you had no further use for him. So I'll take him off your hands." Here, Marcus gave the man a thin, mirthless smile, before adding, "And I will contribute the equal of the amount of his cost to the payment of your fine."

"Oh, you are too kind," the trader said, in a voice heavily laced with sarcasm.

"Indeed," agreed Marcus, unperturbed. "I am. And this way, I accomplish two things. I remove the slave from your tender ministrations" (and here he let his own sarcasm show), "and also thus prevent you from repeating such a lewd act where you had no right to do so, at least not with this particular slave again. And I will tell you frankly, sir, if I catch you doing this sort of thing again with others, you will be in prison shortly afterwards. Believe me, next time I will make it a very public trial, so that all your neighbors, friends, and relatives can see just what type of an immoral and disgusting person you really are. In my opinion, you're not worthy to be called a Roman."

The open-mouthed trader just stared at Marcus in obvious surprise.

"Do I make myself clear? Do you agree to this?" Marcus pressed him in a tone that brooked no dissension.

The stunned man simply nodded his head in mute acquiescence.

"Then unshackle the slave now and hand him over to me. Now, I said!" he added in a more authoritative voice, when the merchant made no move to obey him.

The man sprang into action. After he'd completed his task, Marcus called to the slave and said, "You! Come down here with me. I'm your new master now."

The youth didn't answer. Marcus hadn't expected him to. Slaves rarely spoke, unless asked a direct question. In any case, he doubted if the boy was up to speaking just yet, after the throttling, he'd just endured.

The young man reached down, hesitantly pulled his filthy loincloth up from around his ankles, and settled the minimal item of clothing around his lean hips once more. He did this with a quiet dignity that impressed Marcus. Then rubbing his wrists where the iron shackles had chafed them, he slowly descended the rickety wooden steps of the platform, carefully, one at a time, but with no hands on the railing, despite probably still being groggy from his near strangulation.

Now he came and stood directly in front of Marcus. A very handsome youth, he appeared to be about twenty years of age, or perhaps just a little older.

Close to my age, Marcus thought.

The young man had a shock of raven black hair, which looked tangled and unkempt. Before he'd bent his head forward in the normal attitude of slavish humility, Marcus noticed his striking blue eyes. They were so deep a color, so dark, they almost bordered on violet. Although filthy in appearance, Marcus noticed the unblemished whiteness of his skin beneath all the dirt. He saw now why the slaver hadn't beaten or flogged him in the usual way. No doubt, he didn't want to mar that beautiful skin, depreciate the youth's value in such a way.

Instead, the trader had resorted to choking him. Such bruises, if any, would go away comparatively quickly, while scars from the lash would not. Those were permanent. However, it wasn't just to avoid marring the boy's skin that the trader had choked him, instead. Marcus suspected the ugly slave trader had enjoyed having his sex in such a rough and violent way. Many Romans seemed to like it this way these days—the blood lust of the arena always there now, bubbling just below the surface of the general populace, and so quick to come to the surface with only minor provocation.

"You are part of my household now," Marcus told the youth in a firm voice. "I don't shackle my slaves, nor will I make you, in particular, wear a collar as you're wearing now, so we will have that removed soon. However, I expect absolute obedience from you. Failure to give me such respect and the collar will be around your neck soon enough once more. Do you understand?"

"Yes, master, I do." He raised his head to meet Marcus' gaze directly, in a breach of the usual propriety in such situations. The slave added in a low and masculine voice, "I would obey you now in all things, anyway. You've saved my life and among my people, this means my life is now yours to do with as you please. I'm indebted to you."

Instead of taking offense at this confident statement, so unusual for a slave to dare, Marcus was impressed. "How are you called?" he asked, in a slightly softer voice.

"I have been called Lucian these last three years, since my captivity, master."

"You prefer this name?" asked Marcus.

The youth nodded. "I think you'll find it much easier to pronounce than my real name, which is a Celtic one. The Roman tongue has a very hard time with it, and that's why my former master renamed me."

"And has he," Marcus indicated the corpulent slaver with a quick flick of his right hand, and who was still watching them from the platform, "been your master all this time?"

The slave shook his head, his unruly mass of black locks shifting from side to side as he did so. "No, master, he only recently acquired me just some days ago. My last master lost me in a game of lots. It was his first trip to Rome and he wished to participate in all its delights to the detriment of his purse. He sold me to get his money out of me."

"Your first master, he was from North Gaul?"

The slave dared glance up at him again, in apparent surprise this time, his dark blue eyes flashing at Marcus, before he remembered to lower his head in a respectful attitude once more.

"Yes," he murmured. "May I ask the master how he knew this?"

"You appear to be from the northern regions. Your skin is too pale by far to be from a more southern clime, your eyes too blue. So your former master lost you in gambling?"

"He did, master."

"In my opinion, such gambling may be the ruin of the empire. In reasonable levels, it's harmless enough, I suppose, but I have known men who have lost their entire estates this way. This brings about not only their ruin, but that of their children, as well. The law should not allow such things. True Romans should never sacrifice honor and their respect just for a chance to win at a game of dice."

"Yes, master," the youth said. His head was still bent forward, the unruly mop of jet-black hair still shielding his face.

Even so, Marcus had seen enough. The young man's handsome features impressed him. The straight line of his nose, the firm squared chin, the high cheekbones, and the full, almost sensuous lips, were perfect in their male proportions, as was his body. A little on the lean side, perhaps, for lack of proper nutrition, but still a thing of lithe beauty, with a muscular and angular torso tapering down to slim hips, which in turn were supported by muscular thighs and well-formed calves. Even his feet, though currently dirty, were a remarkable sight, being long and narrow, with beautifully formed toes, as in the classic Greek concept of male beauty.

No question about it, the lad was male through and through, with hard lines and manly planes at every turn. Moreover, Marcus had seen him naked, so he knew the boy's nether parts were well endowed, wonderfully so. His testicles had hung down like twin ripe plums in their pale-skinned and almost hairless sac. His penis had been flaccid, but still it had showed large, projecting out from a small bush of darkest pubic hair, hanging down like some marvelous sexual serpent. Marcus felt the first tugs of a physical longing for the youth at these memories.

"Are you well enough to walk?" Marcus asked, gently.

"I'm mostly recovered, master."

"Good. Then come with me now. There are things I must attend to this day, but I'll keep them as brief as possible for your benefit. You will accompany me for the moment. Later, I'll see you settled in at my house. It is no villa, but even so, it's comfortable enough. You'll have the company of several other slaves there.

Bowing his head in obeisance, Lucian didn't speak. For

Marcus, this was as it should be. He heartily disliked chattering and gossiping slaves. Judging by his behavior so far, Lucian didn't seem to be one of these. Marcus was thankful for that much, at least.

Without another word and without looking back to see if Lucian followed him, he set off down the narrow street once more, heading for his office in the administration complex, which was still several streets over from here.

Lucian dutifully followed him in silence. So quiet was he, it was all Marcus could do, not to look back to make sure he was still there, trailing behind him. Nevertheless, every now and then, the scuffling sound of bare feet on paving stones, assured him the youth was with him still.

At thought of his exposed feet, Marcus realized he must find the young man some clothes and sandals. It wouldn't do for Marcus to be seen in the company of a nearly naked man, one who was filthy into the bargain. Such would not reflect at all well on his office of magistrate. Still, the enticing thought of being able to continue to view Lucian in so exposed a way, appearing so bare before him, was a strong inducement to leaving the youth in his current state of undress.

No, Marcus thought. I must clothe him, for having him so naked will only give me a constant erection. And that wouldn't look good either, for people to see the toga of their magistrate sticking out like a tent in front of him…

Chapter 2 — The House Of Marcus Darius Macro

Lucian felt in a permanent state of amazement. With the brutally attempted rape and then probable murder of him by the slaver, Balbus, thankfully interrupted by Marcus, Lucian just felt grateful to be still alive, and more, was astounded to be. He had been sure he was about to die. Although his time with Balbus had been mercifully short, the man's other slaves had told Lucian how brutal he was, how many slaves died under his cruel hand.

In fact, they claimed it was the reason he was in the wholesale end of the slave business. It was far cheaper to obtain fresh slaves this way, than to have to buy them at final auction for higher prices. So the man had become a seller of slaves. His overall profits from the business more than compensated for the occasional death of one of them. In his chosen line of business, he could easily replace such.

To be out of that creature's clutches was a miracle in itself. Now, being owned by Marcus seemed a wonderful thing in comparison. Lucian was so relieved, for not only was Marcus a striking figure of a man, but he seemed a very fair one, too.

He had tactfully understood Lucian's need for clothing. To walk around virtually naked in the streets of Rome was a humiliating thing and Lucian had cringed at every step of the way. Still, as a slave, he had dared say nothing. However, Marcus had quickly fixed this problem for him. Now, although still filthy from days without a proper bath, Lucian felt much better just having decent clothes upon his back, covering his nudity.

He had been surprised at how kind Marcus had been about it all. His new master had stopped at the first stall on their way that sold clothing. He had selected a used woolen tunic for Lucian, but a clean one and in reasonably good condition.

Then, with almost no haggling, he'd purchased Lucian a pair of leather sandals, as well. They were the plain ones worn by slaves or the very lowest of the free classes, but they were in fair shape, too. They had been worn only a little. Marcus had gone even further. He had told Lucian to place his hands on his shoulder and lean against him, while he'd placed the sandals himself upon Lucian's feet. He'd done that right in the middle of the street, for all to see.

As far as Lucian knew, this was almost unheard of in the Roman world. Masters didn't treat their slaves well, as a usual matter. Even his first owner, a plausibly kind man by Roman standards, would not have literally stooped to do this for Lucian, to perform such an act of kindness. So Lucian had just stood there, first raising one foot and then the other, while Marcus strapped on his sandals for him. All the while, he'd gazed down upon his master's curly, golden locks that shone so like spun gold in the bright morning sunshine. It was all he could do not to reach out and touch that hair.

Then, at another stall farther down the busy street, Marcus had bought him some fresh fruit and bread, along with a small amphora of weak wine to drink. These items, Lucian had consumed while Marcus had gone on inside a palatial looking building, where he said he had to meet with cohorts of none other than Sejanus himself. That man was, for all practical purposes, the current master of Rome. Emperor Tiberius was far away at the Isle of Capri, where they said he engaged most of his time in tremendous debaucheries. These included men, women, and even children. Rumors said he threw those who displeased him off a nearby cliff into the sea. Lucian mentally shuddered at the very idea such a monster of a man could exist, let alone actually do such terrible deeds.

Maybe, Lucian dared to hope, he'd found a home where he could feel reasonably safe. He knew one thing; he owed his life to Marcus. Lucian was determined to pay him back in kind, if possible. In the meantime, in his own way, he would do his best to protect and guard Marcus in every way he could. He would stop at nothing to do this. Nothing else was as important, even his freedom. He would be a faithful servant to the man.

When Marcus finally reemerged from the imposing building, he and Lucian headed toward home. They were now near the top of the Palatine Hill, so this involved them descending it again. Lucian hoped they wouldn't go too far down the slope. That would mean Marcus must live in an apartment down in the crowded ghettoes of the older streets of Rome.

The area was an absolute warren of dismal tiny alleys and shadow-filled, narrow lanes. Too many people of too many nationalities vied for too little space in those constricted streets. Despite the much-vaunted sewers of Rome and the nightly flushing of roads with water, the whole area still smelled terribly. Lucian knew this from being with his last master prior to Balbus, who had rented temporary quarters there while on his short visit to the city.

And the noise could be awful, what with children shouting, peddlers hawking their wares, babies crying, women screaming at them and their husbands, and with men bellowing orders, or letting loose with peals of drunken laughter. With apartment buildings as high as five stories, and often very poor methods of sanitation used in them, the whole place had a general background reek of piss, sour odor of vomit, and the stink of shit, all mixed in with the greasy cooking smells from the street vendors. The entire area was a constant and awful assault on the senses.

Thus, it was with a profound relief for Lucian when Marcus turned to their left and entered a gateway into the vestibulum of his home. They walked the length of this to the main door. Instead of opening it, using his fist, Marcus banged loudly. A slave with salt-and-pepper hair opened the door.

He bowed to Marcus. "Good evening, master," he said. His tone was a servile one, a shade oily sounding. His expression was haughty.

Marcus brushed past the man and entered the atrium of the house. Lucian followed suit, but more slowly. He nodded respectfully to the slave, as he passed him. The man didn't respond, but instead gave him a suspicious glance, a speculative lift of one dark eyebrow.

"Didius, see to getting some real food for our Lucian here, and while you're at it, have them send me my meal. I will be in the triclinium, waiting. I have some documents to peruse. After Lucian has bathed and been dressed as a proper house slave, send him to me. I wish to explain his duties to him."

At these words, Didius lifted both of his thick black eyebrows in speculation, but he made no comment. He merely bowed once more to Marcus and said, "As you wish, master. It shall be done." He said this in that same servile voice, which Lucian now suspected was a professional one, and not really meant to be humble at all, but just superficially to sound that way. The servant turned and walked from the room. As he did so, with a peremptory flick of his right hand, he motioned for Lucian to follow him.

Ah, so the pecking order begins, thought Lucian, sadly. Now that he was no longer with his new master, Lucian had many things to consider, not least of which was to know what his new function in this household would be, the role he was destined to play. This also entailed what status he would have.

Where would he be in the pecking order of the slaves in the household? It didn't matter where, unless it was at the very bottom. Otherwise, those below him would be jealous, and those above him would fear his replacing them. In Lucian's relatively short experience as a slave, it always seemed to be that way.

He could do little about it. Even so, the thought of going through all this yet again, as with his first master's household, troubled him greatly. He was not one for confrontations. He only wished to survive and somehow, someday, to be free.

Above even these desires was the need to protect and take care of Marcus, his golden savior, his Roman Adonis. He had very strong feelings about this bred into him from the time he was a child. His Celtic culture stressed responsibility and duty, and the fulfillment of obligations to others. This was one's highest attainment of personal honor in his homeland. Although he was no longer in his homeland, Lucian was still intent on behaving according to the code of ethics he'd learned there. This was all he had left to cling to, since he'd lost his freedom and everything else.

"Who are you?" Didius asked him in a low voice when they were safely beyond earshot of Marcus. He had stopped in the middle of a hallway, a long one, with tiled floors and walls clad in striated white marble. They were out of sight of their master here and Didius had turned to look at Lucian, although it seemed more of an inspection. "Where have you come from? Why are you here?"

Lucian attempted an ingratiating smile, before saying, "As for where I'm from, I'm originally from across the waters near northern Gaul, from the isle of Britannia, as Romans call it. As for why I'm here, your guess is as good as mine is. The master saw me for sale, and chose to buy me, but he didn't say bother to tell me why. I thought it better not to ask." Lucian deliberately didn't mention the circumstances of the morning's events, being too embarrassed and mortified by what had occurred to want to recount such to this austere and superior-seeming stranger.

"Well, I have a good idea as to why," Didius said, and now he was frowning, deeply. "It doesn't take much imagination to see why he might have picked you, what with the way you look and all."

"What do you mean?" Lucian asked, curious despite himself. "You know why he bought me? If so, please tell me."

"What I may know or not know is of no business of yours. You will do better to mind your own affairs. Is that clear?"

"Perfectly."

"Good. Now I will take you to the cucina. The cook there will provide you with something to eat, and you will take your meal there. When you're done, I want you to come and look for me. I should be in the atrium. I'll show you to the bath. It's not a large one, but at least we have one here. Usually, smaller homes don't have such, and so those people must go to the public ones.

"So you're lucky," he continued, "to have been chosen by our master. He runs a good home and is fair to the servants—for the most part. Here we are," he added, as they entered into the kitchen, or "cucina," as Didius had called it in the Roman tongue.

Lucian looked around him. There was no sign of any cook, but there was a heavy wooden trestle table in the center of the tiled room. Various cooking utensils hung about the place from iron hooks, along with an array of iron pots, copper pans, and pieces of earthenware crockery also adorning the walls. A pit fire with an open circle in the ceiling above it must be for the actual cooking. The place carried the odor of old cooking smells, the yeasty odor of fresh-baked bread, the pungent aroma of imported foreign spices, and sharp scent of garlic.

"As usual, our cook seems to be missing," Didius said, sourly. "No doubt, he's off sipping at a cup of wine somewhere. I'll find him and send him to you. You wait here. Don't wander about. When you've finished eating, come to me directly as I've already told you. Do not delay in this. I don't like to be kept waiting. Is this understood?"

Lucian nodded, but said nothing. To acquiesce too much, only to later on find out his status was higher than this man's, would not be a good thing. However, if his status among the slaves turned out to be lower than that of Didius,' then it would be wiser for him at least to pay some lip service to him for the time being. Again, it was the old pecking order problem.

Until one knew where one stood in a new household, it was best to be very careful, to play it safe. Moreover, Lucian had no wish to make unnecessary enemies. One made them enough, anyway, without even trying. Personal greed, fear of position, and outright jealousy were usually the cause of this. One didn't have to work to acquire enemies. One acquired them as a matter of course, especially, when one was a slave.

Later, after the cook had reappeared and served him, and so having eaten a substantial meal of sizzling roasted lamb, tangy brown olives marinated in heavy oil, and a huge chunk of crusty and coarse bread with olive oil drizzled on it, Lucian went in search of Didius.

He found him, and although brusque, the man was efficient at his tasks. He saw to it Lucian bathed and groomed himself in the proper Roman way, using olive oil and a strigil gently to scrape his skin clean, before a plunge in the caldarium bath. Then, dressed in a clean slave's tunic, one Didius had provided for him, and his only pair of sandals, he made his way to where Marcus waited.

He entered the space to find his master stretched out on a typical Roman couch. These had no backs to them, but used pillows instead, for support. He was lying there on his side, completely naked, facing Lucian, so everything was clearly visible.

Unlike many men under such circumstances, Marcus was truly a remarkable sight, looked even better in the buff, than when clothed. His lean, almost lanky body lay stretched out upon the couch. His uncircumcised penis was soft, but was still impressive to behold, even so. His testicles, like two large and edible mushrooms hanging in their sac, hung pendulously down onto his lower thigh.

Marcus sat up when he saw Lucian, shoving aside his discarded toga and tunic in the process. "Ah, he said, "don't you look much more presentable now. What a striking contrast your white skin and tunic make against such dark hair."

Lucian thought the same thing applied to Marcus, as well, but in a different way. He was all muscle, with a bronze gleaming

- 17 -

sheen of a tan covering his firm flesh. His legs and arms had fine golden hairs covering them in a slight furze. His pubic hair was a lush bush of the same fine-spun gold, and a thin line of this hair trailed upward over his taut belly, climbing towards his chest where it spread out in a triangle there, a sprinkling of gold.

Marcus just watched him as Lucian took it all in. Lucid, brown eyes peered up at him from beneath a thatch of curly blonde hair that lay in a casual disarray over his forehead.

Masculine, firm lips, curled in the slightest of smiles, then parted to say, "You feel better?"

"Better, master?"

"Yes," Marcus said, as he made an impatient gesture with one hand. "I mean, now that you're clean and better fed."

"Oh, I do, very much. Thank you, master, I do."

"And now you would like to know what your duties will be, what I would expect of you?" Marcus eyed him closely with those intense brown eyes of his, as he said this.

"I would, if the master wishes to tell me." Lucian said this in a soft voice, meant to be that of a humble slave who desired only to do his master's bidding.

"Well said. I think you may do nicely here. You're no fool. You watch what you say and how you say it. And you don't say any more than you have to. I've noticed that, too. Did you really mean you felt bound to me? I mean, more than as just a slave, and as you told me earlier in the marketplace?"

The sudden change of subject took Lucian off guard. Nevertheless, he said, rightly enough, "Yes, master I did. You own me. It's true. But I wish to be more than just a slave. If you were ever endangered, it would be my duty to come between you and any harm. This I must do to uphold my personal honor."

"So this is just a duty of yours, then?" Marcus asked of him.

Lucian was silent a moment trying to think of how best to

answer this. "By my people's commands, yes, it's a duty. However, I willingly and wholeheartedly undertake the task. You saved my life. I'm eternally grateful for that favor. I would readily lay down my life now for yours."

Now it was Marcus' turn to be silent a moment. Then, he said, "I see. Good enough. You answer well, Lucian. Now, about those duties I have for you..."

Chapter 3 — The Duel Begins

Marcus hesitated before continuing. He noticed Lucian was staring at him, his gaze seemingly centered on his crotch area.

"Nudity makes you uncomfortable?" he asked, as he pretended innocently to spread his thighs slightly apart, bend one knee upward, as if in search of a more comfortable position. Marcus knew this caused his cock and balls to hang down in midair, instead of draping across his lower thigh. Let the youth get a good look at them dangling there, an unobstructed one.

"If so," he added, "you must get past this, for we Romans often prefer our nakedness to clothing, especially when at the public baths, and I will be taking you along with me there often, as my personal attendant."

Lucian gave a small shake of his head. "I'm not unaccustomed to nudity, master," he said, in a strangled voice, one barely above a whisper.

Marcus thought about this in silence for a moment, then said, "Is it you fear I wish to have your body? And if so, would such an idea be unpleasant, even repellant to you?"

Again, Lucian shook his head. "No, master. I hadn't thought that. But if you wish to use me in such a way, as your slave, I can only willingly do your bidding. My body is yours to do with as you please, of course."

Marcus frowned at Lucian's choice of words. "But given your wishes in the matter, you would prefer not to?" He knew his tone sounded a bit harsher now, tinged with a slight bitterness of what he felt was a rejection.

"I would prefer to have a choice, yes," the younger man said, "but as a slave, I don't, so it's of no consequence." He said this with his head bent forward. Marcus suspected this was not so much out of humility this time, as out of a wish to avoid meeting his gaze. Lucian, there could be no doubt, was now equivocating with him.

Marcus stared up at the slave and just as hard as the youth had been staring down at him moments earlier. "I would have an honest answer from you," he said, pointedly.

Now Lucian did look up at him and there was a hint of defiance in his indigo, blue-eyed gaze—no, rather it was a reserve of personal dignity, a wellspring of some inner strength, Marcus decided.

Either way, it made him feel slightly uncomfortable for having asked the question. He realized he was treating this man as if he were an equal in this conversation. He must remember Lucian was just his slave. He was a very handsome one, admittedly, but still just a slave—a thing to be bought and sold, and used as he wished. And oh, how he wished to use him now, to feel his hard slick cock sliding up between those firm white cheeks, to penetrate that tight ass, plunge his prick deep into the youth's gut, there to fuck him hard.

"Given a personal preference in the matter," Lucian said, at last, "I would prefer not to be used so by you."

Marcus' fantasy dissolved in an abrupt flash. This bold statement took him aback. He wasn't used to being rejected, not by any other man or woman, and yet now by a mere slave?

"You don't find me attractive enough?" he asked, his voice slightly high-pitched in his sheer surprise at such effrontery.

Lucian shook his head, as if confirming this, but then he said, "I find you very handsome, master. You are like a Greek god to me, perhaps even as Apollo might appear in your golden looks, your muscular physique, and your fine-looking features."

Marcus felt somewhat assuaged by this blandishment, as any man with any sense of vanity would. "But despite all this, you just don't like bedding with men? Is that it?" he asked, searching for the cause of Lucian's reluctance.

Lucian gave a slight shrug, before saying, "That's far from being a problem with me. I find it infinitely more preferable making love to men, than to the crude bedding of women, given a choice in the matter. I find men's hard bodies far more appealing, their behavior less complicated, much more direct in their needs than women. Truth is I enjoy a man physically much better than I ever could a woman. Men, to me, are beautiful in their form and shape, whereas, women's soft bodies, their pendulous breasts, are not."

"Ah, so if my being a man is not the problem, then we are back to this matter of a choice again. Is that what this is all about for you, Lucian? Is this your only obstacle? And if I commanded you to wrap your soft lips about my hard cock, to sink your mouth down onto it, there to suck until my juices flow from my balls and down your throat, if I were to demand this right now of you, would you do so willingly?" He spread his thighs even more suggestively, and even as he did this, his dick twitched, lifted slightly, as if a thing with a life of its own.

Lucian started at this, appeared as a victim who might be mesmerized by a cobra's baleful gaze, as he stared at Marcus' awakening cock. His tongue licked suddenly pallid lips. His pale face flushed a crimson red. "I...I would do so willingly," he said, in a halting and hoarse voice.

Now Marcus, enjoying his advantage, purposely squeezed his half-erect cock with his right hand, making the large head pop out from inside the generous foreskin.

"Then you would like some of my cock," he added softly, barely above a whisper. "You want a taste of it now, don't you? You desire it. I can see this. You want to lick at the clear drop that even now appears on the tip of it. Don't lie to me," he added, when Lucian was about to speak. "I can see by the bulge in the crotch of your tunic, you like what you see and want it."

"I—I would do so willingly," Lucian stammered again. "As your slave, it's my duty."

Marcus frowned, let go of his swelling penis. Even so, the thing now stood almost at full attention, wavering slightly back and forth in front of Lucian, who still seemed unable to wrench his eyes away from the sight of the large member.

"You play word games with me when I asked for the truth," Marcus snapped, irritated now. "I ask again; given the choice, would you service me here and now, and fully, of your own free choosing?"

Gently, almost unnoticeably, Lucian gave the tiniest shake of his head. "No," he whispered, and then he licked his lips before adding, "I would not. I would not prefer to do it as a commanded slave."

"But as a freed man you would?" Marcus deliberately narrowed his eyes to mere suspicious slits. "Is that what this game of yours is all about? You inveigle me for your freedom and with promises of willingly letting me fuck you how and as I please, if I grant you this. Is that it? Is this how you reward me for saving you today from that disgusting pig fucking your pretty little ass raw, and choking you to death?"

Marcus gave a little shake of his head, before adding, "Perhaps, I should have let him continue at his pleasures for a while longer. It would make for a good show, you being fucked up the ass like that in public, and in broad daylight! Yes, quite the show it would be, but…so humiliating for you, yes?"

Now Lucian's handsome features had a stricken look to them. "You misunderstand me, master," he said, sounding contrite. "I didn't mean to bargain with you in any way. You asked me for the truth. As the truth, I said I would willingly do whatever you demanded of me as your slave, and because you saved my life today. Neither would I find the task distasteful in any way. On the contrary, I would enjoy such closeness with you, doing you such a service. To adore your body, to worship you in such a way would be a sought-after privilege, not a trial for me."

"Then what's the problem?" Marcus asked, gently now. "What is this question of choice that confounds you so much?" Already, he regretted what he'd said a few moments ago; felt he'd gone too far. At least, he had judging by the painful look now marring his handsome slave's face. He hadn't meant to be so brutal, but he was terribly sexually frustrated.

How his loins ached for this young man. How he wanted to cradle Lucian's head in his hands, his fingers buried in that thatch of raven hair, as Lucian took his bulging cock into this mouth, swallowed him down to his balls, milked him of his hot seed, and swallowed it all! To feel Lucian's throat muscles constricting around the head of his cock as he swallowed—the very thought made Marcus' heart beat faster with anticipation, his cock rise to ramrod stiffness.

"I'm a slave," Lucian reiterated. "And as a slave I have no choice. I'd prefer to come to you as an unfettered lover, out of my own desire and wishes, out of my need for you, man to man, as equals in our love. But as a slave, this choice will always be denied to me. Whatever I do, whatever I say, it could always be construed as a slave lying to his master, just trying to please him, so as not to incur his anger, or to gain some advantage over him."

Marcus was silent again, this time for a very long while, to the point where Lucian began to fidget where he stood, as if in fear he might have said too much, and perhaps had gone too far.

"I see," Marcus said slowly, at last. "And this is not because you really don't desire me or men in general? This would be understandable, if so, since most men are not of this persuasion."

Lucian gave an emphatic shake of his head. "No, master! I do crave men with all my heart. I've never even wished to lay with a woman, nor have I. And you, from the moment you saved me in that street, appeared as a god to me, something to be desired in such a way above all else."

Odd, thought, Marcus. That's just the way I thought when I first laid eyes on him, as being like a Greek god.

"Very well," he said aloud. "I understand how you feel. I thank you for speaking truthfully to me, and as I've asked. Hear me, Lucian, when I say I'll not demand anything of you, of your body in such a way, when it comes to me. You are free to come to me only when and if you ever truly choose to do so.

"But I warn you, Lucian," and here he paused for effect, before adding, "you will come to me eventually. Everyone does that I've ever wanted to lie with. And Lucian, I want to lie with you, badly. I want to feel myself deep inside you, buried between your ass cheeks, to mount you until my cock is high into your belly. Then, Lucian, I promise you, I will fuck you so deeply, my cock will meet up with your yesterday's breakfast!

"Now," he added, in a brusque tone, "Leave me, but send in the slave, Octavos. I'll have him, if I can't have you. His ripe ass will pay dearly for your refusal to offer me yours."

Lucian just nodded, and hesitantly, as if at a loss, turned to leave.

"Oh, and one more thing," Marcus called after him. "Return when I'm finished with him and I'll then go over your other duties with you. And," he added, in what he knew was an almost malicious tone of voice, "if you wish to sneak a look at how well I fuck Octavos, to get an idea of what I can do for you, you're welcome to do so. I enjoy exhibiting my prowess. And it will show you how well I can plow your own furrow for you, if only given the proper chance to be such a considerate farmer to you."

Lucian nodded once more, and then bowing his head, fled from the room.

Marcus smiled to himself. He had seen the look of lust in the slave's eyes, the sudden, unbidden gleam of an aching sexual hunger. Oh, yes, Lucian wanted him well enough…they usually always did.

More than one can play this game, Marcus thought, happily, and I have the upper hand, because if I tire of this playing about, I could simply order him to submit.

However, even as he thought this, Marcus knew he wouldn't do such a thing, at least, not if he could help it. His desire might override this feeling, but he instinctively knew sex with Lucian would be far better if that so perfect body of the slave was not only willing, but also wanting it.

That, Marcus vowed, he would make Lucian do. He would make him want it. The slave eventually would come to him of his own free will. Only after he'd begged on his knees, would Marcus then pleasure himself between those lips and up inside that taut-muscled ass. Before he was through with Lucian, the young man would be trembling with happy exhaustion and walking awkwardly for days to come, into the bargain!

It was then that Octavos appeared, a thin man, who by the look of him must be well above his mid-twenties. He, too, had dark hair, as did Lucian, but it didn't have that almost blue-black sheen to it the younger man's did. Then, in addition, he'd a lot of hair elsewhere, which wasn't overly pleasing to Marcus, who liked his men on the hairless side. Octavos was just the opposite.

Hairy-chested and hairy-assed, to fuck him would not be nearly so enjoyable a thing, as sliding his cock up between Lucian's quivering cheeks. But it would have to do…for now.

Besides, Octavos was good at his job. He knew how to tighten his asshole to milk Marcus and at just the right moments, right as he was about to cum. Octavos could make Marcus shoot his load with just a few tight contractions of his sphincter muscle that way, so good was his sense of timing.

Then, Lucian might well be watching, as Marcus hoped he would, so he was determined to put on a good show, to let him know what he was missing. He would fuck until his very balls tried to enter the little man's asshole. He would make Octavos scream out in a combination of ecstasy and pain as he punched his cock deep into his belly! And with every plunge up that man's vitals, Marcus would imagine he was sinking himself deep into Lucian's love hole, impaling that handsome pale body with his hard shaft, pinning Lucian roughly to the couch like a helpless victim. Oh, Marcus would make Lucian see and feel the full power of Rome that hung between his legs!

Chapter 4 — Treading A Difficult Path

True to Marcus' expectations, Lucian did risk a look at the two men together, Marcus and Octavos, as they copulated with such animal-like heat, it sparked a strong response in Lucian's own loins, gave him an instant and ravening erection.

He had done this by spying on them from a distance, from behind the safety of a gaudily painted column. Only mere minutes had passed since Octavos had been sent to Marcus, but already Marcus was atop his naked body, ass-naked himself, straddled over the smaller man, and fucking him with a wild ferocity, his cock pumping away, piston-like, in a sheer sexual frenzy.

Marcus' powerful thigh and ass muscles strained as he entered Octavos and repeatedly rammed his long prick up the man's hole. Lucian could see how that sphincter muscle seemed to grasp and try to hold onto that lubricated and shining cock of Marcus' and was stretched wide by the sheer girth of that slick member reaming it.

Marcus rode him with incredible power, a brute force, a wild stallion, and the muscles in his ass flexing and relaxing, as he slid his hard shaft of turgid flesh into Octavos' gut and then pulled it out again. He did this over and over. The steady sound this fucking suction made, the rhythmic slap-slap of Marcus' golden balls against the man's hairy ass crack, inflamed Lucian with desire, an intense jealousy.

How he longed to be where Octavos was now, flattened under Marcus' weight, belly pressed into the couch, and feeling that pile-driving cock forcing its way inside his puckered asshole, stretching it wide, ripping it apart, and rutting away inside of him.

Lucian watched in envy as the little man just laid face down there, head turned to one side, eyes glazed with the satiation of lust, an almost serene smile of ultimate pleasure playing about his thickened lips. He had his buttocks slightly raised to allow for deeper penetration by Marcus, as if his ass craved every possible inch of that huge organ within it, clear down to Marcus' swaying balls, and perhaps even them, too. Lucian had no doubt that if he could, Octavos would dearly love to have Marcus' entire nut sac inside him, as well. And it certainly looked as if Marcus was trying hard enough to do just this, the way he plowed away at the man, reamed his asshole.

Now Octavos, who had been steadily grunting with the vigor of each thrust into him, suddenly groaned in what seemed simultaneous pain and pleasure. Octavos was cumming and without having stroked or touched his cock at all, in any way. Was Marcus that good at fucking, that he could do this for someone? How Octavos now groaned, as if in agony! But Lucian knew better.

If this be pain, it's such a wondrous pain, combined with such exquisite pleasure, Lucian thought with real envy. To feel Marcus' hot breath burning the back of his neck, to feel that gleaming, sweating, hard, bronzed body lying astraddle atop of his, fucking him into delirium, would be as a dream come true.

Lucian, suddenly filled with an incredible jealousy, abruptly turned his head away from the provocative scene, and stalked bitterly from the room. He didn't even think to hide his presence by trying to tread quietly, to make a silent escape.

Marcus, although busy with his fierce ass rutting of Octavos, heard the sound of sandals slapping sharply against hard marble flooring. He paused, just a split second in his activities, just long enough to glance over his shoulder. He did this just in time to see Lucian depart. Marcus smiled to himself with satisfaction. And this sight impelled him to finish his business of impaling Octavos by way of the man's tight rectum. He fucked into him again, shoving with all his might.

Octavos might be hairy, but he was always a good, tight fuck. Then, even as Octavos bellowed in ultimate pleasure, screamed out his master's name, Marcus came. He felt his balls tighten like rocks in their sac; the thickly liquid seed raced from there up his shaft, reached the head of his cock, and then exploded into Octavos' gut.

Again, and again, Marcus fucked in and out of him, and with each downward push, he pumped more of his cum up the man's hole. True to his behavior, Octavos helped this along by squeezing his asshole around the fat cock, milking it, juicing it like squeezing some fruit of its precious liquid, the very essence of Marcus. So much did he cum, that Octavos' ass couldn't contain it. The white cum dribbled out around Marcus cock, slid down the slave's ass crevice, onto his sagging balls there, and ultimately onto the couch.

Marcus collapsed on top of the smaller man, panting, sweating, exhausted, and utterly satisfied. He lay there, breathing heavy, even as the slave lay very still beneath him, allowing his master to recover without interruption or unnecessary movement on his part. At last, Marcus slid his cock from out of Octavos' ass, and rolled off him. Quietly, the slave slid the rest of the way out from under him, grabbed his tunic and sandals, and with bare feet padding softly on cold marble, he left the room. He knew Marcus preferred to be left alone now.

It wasn't very much later when Octavos' found Lucian sitting on a stone bench by the square pond in the center of the peristylium.

"The master wishes to see you," he told him.

Lucian glanced up at him. He hadn't heard him come in. The slave's self-satisfied smile annoyed Lucian. He wanted to punch the man in his smirking face! Who did this hairy-assed little monkey of a man think he was? Why should he get the unfettered benefits of his master servicing him in such a magnificent way?

Marcus had been like a stud stallion in his abilities. This thought made Lucian anxious to see him, perhaps too much so, he knew. So, rather than speaking, he just gave a curt nod to Octavos and then left him standing there alone, with that same self-satisfied smile still lingering upon his lips. What infuriated Lucian was that Octavos probably didn't even realize he looked that way!

Lucian went in search of Marcus. He found him where he'd left him, on his couch in the tribiculum, only now Marcus was dressed in his tunic and sitting upright, although Lucian could still see a faint sheen of perspiration on his brow, as a last mark of his recent sexual escapades. Marcus, too, wore a self-satisfied expression, a twin of the one on the face of the smirking little Octavos. For some reason, this irritated Lucian even more than when Octavos had looked at him in this fashion.

Although, Lucian didn't want to hit Marcus, as he'd wanted to hit Octavos. Instead, Lucian wanted to grab this man by his golden locks, roughly pull back his head, and kiss him hard on the lips, force his tongue into the man's mouth and down his throat. That was another way to remove a smirk and a better one when it came to dealing with Marcus, Lucian felt. Give him as good as he gave. At least, doing such would make Lucian feel much better.

"Now we will discuss your duties," Marcus told him, without preamble.

Lucian gave a brief bow of his head, to acknowledge he was listening, but he said nothing.

"I wish you to be my personal attendant in all things possible. Do you understand what this entails?

Now Lucian felt forced at last to say something. "I—I'm not quite sure, master," he stammered. "May I most humbly ask what this means?"

Now Marcus gave a thin little smile, one not much better than his previous grin. Then he said, "I suspect you never do anything quite that humbly, Lucian. But yes, I will explain it to you, if I must. I want you at my side as much as possible. This, of course, may not always be possible, as when I must attend a private meeting with the Lord Sejanus, or those of his subordinates who need to see me on matters of delicate state business, such few meeting of those as I have." He said this last with a wry touch to his words.

"However, even then, when possible, I would like you with me, or at least, very near me. Furthermore, I wish you to sleep in my chamber at nights. That way, if I should need anything, you'll be right there to get it for me. When you leave here after this conversation, you will have Didius put a couch in there for you. You understand?"

Again, Lucian bowed his head in obeisance, but said nothing. What he heard astounded him so much; he couldn't even think to make any sort of comment.

"Good." Marcus nodded his head in a sign of his approval. "Another thing; you will sleep naked. You may have your choice in coming to me when and if you please, but I shall look at you in your bareness anytime I wish.

"Oh," he continued, "and you'll take charge of the household finances, as well. It will be your duty to scrutinize all transactions, to endorse them as acceptable or not. I charge you with taking care of all purchases and payouts for such. I'll give you a daily allowance for this purpose, and at the end of each week, I'll expect an accounting for the money I give you and in detail. Is this, too, clear? This is a grave responsibility I'm handing over to you," he added, before Lucian could speak. "Up until now, Didius has taken responsibility for this. But from now on, it will be you who does this for me, and you will be answerable only to me."

"I understand, master," Lucian managed to say, if haltingly.

"Do you? That's good. Another thing, if there is any shopping to be done you'll go and do it yourself. This means you'll be traveling the streets of Rome, acting directly on my part."

He glanced up and down at Lucian, as if inspecting him. "You'll need better clothes for this purpose, since you'll be my representative. You will wear ones of higher quality than you're wearing now. See to it that the tunics are made of linen and wool. Have them frequently laundered. So one of the first things you will do, starting tomorrow, is buy yourself some new tunics, undergarments, and at least one other pair of sandals. You will keep one of these sets of clothing for your best wear, as for when you accompany me outside this house."

He paused, before adding, "Have one of the other slaves here cut your hair, and see he does a good job of it. As it stands, you look shaggy and unkempt. Also, remain clean-shaven at all times. I want you to look your best in the Roman way and not as you look now."

At this, Lucian felt a mild resentment. He couldn't help how his hair looked. He was a slave, not a master, and had no choice in such matters as when he was to bathe or groom.

"Finally, although everything in the house will continue as it is in other respects, that is, as smoothly as possible, it's you I will expect to see first in the morning, and first thing when I get home in the evening, as well as the last thing I see at night. It is you and you alone who will serve me my food and drink."

Now Marcus stood up, his spotless tunic contrasted nicely where the hem of it cut a white line across the top of his tanned thighs. He approached Lucian. Marcus stopped just before him, his face now within inches of Lucian's own.

"Do you understand all this I'm telling you?"

One more time, Lucian bowed his head and gave a slight nod. Then he kept his head bowed, as a slave should.

"I said, do you understand me?" Marcus' face held a severe expression now, as he repeated his question. He reached out, and cupping the palm of his right hand, he lifted Lucian's chin, so that he had to look at him.

Lucian now stared directly into those wine-dark eyes. "I understand you, master," he said, softly. "Everything shall be done and exactly as you ask. I promise."

"Do you have any questions for me?" Now there was a speculative look to Marcus' eyes.

Lucian had many questions, for never had anyone asked this sort of thing of him before. His other masters hadn't wanted him this close, at least not in such an intimate way, at least, if it didn't involve sexual activities that bordered on his rape. Nor had they given him any responsibility, any trust, whatsoever. Always, he'd been shackled or worn a slave's collar. Now, all this had changed, wonderfully so. But there was one thing he did have to mention.

"The other servants..." he started, hesitantly and then trailed off, not knowing how to continue.

"Ah, the other servants, yes." Marcus looked slightly amused. "You will definitely have trouble there, my handsome Lucian. I imagine Didius, as well as the other servants, even including little Octavos, but to a lesser degree, may not be pleased with the new arrangements, your so elevated status in this household. I suspect you'll have to watch out for Didius most of all, though."

He frowned now, his eyebrows dipping into a V-shape, before adding, "I don't know how far he might go in trying to sabotage your efforts, but I have no doubt he may try. He is of the type. It is one reason I never gave him too much power over this household. Despite the extra effort and cost to me on my time, I have reserved most of the burden of running things for myself. As I think you already know, this is unusual in a Roman household. But I'm no fool. It's better I do it than someone I don't trust."

Here, he gave a soft sigh, and then said, "And I will try to smooth the path for you as much as possible, at least the beginning of it. I imagine in your journey along the road in this matter, that there will be rough times for you. Still, at least, I can set you on the right track. Send Didius to me when you leave here. I would have words with him in private. I hope this will help you in your coming tasks. But don't depend upon the effects of my lecture to him for long. People usually revert to type, slaves more so than most. Now, any more questions?"

"Just one," Lucian hastened to say. "May I ask the master why he's doing this? I don't question your right to do so," he added in a rush, for fear of offending Marcus, "but you don't even know me. Why place so much trust in me so soon? Is this a wise thing for any master to do?"

Marcus still stood very close to Lucian, his face within inches of Lucian's own. So close was he, that Lucian could feel the Roman's warm breath upon his cheeks.

"You're right," Marcus said in the quietest of voices, almost a whisper. "I don't know you. And I don't truly know if it's wise to place my trust in someone like this, under such circumstances. Somehow, I find I do trust you, though, even so. I believe you when you tell me you have my life held in a position high above your own, that you would do anything for me. I have long needed someone I could trust in this way. There has been no one in my life into whose hands I could place this burden. Now I place it into yours, trusting you to take care of these duties and me. You will not disappoint me in this, will you?" The last sounded almost as if a plea.

"I'm new to such responsibilities," Lucian whispered back. He swallowed hard, and then after another moment, he continued by saying, "but I will do everything within my power to please you and to serve you in the best way possible at all times, master."

"Indeed, I expect you will," Marcus was again silent for a

moment after he said this. His clear brown eyes seemed to search Lucian's face for a short while, as if trying to divine something there.

Then he gave another sigh, dropped his hand, and said, "Very well, my Lucian, you may go. But send Didius to me. Later, after he has seen to moving a couch into my chambers, I expect you to go there. I still have some small amount of work to do before I retire, but again, I expect you already to be there, waiting for me, because among your various duties, will also be that of undressing me, and seeing to my other personal needs. Now, you may go."

"Yes, master." It took all his will, all his strength, for Lucian to wrench himself away, to turn from Marcus, and leave the room. He so enjoyed being close to the man.

"Oh, and one more thing," Marcus called after him. Lucian stopped in his tracks and turned back to face his owner. He waited, patiently.

"Never forget you're my slave, Lucian," Marcus told him, almost harshly. "I've raised you up, but I can just as easily cast you down again, should you displease me in any way. Is that, too, clear to you?"

His face suddenly flushing, feeling his cheeks burning hotly, no doubt going a bright red in the process, Lucian managed a tiny nod. "I comprehend completely, master," he said, in a small voice. Then without waiting for further leave, he fled from the room, flustered by his own severe embarrassment and shame.

Marcus, it seemed, could be very much like the two-faced god, Janus, behaving one way, so tenderly and then so abruptly another, as a Roman master normally would. What was more, Marcus seemed to be even more mercurial in nature in some ways than even that ancient god of Rome was supposed to be.

Lucian's mind was as awhirl as he walked away. He didn't know what to think. In fact, he wasn't even sure what he was thinking with, the head on the top of his neck, or the head of his cock. That he wanted to bed Marcus, to make desperate love to him, to give his body up to be used in any way his master desired, Lucian had no doubt. That Marcus had seen this lust reflected in his eyes, Lucian, also had no doubt. Marcus wasn't a stupid man. He was observant. Lucian knew he'd watched him with a keen eye. As a successful magistrate, Lucian supposed he must be that way, so observant. Nevertheless, his feelings for the man were as a power, a power Marcus wielded over him, Marcus, the ever-observant one, could give him pleasure or pain as he chose, it seemed.

And Lucian had only just barely managed not to give in to that power in this meeting, to fully surrender to Marcus' needs, and yes, even his own desires, as well. How Lucian had wanted him at that moment, when he'd seen Marcus lying there completely naked upon the chaise, in his manly splendor, his glorious male nakedness, a golden yet vulnerable god, one so exposed, so vulnerable. It was all Lucian could do not to have fallen to his knees right then, to take hold of Marcus' massive cock, to worship it as such a thing should be worshiped, with his mouth and his entire body.

So busy was he in thinking this, he didn't even realize when he entered the kitchen. Didius was sitting at the scarred trestle table there, quietly sipping from an earthenware goblet full of red wine. He had a forlorn look about him, as if his private world had come crashing down, had somehow been shattered.

Perhaps, it has, Lucian thought, with some compassion, for he didn't like to hurt anyone.

But judging by his morose behavior, it seemed Didius, too, was not a stupid man. He must already feel big changes were in the wind, in his personal fortunes as the ruler of others in this household.

Just how exactly the man might have known this, wasn't a complete mystery to Lucian. He knew that in order to survive as the head of the house, with all the other slaves vying all the time for the same position, Didius must be intelligent, or at least crafty, or he wouldn't have lasted long at the top. Age and experience might not bring wisdom in all cases, but with Didius, Lucian suspected it had to some degree.

Therefore, he resolved to be careful about whatever he said to the man. He would say as little as possible, and when he did, he would say it carefully, but also truthfully. It wouldn't due to be caught in any lies, ones that Didius might then be able to use against him later. But the less information he gave to him, the less Didius could use such information against Lucian in the future.

So, thought Lucian. The battle begins. The struggle for the household pecking order is about to take place for real. And as trivial as that might sound to some, Lucian knew it could also mean a real matter of life and death. For in the Roman world, what little one had, even as a slave, one tended to want to keep. Sometimes, this was at any price, any cost, perhaps even murder, if necessary. And Didius looked the type to do just this, if pushed too far.

"Didius, the master wishes to see you," Lucian told him in a tone he hoped sounded properly servile.

Didius slowly raised his eyes to regard Lucian standing there before him. His stare was a cold one, seemed to pass right through Lucian as if he weren't even there.

"And why does he wish to see me?" the older man asked, quietly, but there was an angry undertone to his words even so, a subtle tension, and not even a sescuncia of servility, nothing at all.

"The master didn't confide in me the nature of what he wished to see you about," Lucian said, giving a deliberately helpless shrug of his shoulders to fortify his statement. "He just asked that I send you to him."

"Indeed, he did, did he? Well, I wonder about that. I know he has taken a liking to you, Lucian. I have seen it clearly enough in his eyes, the lust there plain to see. He looks at you, as he has never looked at any other, whether man or woman. Don't think I'm not aware of this, what it means. But you should remember something."

Here he hesitated just a moment, before adding, "Those that rise so quickly often fall just as swiftly. You would do well to remember this. Obviously, today is not my day. But then again, tomorrow or the day after may not be yours, either."

Lucian just gave a slight shake his head, a gentle negation, and then said, "I neither desire nor want what you want, Didius. I have no urge or wish to battle with you for dominance of this household. My sole intent is to survive, nothing more. I wish to take nothing from you, because I know doing this would endanger my survival in the long term.

"However," he added, "it would be better if we both agreed to declare our neutrality toward each other. We must abide by the master's wishes, true, and I will do exactly what he demands of me, even as you must. If you don't interfere with me in this, I'll attempt to do what I must in a way that doesn't see you humiliated or shamed in any way in front of the other slaves."

Here, he paused, before adding, "Didius, I will attempt to defer to you in all things I safely can. You see, I know I will not be here always, just as you imply, and you probably will be. So I don't look to offend you while I am here. Can we both not make the best of a bad situation; just see this as me passing through here for a while, but ultimately to go?"

"Perhaps, we can," Didius said, sounding thoughtful. "But it remains to be seen. I shall have to think more on this. And now," he said, as he rose heavily from the trestle table, "I must go to see what it is, the master desires." He said this last with a notable sarcasm giving an edge to his words, and a scornful look distorting his features.

Lucian watched him go without saying anything more. He knew the die had been cast. Now, it only remained to see what came up. Either they could be allies of a sort, or they would be outright enemies. He would just have to wait and see. Somehow, he suspected he would not have to wait very long. But one way or another, Lucian was determined to obey his master.

Mercurial, Marcus might be, arbitrary even, but he'd saved Lucian's life. What's more, Marcus had raised him up, almost if not quite, as an equal. And Lucian, in his heart, suddenly knew why Marcus had done this. He wanted Lucian to choose him and he wanted him to do so freely, completely on his own, and as near being an equal as possible, given the strict conditions of life in Rome, the separation of the various classes. This was what Marcus had demonstrated with his lavishing of such honors upon Lucian, that he wanted it to be by his choice, freely given and without conditions.

So having done this, Marcus was waiting for him to decide of his own free will. Even in this, there lay a possible trap. Once he gave himself to Marcus, would the man then lose interest in him? This often happened, Lucian knew. Men, as well as women, could grow bored and sometimes very quickly. They could be fickle. This was because it often was their wanting, rather than finally their having, that kept a lover's interest. For once satisfied, interest often faded.

Then where would Lucian be? Where would he be when Marcus married, as he must soon do, for he was of that age? How would Lucian end up then, even if he were still the favorite, with a jealous wife living under the same roof? To protect his master, Lucian had sworn to do, even if it meant the taking of his own life. But this didn't preclude him trying to stay alive, to survive in his own right. His life was still important to him, at least.

Still, his need to protect Marcus and survive was all he should need. In such uncertain times as existed in Rome, this was no easy matter, not for him, not for Marcus, or anyone. Even slaves knew this. They had to, if they wanted to keep living. Otherwise, their short lives would be even shorter than they already were…

Chapter 5 — A New Status

Lucian did his best to settle into his new role. As Marcus had demanded, he was there in the sleeping chamber when Marcus was ready to retire. Already naked himself, he helped undress his master, who preferred to sleep entirely naked, as well, without any undergarment to hinder him.

He made Lucian remove every single item of his clothing himself. Lucian felt sure this was to tease him and it did, terribly. To be so close to this man, to have his fingers brush against his taut skin, to trail them lightly across that treasure trail of fine golden hairs on his chest and belly, to feel the play of those solid muscles beneath his hands, did fire Lucian to an almost uncontrollable sexual heat.

How he wanted to caress that body! How he longed to move his lips over that magnificent torso and let his tongue linger on those hard nipples. But he managed to restrain himself. At times, by literally gritting his teeth, Lucian made it through his assigned tasks without trespassing into what was for him a self-imposed inviolate territory.

He didn't want to blur the line between the roles of slave and master if he could help it. Yet, being entirely nude himself, he couldn't hide his burning erection. Often his cock was in the way when he tried to do his duties so big was it, so straight did it stick out. Marcus always noticed this. Then, often, a sly grin formed on his face as he caught sight of Lucian's swollen prick.

Besides undressing and dressing Marcus, Lucian had to hold the chamber pot for him while Marcus urinated. Bent forward to make sure the golden stream of urine stayed within the confines of the pot, Lucian's face was often just inches away from Marcus' exposed cock, those wonderful balls hanging there like forbidden fruit hidden in their sac.

Moreover, there were times when he had to bathe with Marcus, so that he could lathe his master's back, rub his body all over with one of the expensive sea sponges imported from Greece Marcus owned. At such times, Lucian could barely control himself. Often, he would notice again that tiny grin, that small smile, or even a slight leer flick across Marcus' face.

That he was being teased, Lucian knew very well. That the teasing was getting ever more effective in inducing an embarrassing response in him, he also knew. Lucian constantly had to fight an erection, and often, he simply failed. It was becoming ever harder, literally and figuratively, for him to restrain himself and his straying hands, as well. Frequently, only at the last moment, he would manage to snatch his fingers away, from where they trailed lovingly across Marcus' hard body, just barely keeping them from straying into those forbidden regions. He knew Marcus noticed this, too, although he never commented on it. The man was shameless, a veritable demon from Hades.

However, Marcus was true to his word with regard to everything else. The night he'd been told of the new role he was to play, Didius had come back into the kitchen shortly later, looking white-faced, and stricken. That Marcus had spoken to him in ultimate terms seemed apparent. What he'd said exactly, was a mystery still to Lucian, but it must have involved some sort of dire threats. This seemed apparent, for Didius was subdued for days after that. In addition, he tacitly seemed to agree with Lucian's earlier proposal of a neutrality of sorts between them.

So although Didius still appeared to be the nominal head of the household still, Lucian was in fact, the true power. Nevertheless, Lucian was always careful to appear to defer to Didius when in front of the other slaves, to maintain the illusion of the man's supremacy over him.

Still, some things couldn't be hidden. Lucian didn't wear the slave's collar, for instance, while all the others did. He sported newer clothes, of the best quality. He could come and go as he pleased, and he alone dispensed money for the slaves to use to buy household items.

Often, Lucian would leave the house to do the shopping himself, or run various errands. On some occasions, he would take Didius with him. This was for more than just show. Although it looked better if Didius had a hand in these affairs, helped to bolster his position as the seeming head of the house still, Lucian also relied upon him to aid him in finding his way around Rome. Whether it was to the ironmongers, or just general shopping stalls for meat, fruits, vegetables, and bread, Didius was a big help in picking out the ones with the best prices. Although the two certainly didn't become fast friends by any means, they did seem to acquire a certain respect and cordiality for each other, an understanding.

There was one thing, however, which just couldn't be hidden from the other slaves. This was Lucian's exalted position with Marcus. Always, he seemed to be at the side of the master. From the time he came home, Lucian was always in his presence or doing something for him. The fact the two virtually slept together in the same room was blatantly obvious, as well. Rumors were rife. Snide remarks were common. Octavos even went so far sometimes as to voice such comments to Lucian himself. Obviously, the little man was jealous.

Lucian never overtly reacted to these remarks. He never lost his temper. He would simply state that as a slave he had no choice in the matter, but to do his master's bidding, even as Octavos must do. After all, they were both just slaves, weren't they?

To this, Octavos had no ready reply. What could he say? Lucian was right, of course. No matter how good things might be for Lucian right now, slaves were still just slaves. Their lives and futures turned on the whims of their masters desires. Knowing this, Octavos began to relax, to put aside his envy of Lucian.

One day, just a couple of weeks after his elevation to his new status, Marcus told him to be ready on the morrow, for

Lucian had to accompany him to the offices of none other than the mighty Sejanus himself. Although outwardly he remained calm, inwardly, Lucian was mentally quaking. Sejanus was the most powerful man in all of Rome, practically the empire. He was the head of the newly expanded Praetorian Guard, as well as sharing the Office of Prefect with none other than Emperor Tiberius, himself.

Nominally, Praetorians were supposed to protect the emperor, be his personal armed forces, bodyguard, but with the emperor away in Capri, they instead served as the real police of Rome. They carried great power. And as their commanding officer, Sejanus carried even more authority, because of this fact. He was, for all practical purposes, the embodiment of the Emperor Tiberius while he was absent from the city.

So dressed in his best clothing, his finest pair of sandals, and once they were out on the open street, Lucian walked respectfully a pace behind his master. Marcus led them up the lane, toward the peak of the Palatine Hill.

Yet with every step, Lucian's trepidation increased, his nervousness grew. Many stories flew about the city concerning the mighty Sejanus. Some said those who he summoned to see him sometimes never returned. They simply disappeared or ended up in the arena as bait for the gladiators. So Lucian was afraid, but not for himself, but for his master. He didn't know how he could save him it such a fate suddenly befell Marcus. But he knew he would have to try…somehow.

They toiled their way up the Palatine Hill. It grew ever steeper as they climbed. The streets were narrow and sometimes serpentine here, as they bent to avoid dead-ending at the vast grounds of the Imperial Palace. This street plan was not the norm. The Romans were fascinated with the idea of logically planned cities. They seemed to love using the grid pattern for laying out their towns. The results of this were apparent in places as far away from Rome as the very borders of northern Gaul.

Nevertheless, for Rome itself, it was a different matter. This city had grown organically. There had been no plan. So the Romans of today had to deal with what already existed. Rome was such an ancient city, and with such an existing labyrinth of streets and roads. One could not straighten them without demolishing huge blocks of apartments, various temples, and other public buildings. In addition, it would mean the rerouting of sewers, aqueducts, and other essentials. Not only would this be an extremely expensive proposition and difficult to do, but the Roman citizens would not take too kindly to such an upheaval, such a great inconvenience to them.

And when disturbed or angered in any way, the citizens had a propensity for rioting. One didn't mess with the mob, not without trying, at least, to consider the consequences to some degree, because those consequences could be great in violence and damage.

As they approached the Imperial grounds, the number of troops coming and going increased. In their splendid armor and bright red capes, they marched in small groups of eight, or contuberniums, as the Romans called them, up and down the streets intent on their various and unknown missions. Once, the two of them even passed by a full centuria. Intimidating with the clank-clank of their armor, the rhythmic crunching of all those sandaled feet on gravel as they marched in unison, their passage was an unnerving sound at the best of times.

With eighty men or more in this group, the noises held a new significance for Lucian, for there were so many more soldiers here, than he was ever accustomed to seeing. Anonymous in their shining helmets with red plumes, they made for a daunting display. Now Lucian could see why the very sight of them raised such fear in Rome's enemies.

When the centuria marched by them, Marcus and Lucian were forced to step to one side of the road to allow them to pass without problem. This meant flattening themselves up against the front of the building nearest them, since the road was so narrow here. The two of them had little choice in the matter, it seemed. The soldiers were not about to give way or stop for them. This much was certain to Lucian.

Finally nearing the palace proper, they made a sudden detour from what Lucian thought was to be their route.

As if sensing his unspoken question, Marcus said, "Sejanus does not work from the palace. His administration is in a new wing of the Praetorian Guard's barracks. He has had them expanded. They're quite luxurious, ostentatious, even, but he won't have anything to do with the palace itself. He is very careful of the Emperor Tiberius' feelings in this matter. He wishes to avoid angering him in any way, as in assuming too much authority for himself, such as occupying the palace. That edifice belongs to Tiberius alone. One must tread carefully when it comes to the emperor."

Lucian didn't say anything by way of a response. None seemed required.

They made it to the gate of the barracks' grounds. Here, two towering guards stopped them. In full dress uniform, they stood in front of the gateway, blocking their progress. Again, it was an impressive, if still intimidating sight.

"I know you, of course," said the slightly taller of the guards, the one on the left of the entrance. His eyes flicked over Marcus in a blatant assessment. Despite the helmet, Lucian saw the big man's face looked as hard as chiseled granite, all harsh angles, and severe planes, with gray, flinty eyes to match. He looked as if he would kill someone at a mere wrong glance. Lucian had no doubt this might be true, if the soldier felt so provoked.

"Who is this?" The guardsman asked roughly of Marcus, as he shifted his gaze to appraise Lucian. "Him, I don't recognize."

"Oh, you wouldn't. He's my new slave and my personal

attendant," Marcus said, smoothly. "This is the first time I've brought him along, Petrus." He spoke in an easy and familiar manner, as if he knew the soldier, which, since he seemed to know the man's name, must be the case.

This made Lucian wonder about Marcus' past. Just who was he? Where was he from? How had he come to such a position of relative power, such as being a magistrate? That it was an elected position, Lucian already knew. However, in Rome, no one won elections without support from other government officials, or the powerful patrician class, the nobility that ruled Rome.

Marcus must have friends, perhaps powerful friends. If he was to serve his master better, Lucian realized he must find out more about his background. This would not be easy, because he wouldn't consort with the other slaves of the household when it came to rumor. Lucian kept himself completely apart from such behavior. He never wanted to hear gossip, be a part of spreading it, or have it ever reported to Marcus that he was the subject of such gossip, although over this last, he had no control. He was certain they talked about him and not necessarily in a kind way, but Lucian could do nothing to stop that.

Still, he abstained from sitting around the kitchen table. He didn't drink wine with the others and talk about household events, as they did. And without this source of knowing what he couldn't divine by direct observation, he simply couldn't know everything. But Lucian studied and practiced to be a good observer, to learn as much as he could in this way. It was his only other option.

After submitting to a weapons check, one handled with obvious respect when it came to Marcus' person, but much more roughly and invasively handled where Lucian was concerned, including a rough squeeze of his crotch that caused him to wince, the guards allowed them to enter through the gate.

"Come along," Marcus said, sounding slightly irritable now.

"If we don't hurry, we'll be late. And Sejanus most definitely doesn't like people to be late. It puts him in a foul mood. But then, many things do."

Lucian took him at his word, and so quickened his pace to match that of Marcus' broad stride. Now, he saw Praetorian Guardsmen everywhere. They seemed intent on their missions, whatever they were, and looked like so many red ants swarming about an anthill, dressed as they were in full uniform with their ubiquitous red capes.

Passing a cohort of soldiers marching in the opposite direction, their sandals crunching noisily as usual on the graveled walk, Marcus and Lucian finally came to the steps of the headquarters of Sejanus. They mounted these marble stairs. Here, after being examined by and then moving past yet more guards stationed on either side of the entrance, they entered the main hallway, one flanked on either side by colossal Corinthian columns of red-veined marble. Inside, was even more marble. It was everywhere in evidence.

White Carrera panels of marble completely covered the walls, and tiled squares of the same marble formed the floors. Pedestals with busts of various Roman nobles lined either side of the long, wide corridor, fading away to seeming infinity in the distance. High above, an endless-seeming series of arches created a vaulted ceiling that stretched away down the hallway. Built to impress, the place did! Lucian had never seen its like before.

An endless seeming succession of brass-covered doors opened off to the left and right, as one walked down the echoing length of the corridor. Where or what they led to, Lucian couldn't say, nor did he really care. His thoughts circled around the upcoming meeting with Sejanus, too much so even to consider anything else just now.

At last, after a long walk down that grandiose corridor, they approached a doorway on the right. Yet two more of the guard stood stations outside of it, to either side, barring the entrance.

Once more, the two of them submitted to bodily searches. The dour-faced soldiers were intent only upon their task, it seemed, and nothing else. Marcus didn't even attempt any conversation with these two. Lucian feared they wouldn't have bothered to answer him if he'd made the attempt.

Finally, they were ready to enter. The soldiers pushed on each side of the gleaming brass doors. They swung open. Marcus first, followed respectfully by Lucian, stepped into a large room, also with marble-tiled floors. It was a vast room, and gaudily painted columns supported the high vaulted ceiling above. Here and there, scattered about its vast expanse, were ornately carved, wooden chests, tables, and even a few "sella," those favorite chairs of the Romans.

Lucian noticed a slave standing at attention in the far right corner of the chamber. Dressed all in white, sporting a splendid tunic, he stood ramrod straight, his face holding no expression whatsoever. It was as if he was a living statue, and he was just about as anonymous.

In the center of the room was a large table, one made of what looked to be cypress. On top of this, spread out, was what appeared to be a map drawn on a thick sheet of vellum. Just what it was a map of, Lucian couldn't say. He couldn't make out the features from where he stood. He supposed it was a map either of the city of Rome proper, or of the empire as a whole.

But this didn't command his attention for more than a moment. For there, on the far side of the table, standing next to an ivory curule, the favorite chairs of Roman senators, was the man who must be the all-powerful, the mighty Sejanus, himself.

Chapter 6 — The Great Sejanus

He appeared at first glance as a rather unassuming looking man, despite the full toga he wore, one hemmed with a red stripe. He leaned over the map, supporting himself there by having placed the palms of his hand flat upon its surface. In this position, with head bent forward, Lucian could see he was developing a pronounced and gleaming bald spot.

They hadn't been announced, yet the man glanced up as the two of them entered, apparently alerted by the opening of the great doors. Lucian suspected there was no reason for anyone to announce them. He was certain the man, who now looked at them, had fully expected their arrival and at this precise time. So who else would be here now, but the person he'd requested? Lucian knew he didn't count as a person, not when he was a slave. He figured Sejanus probably didn't even know he existed until now, for that matter.

Sejanus quickly disabused him of this notion, for after his master said, "Hail, Lucius Aelius Seianus." Sejanus responded by saying:

"Greetings, my faithful centurion," He said this in a hearty way, as if they were old friends. "You are hale and fit?" He didn't wait for an answer, but instead added, "Come, stand beside me. I wish to discuss something with you. Your slave there, is it? He may remain where he is."

So much for not knowing who I am, or more correctly, what I am, Lucian thought without humor. And this, despite his not wearing clothes obviously belonging to a slave. He remained where he was, as told to do, standing just inside the doorway. He didn't dare do otherwise.

Marcus crossed the wide space of floor separating him

from Sejanus. He moved around the table and took up a position on the right next to his superior. There, he towered over the shorter, nondescript-looking man. Sejanus seemed undeterred by this difference in their height and appearance. He casually reached up, placed one arm across Marcus' left shoulder in a gesture of familiarity.

As he did this, he said without looking at Marcus, "Look, you here, my centurion." With his free hand, he stabbed a forefinger at the bottom portion of the map. "Do you recognize this?"

Marcus looked down at the drawing for a moment without saying anything. "Yes, I do," he said after several seconds had passed. "It is the last of the new barracks, the one by the Tiber River, isn't it?"

Sejanus nodded approval, and then said, "Indeed, it is. And do you know what this means now that it's finished and fully occupied?" he looked up at Marcus as he asked this.

Marcus nodded. "It means your plan for placing the Praetorian Guard strategically throughout the city is now completed," he said.

"Indeed," acknowledged Sejanus, he glanced up at Marcus again, as if seeking approval. Then he dropped his arm from Marcus' shoulder, and once again turned his full attention to the map. "And with the soldiers now able to make regular patrols throughout Rome down there," he continued, "we shall have much less problem with the local gangs." He said this last with an obvious relish.

"Have they been of more trouble there?" Marcus asked.

"You tell me. You're a magistrate. How has it been with you of late in your district? What matters do you mostly preside over these days?"

"Ah…" Marcus murmured.

"Ah, indeed," Sejanus said, and then a slight smile played

about his thin lips, before he added, "You see? It's as I thought. Haven't you also had many cases of extortion of merchants by local gang members recently? Aren't they on the rise? Other magistrates complain they've been. The issue has become like a plague for them. They say they can hardly keep up with the workload, because of it all."

"I've had much the same problem," Marcus admitted. "But will the addition of so many soldiers to the Praetorian Guard really be of much help in this matter? May they not simply demand the same extortions from the same merchants, just in place of the gangs doing this?"

"To some degree, I suppose they will."

To Lucian, Sejanus didn't look in the least bothered by this odd admission.

"And this does not particularly bother you?" Marcus looked perturbed now, for his eyebrows had furrowed into a slight frown.

Sejanus shrugged narrow shoulders. "It is not in anyone's power to completely stop corruption in Rome, my friend. All we can do is to try to determine who commits such crimes, as well as who controls such corruption, and maybe to a lesser extent, to what degree it all flourishes. But to stamp it out entirely—that is nigh impossible.

"In any case," he added, "with so many soldiers of the Guard on the streets of Rome, the acts of violence so frequent these days should diminish. Everyone should feel generally much safer. That, in and of itself, should make the merchants and the general populace happier. And even more especially, it should please our dear friends, the noble patricians. They complain it isn't safe to move about the streets of Rome these days, that they are accosted and assaulted by the rabble, thieves, and gang members, on an almost daily basis if not accompanied by enough bodyguards.

"And after all," he continued, "we must see to it the members of the aristocracy make it to their orgies on time. The Gods forbid anything should interfere with that particular goal of theirs."

Lucian didn't miss the man's profound sarcasm here. Born of the equestrian class, Sejanus, despite his immense power granted to him by the Emperor Tiberius, would never be a member of the true aristocracy, the privileged ruling class of Rome. Even through marriage or such means, his would be only a marginal acceptance at best, although the children of such a union would fare better.

"And my part in all of this?" Marcus asked, and to Lucian, his tone made it sound as if he felt uncomfortable with the way the conversation was going.

"Two things," Sejanus said. "First, I'm extending your jurisdiction as a magistrate. I want your region to cover all the area right down to the Tiber River. In this way, you will—"

Marcus interrupted him by saying, "I'll be the magistrate for the entire area that the guards of the new barracks now patrol. Is that it?"

"I knew I picked the right man." Sejanus said, and then he smiled before adding, "You are a quick study, Marcus. Yes, I want you to have jurisdiction over this entire district as a magistrate. That way, if any matters come up for trial, any problems as with merchants or civilians in conjunction with the Guard, you will have the power to decide such cases. We need have no other magistrates involved."

Marcus was silent a long moment. Then he said, "And you will wish me to decide those cases in favor of the Praetorian Guard? Is that it?"

Sejanus shook his head. "No, not all of them, that would be much too obvious. We must consider the sensibilities of our soldiers in such matters, most certainly, try to keep them content.

Nevertheless, you must use your discretion in deciding the outcome. In such matters, it would be best, I think, if you were to consult closely with the Commander of the Barracks. He can guide you better in these matters. But on rare occasion, I have no doubt it will be necessary to throw one of our soldiers to the mob just in order to soothe and appease that rabble and to make it appear as if justice is being done. If we didn't do this, it's doubtful your reelection as a magistrate would ever happen. And we can't have that. You're too important to me."

Again, Marcus was silent. Finally, he said, "As you wish. So it shall be."

"My request doesn't bother you overly much?" Sejanus had an unconvinced look about him.

Marcus turned to face him full on. "You and you alone have raised me to my current high station. It is to you I answer and have to thank for this. You gave me my house to live in, free of a rent I could ill afford. Your making me a magistrate made it possible for me to live comfortably and with enough slaves to do my bidding. So how could any request of yours ever bother me?"

"I knew you were loyal. I knew I chose well with you, Marcus. And never fear, your advancement will not stop with just being a magistrate. Again, you're too useful to me to leave it there. But for the moment, I need to be assured any friction between the patrols and the citizens is kept within bounds, and that the Praetorian Guard is not angered too much or too often by its soldiers being found guilty. We have created a huge and powerful force at our disposal by expanding the Guard. But we don't want this great new beast to turn on us. We must be willing to placate, when necessary."

"Never fear," Marcus said in a firm voice. "I'll see to it that your will is done."

"Very good. And now," Sejanus said, "I must ask to take leave of you. My next appointment will soon arrive and I'd rather he doesn't see this particular map. He's a senator, and they seem to have some qualms about my expansion of the Guard." So saying, he gestured toward the silent slave who had been standing so faithfully, so quietly in the corner. Immediately, the man jumped to do his master's bidding. He hastened toward the table and the map laying there.

"Fare you well," Marcus told Sejanus, even as the slave began rolling up the drawing.

"And you, my centurion." With that, the powerful man turned his attention to the removal of the map, as if he'd already forgotten Marcus. Taking this as an obvious signal to leave, of his dismissal, Marcus strode toward the door. As he approached Lucian, he raised his eyebrows, as if to signify he'd just been through a particularly harsh ordeal.

Later, as they strode down the Palatine Hill together, heading down the steep street for home, and doing so at an unnaturally fast pace, Marcus asked of him, "What did you make of the meeting?"

Lucian didn't wish to answer this question. So instead, he said, "It's not my place as a slave to comment on such matters, master. In any case, I don't really understand such affairs of state."

Marcus paused in his walk to turn to Lucian, who immediately stopped, as well. Gazing at him full on, Marcus asked, "Do you really expect me to believe such an equivocation from you, Lucian? Do you take me for such a fool?"

Lucian felt himself blushing. "I—I—I" he stammered, "certainly didn't mean anything of the sort. You're my master. The last thing I would ever call you is a fool."

"Then the truth, now," Marcus insisted. "Tell me what you thought of the meeting." He began striding down the hill again. Lucian quickly followed suit, not wanting further to irritate his master by keeping him waiting.

"I'm only a clansman from a small clan," he rushed to say,

between gasps of breath, as he hurried to catch up. "But it seems to me you're being asked to compromise your commission as a magistrate, the very justice you've sworn to uphold. Doesn't this represent a grave danger for you if this is so?"

Marcus kept rapidly walking, but he gave a curt nod of his head by way of a response. "Indeed, it most certainly does," he agreed. "If for some reason things ever should go badly, and there is trouble, it's I who will be sent to the coliseum for being a corrupt judge. Sejanus knows this, too. And he knows that I know it, as well. Even so, he fully expects me to comply."

"And if you hadn't?" asked Lucian. He now walked side-by-side with Marcus, having forgotten to stay one pace behind him, as a slave should. Marcus didn't seem to notice this.

"If I didn't, then I would have been arrested on the spot on trumped up charges of treason or something, and then sentenced to death. I would have ended up as fodder for some gladiator in the arena, and probably before this day is out. So you see I had no choice but to comply."

"But he spoke of you as 'my centurion' and so sounded as if he was an old friend of yours. Isn't this the case?"

Marcus shook his head. "It isn't. A few years ago, when I was still in the legions, he raised me up to being a centurion. It was a battlefield promotion. He has never let me forget it, either. Then, I'm truly grateful.

"You see," and now he glanced at Lucian, before continuing, "I'm really nothing special. I was born a free Roman, but other than one tenuous link to a noble family through a third cousin, I'm a true nobody. If it hadn't been for Sejanus' favor, I would be living in one of those horrible apartments below the hill here. I would spend my life in filth and squalor, along with many others, always having to take my meals from the street vendors. Sejanus alone has made my present life possible."

Lucian nodded, although Marcus didn't see this, being too

busy watching the rough paving stones ahead of them as he walked. "It's only right you should be grateful," he said.

"But it's not right he asked me to be dishonest." Marcus shook his head in obvious disgust. "When he asked me to run to be elected as a magistrate, he said it was because he wanted an honest judge he could rely on. Like a simpleton, I believed him. He lavished favors on me after that, such as my house. I thought it was out of a real friendship and appreciation. I was a fool. I should've known better. Nothing in life ever comes without a price. I know that only too well now."

"You have my complete loyalty and it comes without any price."

Marcus stopped in his tracks again. Lucian did the same. Now his master turned to him, looked him square in the face, as he said, "I know that, Lucian. I know I can trust you completely. Somehow, I've known it from the very first. That's why I brought you along with me today. I needed someone I could implicitly rely upon, someone to act as a witness for me. You see, they say Sejanus never calls on people unless he wants something of them. So I suspected I might need a witness to events, just in case, for whatever good it might do, should I get in trouble for doing his bidding, should I go to trial later for some reason."

"And you figured a mere slave wouldn't attract his attention enough for him to think this the reason for bringing me." It was a statement, not a question, and said with some bitterness by Lucian.

Marcus seemed aware of this. "Lucian," he said, in an almost gentle tone of voice, one Lucian never heard him use with the other slaves, "I chose you, because I trusted you. I've just told you that. The fact you're a slave and so go less noticed was just an extra in my favor.

"But I'll be honest," he added. "I wished you along for another reason, too. I know Sejanus is aware of what I do, because he makes sure to be aware of everyone he uses in this way. But I didn't know how closely, until just today."

Lucian had a sudden insight. "You mean, because he knew I was your slave without asking, for I'm not dressed obviously as such, and don't wear the collar?"

"Exactly," Marcus said, and then he smiled a grim little smile, before adding, "And now I know he watches me very closely. He knows far more about me than I'd ever expected he would. I would put nothing past his spies. Yet, for him to know so much, means someone in the household is a spy, a paid informant, perhaps. If this is true, it's even possible Sejanus may already know I'm in love with you." Having said this, Marcus continued with their walk, as if nothing so extraordinary had ever been uttered.

Lucian followed in silence, now one full pace or more behind his master. He was too stunned to speak. He was too stunned even to really think. By the Gods! Marcus had just admitted to loving him! He, a poor slave captured from just beyond the border regions of the mighty Roman Empire? Lucian knew he was physically pleasing to many eyes, both male and female, but he'd never thought, never dreamed, and never dared hope a powerful Roman could love him.

And such a Roman! Marcus, who in Lucian's eyes was the physical embodiment of the Roman God, Apollo, actually loved him! Now what in the name of the Gods was Lucian to do about it? As a slave, what could he do? If Marcus cared for him so, then Lucian must do his bidding, be willing to be bedded by his master, if he so wanted.

Then he remembered. Marcus had given him freedom of choice in this one thing. Now more than ever, Lucian must exercise this right, because he was too confused to reach any decision right now. He must have time to think, to work through all this. Lucian must consider all the eventualities.

For instance, was Marcus telling him the truth, or was this just a ploy, a base manipulation to gain his sympathies, and so his agreement to willingly become Marcus' lover? Lucian didn't think so, but who knew for sure? Yet somehow, and as Marcus had said about him, he instinctively knew his master was telling the truth. He did love him.

But what did this entail? Would it help their situation, or endanger Marcus more? For now, as Lucian contemplated all this, he was convinced more than ever, he must consider Marcus' safety first. It was a duty he had imposed upon himself, and it must come above all others.

More importantly, he knew why he had to do this. He loved Marcus, too. He admitted this to himself now and it was as a personal epiphany for him. That he lusted for Marcus, wanted him sexually, craved his hard male body to become part of his own through the act of fucking, that most intimate of acts, Lucian had already admitted to himself. At this instant, he realized it was more, much more than just this. He loved Marcus, even as a man might love a woman.

I must do whatever I think best for him, no matter what, even if it's to my own detriment, Lucian thought, as they walked on together in an awkward silence. Now I'm not only bound by my honor to protect this man, I must also defend him above all else, because I love him.

And although this thought pleased him beyond belief, gave him a new and profound feeling about what was truly important in life, it also oddly dismayed him. Lucian realized that now, more than ever, he was truly a slave, this time, a slave to love. It would have been some consolation to him, had he known it, that his master, Marcus, was thinking exactly the same thing and at the same moment.

Chapter 7 — A Frank Discussion

When they reached Marcus' house, his master paused before opening the heavy gate. He turned to Lucian. "I know what I said on our walk here may have surprised you," he said in a tender-sounding tone of voice, "and I know you need time to think about it, adjust to it. As I also need time to think, but about other matters. What I said to you, I haven't changed my mind about. But with regard to Sejanus, there is much for me to consider there."

Lucian merely nodded, not trusting himself to speak.

"So I'll need some time alone," Marcus added, almost as an afterthought. "I'll leave you to your own devices for the next several hours. However, I would speak with you later, after you've had time to consider. When you bring me my evening meal, will you also bring enough for yourself, as well, and stay and eat with me? This is a request, Lucian, and not a command. I just desire your company, if you're willing."

"Of course, master, I will." Lucian had no hesitation about answering in this way. Marcus was right. Although, he didn't need time to think for himself, he could see Marcus was troubled. So he could wait, give the man time to consider his problems with Sejanus. Being invited to share a meal with Marcus, as if he were a true equal, to discuss things with him in private, was a chance Lucian couldn't pass up. The fact Marcus had also couched it as a request and not a command, pleased him a great deal.

"I would be honored," he added.

"Good," Marcus said. He touched Lucian briefly on one shoulder, a light, but affectionate gesture, before he opened the gate and entered the vestibulum. Already deep in thought, Lucian followed.

That evening, Lucian was as good as his word. He brought

his master a tray of food. It held a platter of roasted garden vegetables mixed with a small amount of browned, diced rabbit. Along with this was a bowl of marinated olives, a loaf of fresh bread, and another small bowl, this one containing pepper-spiced olive oil to drizzle over the bread. He placed the tray on a low table before the couch where Marcus reclined, waiting.

"You still intend eating with me?" Marcus asked, as he looked up at Lucian, his dark eyes seeming to watch him intently, as if afraid that Lucian might give the wrong answer, not the one he wanted.

Lucian gave a small nod, and said, "Yes, master. I will return in a moment with my own food and some wine for you."

"Hurry then, please," Marcus told him. "I'm anxious to speak with you."

"Yes, master. I'll hurry."

Lucian hurried to the cucina to retrieve his own food and a flask of red wine, along with one empty goblet. The master hadn't invited him to drink with him, so Lucian thought it best not to look too forward by bringing a goblet for himself. Picking up the tray, he placed the leaden cup upon it, and returned to Marcus. There, he placed the second tray beside the first on the low marble table.

"Sit you down," Marcus said. With a blithe wave of his hand, he gestured toward the empty couch opposite his own. "And for the duration of this conversation, please don't call me 'master.' It would only serve to get in the way at the moment, I think."

Lucian nodded and did as told, taking a seat on the lectus, or couch, on the other side of the table. He reclined on his side there, as in the Roman fashion, using an elbow to support himself, so that he had his torso slightly raised at an angle, the better to eat. Now he waited.

Marcus picked at the olives in the little bowl in a desultory fashion, but didn't eat any. It was as if he was trying to find his words.

Then he said, "You, no doubt, remember what I told you this afternoon?"

Again, Lucian nodded. "I do mas...Marcus."

"And what did you think of what I said?"

Lucian paused a moment before saying, "I was most flattered."

Marcus raised one speculative eyebrow at this statement. "Is that all?" he asked. "You have nothing more to say on the subject?"

"Only that I return your love in full measure," Lucian said, and without hesitation. "I believe I have loved you from the first moment I laid eyes upon you, Marcus. Only then, I confused it with a physical love, or lust, as some call it. Now I know it's much more. It's not only with my cock I want you, but with my heart as well. I see that now."

"You don't say this just to please me, to avoid my displeasure or any punishment?" Marcus asked him, and there was urgency in his voice, although he spoke in a low tone, one barely just above a whisper.

"I would not say such a thing to please anyone," Lucian told him, firmly. "I might say it, if only out of a real fear, but I don't fear you in this matter. I know you're a just man, wouldn't demand the truth of someone and then punish them for telling it. It's one of the reasons I think I do love you. You're an honorable man."

"In that, you may have misjudged me terribly, Lucian," Marcus said, and now he spoke with a bitterness tingeing his words.

"How can this be so?"

Marcus gave a sharp shake of his head, as if in acute

frustration, before saying, "I thought of myself as a fair and just man, too. That is, I did up until this afternoon, until I agreed to do what Sejanus demanded of me, out of fear for my life."

He shook his head, before adding, "Now I simply don't know. I have yet to face the problem of how I'll decide if I know a soldier of the Guard is guilty. However, I suspect I'll do just as Sejanus asks of me. To do otherwise would mean my death. So you see I'm only fair and just until my life is involved, and then my behavior changes decidedly for the worse."

At these words, Lucian sat upright, his food forgotten. "How can you condemn yourself for Sejanus putting you in the middle of such a terrible predicament, and without any prior warning?" he hotly asked of Marcus. "This is none of your doing, surely? And if you refused him, he would simply arrest you, have you executed. Then would he not replace you with someone more willingly do his bidding? Isn't this so?" Lucian said, pressing him.

"Yes, it's so, no doubt." It was as if Marcus were speaking to himself, for he was looking down, instead of across at Lucian. "But I'm a Roman and a former soldier," he seemed to be saying to the floor. "I was a centurion, no less; I have my honor to consider."

"Sejanus may call you his 'centurion,' but this is no longer so. You said you left the legions several years ago. That means you have no military honor in that sense you must still maintain now."

"No," and now Marcus sounded bitter again, his words biting. "I have only my personal honor, which I held even more dearly. That is, until today."

"Do you think I'll think less of you, if you do this thing?"

Marcus just looked at him with stricken eyes, but he didn't answer.

"For if this is so," Lucian continued, smoothly, "You

needn't have any worries on that score. You saved my life and you needn't have done so. You bought me, spent money to make sure I would continue to live. You brought me into your home and gave me the highest status any master could give a slave in Rome, short of freedom. How could I not consider you an honorable and fair man under such circumstances? Everything you've done, everything you've demonstrated, tells me all this is true. And you must know that nobody is a match for Sejanus and his power, not any of the patricians or senators. And in this life, we must all make compromises. Often, it's the only way we can go on living."

Now Marcus sat up, too, his meal abandoned, apparently. "You, as a slave, would know this better than anyone, I suppose," he said, but in a kind way, "what with the compromises you must've made just to stay alive. But I'm no slave, Lucian. I'm a full and free Roman citizen, born so. As such, I've been taught my honor is very important to me. And being free, I've no real reason not to exercise it to the fullest extent."

Now Lucian felt hurt. "You think because I'm a slave I have no sense of personal honor? Therein lays the difference between us, Marcus. You are free to choose, to exercise your honor as you please, and at any time. Slaves have no such choice, never do. We may have our honor, but if we try to exercise it, we most likely will end up dead soon enough. So only those slave, the ones who swallow their honor are still around today to be alive, even if only as slaves. All the others are already dead. And I can tell you, Marcus, that a dead man has no honor. He has nothing. He simply rots in the ground. That is, if he was lucky enough even to have been buried."

"A slave now lectures me on honor?" Marcus gave a humorless chuckle at this. "Are these the depths to which I've sunk, that a slave must lecture me on how I go about my duties?"

These words stung Lucian even more than Marcus' last ones had. "You asked me to speak freely, master," he reminded him.

"So now you go back to using the word 'master' again with me? How quickly we seem to revert to type, you, and me. And it's always about choice with you, Lucian, isn't it? You can never let go of that. Has my earlier declaration of love for you then no real meaning? Is your precious need for a choice the more important than my love for you?"

Lucian didn't answer immediately. He had to think and he knew he had to choose his words carefully at this point. "Your love for me means a great deal," he said. "And you give it freely and completely, I know. But you can do this without consequences, as a free man. For me, as a slave, there are always consequences."

Marcus frowned. "You think my love for you isn't real, not lasting, and I'll eventually throw you over for another? Is that it?"

"I think you believe it to be lasting," Lucian replied, carefully. "But as a master, you can freely give and then just as freely take away, if you so choose, and at any time, without repercussions. In this, I cannot meet you as an equal, not as a slave, and so I must be careful, very careful, because I've no choice in the matter."

"Choice!" Marcus shouted. His face darkened, held a suddenly thunderous look, as if a storm were about to break, lightning about to flash in his eyes. "Always with you it's about choice, your right to choose. Do you never let go of this argument? You have no real love for me, do you? You just use me for your own purposes, to gain your freedom. That's it, isn't it? You hope I'll grant you your freedom and so you play with me like this, toying with me, my love for you.

"Well, I won't have it!" he continued. "I love you, and by Jupiter's balls, I won't let you go and so my slave you will continue to be, forever, if necessary! Do you hear me? And I'll have you and without breaking my promise to you about your precious right to have a choice in the matter. See if I don't and soon!"

He paused, breathing heavily for a moment, his chest rising and falling with the effort. Then he added, in a cold voice, "Go, and summon Octavos. I want the two of you to meet me in my sleeping chamber. And be prepared, my handsome slave. For there, I will expect more of you than just empty promises! Now go. Get out of my sight! And don't return until you have Octavos with you."

Shaken by this display of fury on Marcus' part, Lucian jumped to his feet. With a curt nod of his head for a bow, he fled the room, intent upon doing his angry master's bidding.

That is just what he is, Lucian thought cynically to himself, as he went in search of Octavos, my master. It was my mistake in ever forgetting this, for allowing myself to forget. Well, I shall no more. I'm a slave. I'll remember that at all time from now on. And he is my master, no matter how much I may love them. But so help me, by the great Gods above, love him, I do! In the name of the Gods, it's like a terrible sickness from which I can't seem to recover, no matter how hard I try!

Chapter 8 — A Spectacle For Marcus

Marcus was waiting for them in the bedroom. He was stark naked, totally exposed, just standing there with legs spread slightly apart. He was magnificent in his lean nudity, tanned, a bronzed god of male lust, his chest heaving with excited breath, his cock, and balls hanging between sturdy thighs. They looked like so much forbidden and meaty fruit just dangling there, waiting for tasting, fondling, and adoring.

He wore a lascivious grin upon his face. Lucian couldn't help but feel it was an evil sort of smile, demon-like, but one that tempted, invited, made one lust. To bow down before this man, to do his absolute bidding in any way and to any extent he wanted, was a powerful compulsion for Lucian.

"Good," said Marcus when he saw them. "Now, at last, I shall have my way. Lucian, although you may have a choice when it comes to me, you don't have one when it comes to Octavos. You will fuck him as he has never been fucked before. You will fuck him raw, rip his hole until his ass drips out your cum, and you will do it all in front of me. I want to see your cock stick him deep up his hole. You understand, I want to watch as you plow his tight furrow until he cries out for mercy, begs to be allowed to cum!"

"But—"

"No!" Marcus said, in a strident but deep voice. "Say nothing more. I order you. Just do as I told you. Now," Marcus added, "you, Octavos, my so willing little sacrifice on the altar of Priapus, you will lie on your back on the bed. But before you do, I want the both of you to strip! I will have no clothing here."

Lucian was furious, but he could only comply. He had no choice. So doing as told, he jerked off his tunic, and dropped it to the floor. He hesitated a moment at that point, standing there, his chest heaving in anger.

"All of it," Marcus said in a firmly persistent voice. "All of it, so I can see you standing there naked before me, with nothing to hide behind. I want you completely vulnerable, Lucian."

Even as Lucian pulled off his subligar and undid his sandals, Octavos had already removed his clothing, was even now clambering, completely nude, onto the bed. Lucian couldn't help but focus on his hairy ass as he did this, one he was sure he'd soon be entering.

"That's better." Marcus was staring at him now, as Lucian stood there stripped, exposed, and feeling humiliated. Marcus wore a hungry, almost feral expression.

Lucian just stood there with his head bent, so he would no longer have to look at his master. This meant his gaze was at the level of the other man's crotch. Lucian couldn't help but notice Marcus' big cock was already becoming erect. It twitched and lurched upright, in swift jerks, like some serpent preparing to strike. The head of the dick peaked out of the foreskin as his prick swelled in size. The skin tautened and stretched, pulled away from that mushroom-like head. Then it was free, a massive battering ram, that could well rip Lucian's ass apart, if it so wished. That Marcus was well endowed, Lucian already knew, but even so, seeing the enormous organ again now, under these circumstances, made for an impressive and rather frightening sight, for he had no idea what was coming next.

"Get onto the bed," Marcus ordered him. "Straddle Octavos' face. Octavos, use your mouth to make Lucian hard. Lick his balls. Tongue his asshole until he squirms with pleasure.

Knowing by this point, his face must be turning a deep shade of red with his embarrassment; Lucian moved to do as ordered. Carefully, he placed one naked knee on either side of Octavos' head. Then he settled back on his haunches, resting his smooth bare ass only lightly on the chest of the little slave. Lucian could feel the lush hair their tickling his butt cheeks. His ball sac rested just on the bottom of Octavos' chin. His fat, but still-flaccid cock, lay against the man's slightly parted lips.

Octavos wasted no time. He opened his mouth and sucked in the top part of Lucian's foreskin, nibbling gently on it. Then Lucian felt the man's tongue running around the inner edge of it, delicately probing the area between the foreskin and the head of his dick. Instantly, his cock reacted as if it had a life of its own. It began to swell, to grow, the head telescoping out of the protective ring of foreskin.

Octavos became more active. He lifted his head slightly off the pillow to better engulf more of Lucian's prick. Up and down, he moved now, sucking on Lucian's rapidly emerging member. His tongue traveled the full length of the underside of it, wetting the cock with his spit.

Involuntarily, Lucian gave a low groan of deep pleasure. It had been long since he'd felt a man's mouth on his cock. He was determined to enjoy the moment. So he forced the thought of Marcus standing there behind him, avidly watching him, and no doubt stroking his own prick while doing so.

Actually, the mental image of Marcus jacking himself excited Lucian even more. Now Lucian's cock was rock hard, stuck straight out, and wavered back and forth, from side to side. Octavos leaned forward, lifting his head completely from the mattress, and sucked on Lucian's prick for all he was worth, trying from that position to take as much of the thick shaft down his throat as possible. He made gulping sounds and wet slurping noises. Octavos kept running his tongue around the underside of the cock head. He teased the glans there. This excited Lucian even more. He began to pant heavily with sexual excitement.

Lucian raised himself, so his knees took all his weight again. He leaned forward, and using his hips, pushed his throbbing member further into Octavos' mouth, even deeper down the little man's constricting throat.

- 69 -

Octavos gulped and gurgled. Then he made gagging noises. Lucian, despite his lust, pulled back slightly, in order to allow Octavos to breathe a little. But it was only for a moment, before he again shoved his prick down the man's tight, warm, and wet throat, his balls making a meaty slapping sound against the man's chin as they swung back and forth, as he fucked the man's face.

They established a rhythm. Lucian would pull his dick almost completely out of Octavos' mouth, until only the head of his cock remained just inside the lips. This allowed Octavos to take a quick breath, and then he would thrust into him again, fucking him hard. The slap-slap-slap sound of his testicles against Octavos' face came faster now, as Lucian sped up.

The sole area of concentration, Lucian's only focus, was on fucking Octavos and shoving his cock deeper into the man's mouth and down his throat. He strained to do this. Octavos was just a thing to fuck now, his lips acting as suction, mouth a hole of hot meat, throat just a warm moist tunnel in which to spill his boiling sperm.

Octavos worked with him. He raised his head each time to receive Lucian's thrust. Then he would drop it again, as Lucian withdrew. To say that Octavos was a willing accomplice to Lucian's oral rape of him was to put it mildly. Octavos was an active participant, a willing sexual slave, and happy to do everything in his power to milk Lucian of his seed, to drain him of his cum. Lucian was getting so close to doing this now, could feel his nuts squirming in their sac, the sac itself drawing up tight.

"Stop!" The word echoed through the room with its power and force. Without even thinking, Lucian ceased his actions, froze in place. He had stopped in mid-stroke, with his turgid prick buried deep into Octavos' hot mouth. As a sudden afterthought, he withdrew, pulled his cock, dripping with saliva, free of Octavos, allowing the man to breathe easier.

I have even the mind of a slave now, Lucian thought, sadly, when he'd done this. Even deep in the middle of the most primitive thing a man can do and that which gives him the most joy and pleasure in the world, the mere word of my master is enough to make me cease fucking.

But Lucian knew there was more to it than just that. As wrapped up in his own sexual pleasure as he was, never for a moment had he forgotten that Marcus was standing there right behind them, watching them, and undoubtedly pleasuring himself by stroking that massive cock of his.

And that thought had added to the thrill to what he was doing. Lucian was performing for his master, exhibiting himself in all his nakedness and sexual heat. He was performing bare-assed, fucking for him, for his Marcus, the man for whom he lusted. And that added an excitement, an extra fillip of raw sexual gratification to his act of screwing another man in the face, to be able to do it while his lover looked on, was turned on so by his lewd performance.

In his own way, he was bringing Marcus to a heated sexual conclusion, Lucian realized. He had been having sex with him, if only by proxy, through this means. He realized now this was exactly Marcus' intention. He must have thought the same thing and this was why he'd arranged this whole scenario, this coarse exhibition of Lucian fucking Octavos. It was his way of fucking Lucian by proxy, in return.

"I want you to fuck him in the ass now," Marcus said, and his words had an almost strangled quality to them, as if he could barely restrain himself from climaxing.

Again, Lucian did as told. He clambered off Octavos. And purposely turning around to face Marcus, he moved to the bottom of the bed to reposition himself between the little slave's thighs. As he moved, his spit-slick, cock wavered back-and-forth, like some cobra swaying, as if trying to mesmerize its victim before striking.

The effect was not lost on Marcus. By the light of the oil lamps, he gazed at Lucian's swollen prick. His dark eyes were glazed, and he stared with intensity, a concentration Lucian had never seen him use before. Looking as if it was an unconscious act, Marcus licked his blood-filled lips with the tip of his tongue. It was the gesture of a man hungry for sex, cock, ass, and one who was lusting to fuck and cum.

This encouraged Lucian. He made a show of turning about, exposing his own naked ass to his master, as he prepared to mount Octavos. However, his own urge to stare back at Marcus interfered with this tactic. So tall was his master, so lean, slim-hipped, and so finely muscled, it was all Lucian could not to rush over to him, fall to his knees there before that erect monster of a cock standing up so proudly, with its mushroom head bulging at the top, the whole thing sticking straight up from between Marcus' muscled thighs. How he wanted to worship that prick, to lick it, taste it, and touch the one clear drop of lubricant hanging there on the very tip of the head of it like a silvery drop of morning dew. How Lucian wanted to make love to that cock with his mouth, to suck those marvelous balls!

It took all his power to complete his turn and once again face Octavos. The man lay sprawled on the bed, waiting. His hairy chest heaved with his recent exertions. His thighs lay sprawled apart, as if waiting there like some wanton whore's legs to be grabbed and lifted, raised high so Lucian could take aim at his ass, pierce his asshole without hindrance. There was an expression of intense sexual joy on Octavos' face, a look of primal anticipation, of physical rapture.

Octavos' cock surprised Lucian, now that he saw it fully erect. For a man so small in stature, one just barely over 5 feet, he, too, was well endowed for his size. Olive-skinned and dark featured; he lay there, like some handsome demon from the underworld, waiting for Lucian to do whatever he wished with him. Again, excitement built in Lucian to a fever pitch. He climbed onto the bed once more, his bare buttocks facing toward Marcus. He crawled forward on his hands and knees until he was well between Octavos' splayed legs.

"Yes, fuck him," Marcus whispered harshly from behind him. It came across to Lucian as a low hiss of a message.

With this encouragement, and wanting to show off in front of his forbidden lover, Lucian grasped Octavos by the ankles, and lifted his legs high into the air, completely exposing the target of his unprotected ass. He slung one leg over each of his shoulders. This allowed him to move much closer to the bull's-eye of Octavos' asshole. What's more, it raised Octavos' ass even higher off the bed, made it completely vulnerable to his coming attack.

The firm cheeks were now in plain sight, the view of them unobstructed. His hairy ass crack was like a narrow crevice of debauched darkness. It was a tight canyon of warm human flesh leading to his asshole, a tight sphincter muscle waiting for forcing roughly open, for ramming by Lucian's straining cock.

"Do it!" Came the hungry command from behind him. Marcus was louder now. "Fuck him! Shove it in!"

Lucian didn't hesitate. He obeyed Marcus' command. He didn't even bother to spit into his hands and apply the saliva to his cock as a minimal lubricant. Let it burn Octavos' hole a little, let him feel the rough friction of Lucian's prick burning up him— it was all to the good. Pain was an inseparable part of man-on-man pleasure, he knew. So instead of wetting his cock, he just positioned himself carefully, lined up his cock, centered it on the man's ass crack. The fat, reddish head of his engorged penis was now ready to enter deep into Octavos' vitals.

Without waiting for any further commands, Lucian pushed forward. He jammed his hips against Octavos' tight ass, his cock pushing deep into his crevice, and on the first try roughly forcing the man's sphincter muscle to give grudging way, to reluctantly open up to Lucian.

Octavos groaned loudly at this raw and violent intrusion of his gut. It came out as a low, male groan. His face contorted, as he winced in sudden pain at the blunt penetration of his body.

Lucian had no consideration for the man's sensibilities now. He didn't care how much it hurt him. He was enthralled with his own lust, only intent on satisfying himself, his needs, to spew his hot sperm up the man's ass tunnel.

Without waiting for Octavos to adjust to the new situation, to acclimatize himself to the thick staff of hard meat now jammed deeply up his ass, Lucian began to fuck him. He went slowly at first. He would withdraw almost completely, until only the head of his cock remained just inside the straining ring of the man's grasping asshole.

This meant Lucian's own ass rose high into the air as he did this, his balls hanging pendulous between his firm thighs, swinging back and forth there. He knew this would give Marcus greater pleasure, to see him so. He also knew, instinctively, it would cause Marcus much pain, as well, since he couldn't touch Lucian's butt without breaking his promise, couldn't fuck his ass, as he so wanted to do.

For once, I'm totally in charge, Lucian thought. Then the realization came to him that this was how women must feel, even prostitutes, when they had their men in these circumstances. For a little time, at least, they had complete control of them through their cock, their lust, even if it was only short-lived, until the man had spent himself deep within her.

So, Lucian thought, I'm in the same predicament as a woman. Well, then, I'll do what they do in such situations and use it to my advantage. A show he wants, a show he'll get. I'll make him want more!

Now he increased his tempo, speeding up his strokes, slamming himself into Octavos, grinding his hips up tight against that hirsute ass of the little man, as if he wanted to physically meld with those butt cheeks, become one with them. His thighs and ass muscles tensed with the effort of driving his slick prick forward, deep into the little man's stretched hole. Repeatedly, he plunged into Octavos, fucking his gut, raping his hairy hole.

Yes! Marcos is having a good show here, Lucian thought, even as he continued fucking away at Octavos, faster now. But not a thought did he give to the little man. It was as if he was just a piece of meat, hot flesh wrapped tight about the pole of his swollen cock, only a means to a sexual end, a vessel to be used to contain Lucian's erupting sperm, something to spend his pent-up lust upon.

The steady, slap-slap-slap of his hips and thighs against Octavos' flexing ass increased in tempo and loudness even more now, and Lucian, in an almost feral frenzy, fucked away at poor Octavos. The man beneath him grunted loudly with each hard thrust. His body rocked continuously. He gasped constantly without letup, as he struggled to absorb the foreign monster invading his belly, the impact of huge cock in asshole.

Lucian hunched further over him, pulled him up higher by his ankles so he could raise his ass even more, and so could shove into Octavos even more deeply. His muscled, smooth belly slammed against Octavos' flat hairy one and Lucian could feel the man's cock, now so rock hard, squeezing between the two of their stomachs with each such impact.

Octavos began to moan in a grossly lewd pleasure. The sound carried even above the vulgar fucking noise, the suction sounds made by Lucian's cock pistoning up the little man's butt, reaming out his very vitals.

This new sound of Octavos took Lucian aback for a moment. Was the man really going to manage to cum just by the rubbing of his cock between their two bellies? He sounded like it would. Then, grimly, Lucian realized this was probably the only way the man was usually allowed to cum. He was sure Marcus hadn't given any thought to Octavos' pleasure, but only his own, when fucking him. Octavos, it seemed, had learned to derive his sexual sensations from the repeated meeting of belly slapping against belly, as a massage to his prick, a form of masturbation that allowed him to climax.

Very well, then, Lucian would see to it that Octavos enjoyed this fuck to the hilt, literally, as he slammed his cock into him balls deep. He pressed close to the man, ground his belly against his and his trapped cock there with each forward push, their sweat mingling there, acting as lubricant for Octavos' prick.

Lucian knew his own balls had drawn up tight in their sac now, were hard as rocks, as he came closer to exploding his sperm. He wriggled his ass some, as he ground away at Octavos. This gave Lucian even more pleasure, more excitement, as it caused his cock to twist and turn, to bang in the walls of Octavos' rectum. Lucian felt it just might be exciting to Marcus, as well, because he could hear the loud slapping sound of the man flailing away at his own cock with his fist. Lucian could just visualize Marcus' straining fist, pumping up and down his great piece of hardened meat.

He pressed his belly tighter, closer, and ground harder against Octavos' stomach, rubbing them together, feeling the man's sweat-wet hair there against his own smooth, but also perspiring skin. Lucian was determined to make the little man cum. He buried his head in the hollow of the man's neck, where he could hear Octavos grunting, groaning, positively moaning like a bitch in sodden heat, and even making little mewling noises with sheer animal pleasure. Octavos sobbed with apparent enjoyment. Lucian turned his head slightly, nibbled at Octavos' left ear, and then drove his hot tongue into it, probing.

This threw Octavos into an absolute frenzy. He became spastic, twitching, and jerking. Lucian knew he was about to cum. Distantly, as if from another room, he heard Marcus moaning, as well, the deep guttural groans of man fast approaching a powerful climax. Lucian's own breath, too, was coming in heated short gasps, sounded loud in his ears.

The moment approached. Lucian could feel the base of his shaft swell with the coming eruption of his sperm He felt the cum churning in his balls there, wanting release. Now he groaned, and pushed wildly, repeatedly into the little man, fucking him as hard as could, impaling him on his prick, shoving his cock as far up the man's asshole as he could, straining with his hips so he could thrust as deep as he could with his prick into the man's hot, moist, and tightly grasping gut. The asshole felt like a living glove now, massaging and kneading his cock.

Then, as his toes curled with the intense wave of physical pleasure that now engulfed him, the pure sexual ecstasy that rolled over him, he slammed once more deep into Octavos, as if trying to split the man's hairy ass cheeks apart, rip his asshole asunder, disembowel his with his prick.

Octavos gave a throaty groan, half with release of his breath from the force of the impact, and half from pure satisfaction. He turned his face sideways, licked swollen lips, as his cock shot its load. Boiling sticky cum burst from the head of his trapped cock, spurted onto his belly, coating Lucian's stomach, as well, as he continued to fuck away. Spurt after spurt of pearly hot cum jetted from Octavos onto their sweat-slicked bellies.

This was the final straw. It was all Lucian needed. He thrust in once more, penetrating as deeply as he could into Octavos. His sperm rocketed up his shaft. Then the head of his cock erupted cum. He ejaculated his sperm, felt it shoot out of his prick, shoot high into Octavos' bowels. Wave after wave of physical relief, a pure fucking joy washed over him, drowned him in its incredible power.

Still, Lucian would partially withdraw and then thrust again, and again, and each time more of his seed spurted forth, spilled inside, and filled Octavos' ass and gut. With each gush, Lucian felt another wave of indescribable delight, even as he felt some of his cum dribbling out of Octavos' asshole, lubricating, and dripping out around his swollen cock.

Behind him, he heard Marcus give a loud groan, as if in great pain. He heard the rapid and repeated sounds of his fist fucking his own prick. Marcus groaned again, more loudly still, and Lucian knew he was cumming. Then, he felt a hot globule of liquid strike his back, start to flow down his spine there. Then another great gush came, and another, the thick liquid splattering hotly over his bare skin. Marcus was spilling his seed upon him, in buckets by the feel of it.

Lucian collapsed forward onto Octavos, breathing heavily, totally spent. He lay sprawled there. Octavos continued to use his sphincter muscle to gently milk the last of the cum from Lucian. And Lucian could feel the cooling trickle of Marcus' sperm dribbling down his back, oozing over his flesh and down the sides of his ribs.

"Thank you, Lucian," Octavos whispered into his ear. "Thank you for thinking of me, for making love to me, as no one else has ever bothered to do."

Overcome by the little man's gratitude, Lucian turned his head from where it lay still buried in the crook of Octavos' neck. Using his elbows, he lifted himself slightly. Then, tenderly, he pressed his lips to those of Octavos, kissing the man full on his mouth. He did this repeatedly and Octavos responded, opening his mouth, letting Lucian slide his tongue into it, probe his mouth and the opening to his throat. But this was not a heated kiss, but rather a languorous one, a thing of contentment, deep satisfaction, and gratitude, of afterglow.

"Enough!" Marcus exclaimed, and Lucian felt a rough hand seize one of his naked feet, as Marcus grabbed him and pulled him toward the bottom of the bed, tearing him away from Octavos and their kissing embrace, forcing his now half-limp cock to slide out of Octavos' asshole.

Lucian twisted around to face his master, who now leaned over him, still completely naked, his cock dripping the last of his pearly-white, liquid seed onto Lucian's right knee.

"Did I not do as you commanded, master?" he asked innocently, gazing up at Marcus' furious face, his flashing dark eyes, as he did so.

Marcus raised his right hand, as if he was about to slap Lucian hard across the mouth, but then he dropped it again. The arm hung listlessly at his side. "You did," he said, "and far better than I thought possible, better perhaps, than I even wanted you to. Now go, the both of you. Get out!" Although he no longer sounded angry, he did sound very tired, even defeated, to Lucian.

"Would you have me sleep somewhere else this night?" Lucian asked, as he gathered up his subligar and tunic. Again, he tried to sound as innocent as possible. He glanced pointedly at Octavos, who was out of the bed, and already hurriedly dressing himself. He seemed intent on obeying his master to the letter, to depart from his view as soon as possible.

Marcus followed his glance and then he frowned, a ghost of anger again sweeping like a dark shadow over his chiseled features. 'No," he said, thickly. "You will sleep on your couch right here, as usual, at the foot of my bed. First, bring a basin of fresh water and some cloths. I would have you clean me," he said, and looked pointedly down as his once again flaccid, but sticky member. "Only when you have seen to me, made me completely comfortable and ready for sleep, may you then clean yourself and retire...slave!"

Chapter 9 — The Morning After

As was his usual behavior, Lucian rose before daylight the next morning. He had slept only fitfully the night before. Judging by the sounds he'd heard emanating from the bed nearby, Marcus, too must have not slept well, for Lucian had heard coughing, the sounds of someone constantly shifting position, tossing and turning.

However, toward morning, exhausted, Lucian finally fell into a troubled sleep, only to arouse by force of habit just a short time later in time to take care of Marcus' morning needs.

So cleaning and dressing himself, he slipped from the bedchamber. He made his way to the cucina. There in the kitchen, he supervised the sleepy cook, as he made a fresh breakfast for Marcus. His usual morning meal, as with most Romans, was a simple bowl of hot oatmeal, with a liberal amount of olive oil mixed in with it. Added to this was a small amount of salt, spices, and diced green olives. Besides this, Lucian saw to it there were several slices of fresh bread cut. As always, the small, but ubiquitous bowl of seasoned, dark, olive oil was on the breakfast tray. Then, with the addition of a small cup of watered-down, red wine, the meal was complete.

With some considerable trepidation, because he didn't know how Marcus would react to him in the light of day, he made his way, carrying the laden tray to the triclinium. His master shouldn't have been there, but still in the cubiculum, at this time of day.

The usual custom was for Lucian to set the tray down in the dining room, and then go to the bedroom. There, Lucian would help Marcus to rise, since he seemed to love having Lucian bathe and dress him. This had become a usual habit with Marcus, to make Lucian do this, and Lucian was sure it was to titillate him, make him physically want Marcus even more, as he'd have to rub a wet cloth over the man's entire body, move a sponge to places so intimate and personal on Marcus' person. Then, he had to apply oil and use the strigil. Always, Marcus would be gazing steadfastly at him all the while he did this, and with a most provocative and pointed look.

However, this time, Marcus was already up and completely dressed in tunic and toga, and waiting for him in the triclinium. He was partially reclining on a couch, waiting for his meal. Lucian murmured a soft greeting to him and set the tray before him on the low table. Then he stood at attention, waiting for further instructions or orders from Marcus.

"Leave me," was all Marcus said in a quiet voice.

Feeling thoroughly rejected, Lucian did so.

Later, having finished his meal, Marcus had Octavos summon Lucian once more.

"I should be gone all day, today," he told him in crisp, businesslike tone. "I presume you can keep yourself busy here with various tasks without my presence being needed to oversee them?"

Lucian nodded, but didn't speak. He was careful to keep his head lowered in the usual gesture of humble respect for his master.

Despite this, at the upper corner of his vision, he could just see Marcus gazing at him in silence for a long moment.

Then he said, "Good. See to it that my evening meal is prepared, waiting for me, and kept warm, mind you. I may be late. I have decided to visit the Lady Flavia Publia Nimachis today. She has repeatedly sent me invitations. Now, I've changed my mind about considering them. I think it past time I met with her."

Lucian still didn't speak. Marcus hadn't asked a question of him.

"You understand my commands?" Marcus asked him and there was now a frown upon his broad forehead.

"I do, master." Lucian said this without looking up.

Now there was a silence so long, he dared risk a quick glance to see if Marcus was even still there, although he knew he must have been, for he'd heard no sounds of movement. Yes, Marcus was still there and he was staring back at him. Lucian swiftly lowered his eyes again.

Marcus was silent for another moment, and then he finally said, "Sometimes...sometimes, I despair of you, Lucian. I wonder if it wasn't a terrible mistake saving your life and bringing you here." The last he said with an overt bitterness, an underlying tone of glumness.

Lucian still didn't speak. Again, Marcus had asked no question of him. Moreover, right now, Lucian thought it much wiser not to breach the etiquette of interactions between a slave and his master. He was sure such would only anger Marcus further. He had no desire to irritate the man. All he wanted was to love him...well, that and fuck with him.

After Marcus retreated in what was obviously a sulky departure, Lucian threw himself into his household duties as a means of trying to keep numb, to keep him from thinking. Even so, he had much on his mind and not all of it concerned Marcus directly, although he often figured prominently in Lucian's thoughts.

Yet, there was the matter of running the affairs of the house smoothly. There was also another matter. If Marcus was correct and there was a spy in the household, Lucas was determined to find out who it was.

Upon first hearing the news, he'd suspected Octavos. After all, the little man was much around Marcus, especially of late, and so would have knowledge of Marcus' activities, activities that he could report to Sejanus.

Yet, after last night, he was convinced Octavos was loyal. The look in his eyes, the slight touch of his hand against Lucian's as he was just leaving the room, a tiny parting gesture, convinced Lucian he'd no ultimate designs, that he was nobody's spy, and he was totally loyal to Marcus.

It seemed Octavos was a simple man. Those he gave himself to, he seemed quickly to fall in love with. That he loved Marcus, Lucian was sure of now. He also suspected Octavos was very fond of him, as well, for much the same reason. So Octavos was probably not the spy, or so Lucian hoped.

That left four other slaves besides him. There was Didius, nominally still head of the household, but now mostly in name only. There was the fat and often belligerent cook, Albius, who acted like an aging patrician lady. Then there were also the two slaves who did most of the housecleaning, Libo and Scipio. They were both in their very late teens, perhaps even early twenties, but pimply-faced boys, and typical in behavior for their age. It was hard to get them to do anything, and then to keep them at it, once they'd started. Lucian traditionally relied upon Didius to hold those two in line, because he found it personally just too aggravating to keep after the boys all the time himself.

The final slave in the household was the one who maintained the small garden around most of the exterior of the house, and the planted area in the open space at the center of the peristylium. His name was Capito. Possessing a malformed right leg, presumably caused by some accident to him in the past, it was all the man could do to complete his assigned tasks, relatively light as they were, for he had a pronounced limp.

Lucian suspected Marcus only kept him around out of pity and a sense of responsibility. Even so, the man did do his job well enough and Lucian could find nothing wrong with his behavior. He kept himself to himself. He did his job. He was a quiet man for all practical purposes and seemingly devoted to his work, for the plants always looks so perfectly maintained.

But this matter of a potential spy wasn't all Lucian thought about. There was also the subject of Marcus' intended visit with the Lady Flavia. Lucian didn't like the sound of that at all and he suspected this was exactly what Marcus had intended him to feel when he'd mentioned the planned visit.

Lucian wasn't stupid. He knew Marcus had done it, at least partially, as a deliberate act to make him jealous, and no doubt, also to make him worry. Marcus, it seemed, could at times be petty when thwarted in his desires and somewhat cruel, as well.

Lucian knew his behavior was out of a feeling of rejection, his having so lovingly kissed Octavos, and the painful sting such an emotion entailed for his master. This was why Marcus had done this, made an appointment to see the Lady Flavia. At least, Lucian hoped this was all there was to it. He prayed to the Gods that Marcus was not seriously considering marrying the Lady Flavia.

No slaves in the household were currently female. Lucian liked it that way. He suspected Marcus, with his predilection for men, also preferred it this way. Lucian shuddered at the very thought of a woman coming into the household. What if she married Marcus and he brought her home here as his wife? What if the two of them had children? What a terrible idea!

Would Marcus eventually fall in love with her under such circumstances and dote on the spawn of his loins, any little monsters the bitch might whelp for him? How long would Lucian manage to survive here in such a situation?

Women were very keen observers when it came to their men folk. She would learn quickly enough about how Marcus felt toward Lucian, and no doubt, vice versa. Moreover, women didn't like competitors for their husbands, especially if they were other men. She could make life very difficult and miserable for Lucian with her being the woman of the household, Marcus' wife, and him just being a measly slave. She could even end up by putting an end to him! Poison wasn't unheard of in such situations.

People said many noblewomen of Rome were adept at this, using it as the ultimate way to get around Rome's strong system of paterfamilias, where the head of house was always a dominant male. There were those who spread rumors that such clandestine behavior had even included the wife of Caesar Augustus, the Lady Livia Drusilla. Many Romans, slaves and freeborn alike, murmured that she murdered the great emperor with poisoned figs from his own tree, although nothing certain was ever discovered in this regard.

Lucian shook his head. Such thoughts were stupid. Surely, Marcus would not go to such extremes, nor would the Lady Flavia. Most likely, they'd just have him auctioned off. This was the most likely outcome of such a union, probably...

After all, almost all Roman men married eventually. It was necessary for them. Regardless, of how they might like their sex, whether they preferred hard cock to soft pussy, Roman males had to marry and produce offspring.

With the slave population being so huge throughout the empire, everyone free wanted their group to have more children, and at least maintain the current freed man versus slave ratio. Caesar Augustus, himself, had worried about this with regard to the nobility, and had passed laws favoring the birth of more children by the aristocracy. These efforts had only marginally been successful.

It was as Lucian was going about his duties, and thinking these various things, that Octavos appeared in a doorway and then diffidently approached him. With head bent and a slow step, his body language loudly proclaimed he was uncertain of his actions.

Immediately, Lucian felt sympathy for him, for he came to Lucian as if we were approaching a master instead of just another slave like himself.

"May I speak with you, Lucian?" he asked, in an almost inaudibly low voice.

Lucian was in no mood to discuss the events of last night, and truth be told, was a little embarrassed by his behavior then. He could see how Marcus might feel now. In the light of day, his actions now struck him as tawdry and unworthy.

Even so, Octavos had allowed him to use his body as he pleased, and had given him great joy. For this, Lucian was very thankful. "What is it you need?" Lucian asked him, gently.

Now Octavos raised his head slightly, dark eyes looked at him, as he said, "First, I wish to thank you for last night. You treated me as if I had needs, too, like an equal in bed. I thank you again for that." Now he gave Lucian a hesitant little smile.

Lucian grinned back, a bit out of embarrassment, and then said, "You needn't thank me. I should be thanking you, for you brought me much relief and joy. It has been a long time since I have known another person as I knew you last night."

Octavos smiled more broadly at this statement. Somehow, his slightly lopsided grin struck Lucian as being poignant, shy, so out of proportion to what he'd done for the little man.

Then Octavos said, "It brought me great joy, too, Lucian. I had some small trouble walking normally this morning, though." Then he grinned again, teeth gleaming, to show he was only joking.

"Was there something else you wanted to speak about?" Lucian prompted Octavos, when the man just continued to stand there, beaming at him.

"Oh, yes, there is. Are you planning to go to do the household shopping today?"

"I wasn't thinking to. Why do you ask?"

"Well, I just know you're new here and have only been here a short time, so I thought it might be a good idea if…if you went to do the shopping today."

Lucian noticed a curious quality to the man's voice, as if there was an underlying stress to his words. No, that wasn't it. Octavos was trying to tell him something, something more than was just put into his actual words.

"You think today would be better than some other day? Is that it?"

Octavos nodded. "I do, Lucian. It is that you may learn something interesting if you do."

Now Lucian felt slightly suspicious. "It isn't because you or some of the other slaves want me out of the way, is it?" he asked, sharply.

"Oh, no." Octavos shook his head vigorously in denial. "I would never treat you that way, Lucian."

So earnest did he sound, Lucian felt regret at having even asked the question. "All right, I will take your advice and go today," he said, relenting. "I would have had to tomorrow in any case, so why not just make it a day sooner?" He gave Octavos another, briefer smile. "Does that satisfy you?"

Octavos nodded at him. Then, he said, "It does, friend Lucian."

So shortly later, having taken the little slave's odd advice, Lucian set forth down the street, heading for the main part of the city, the forum. As he walked, he pondered what Octavos had said to him, and what it might really mean. That the little man had meant more than was stated was now obvious to Lucian. In addition, he had no real belief that anything was going on behind his back while he was gone, at least not as far as Octavos was personally concerned. He had fully believed the man when he said he would not behave so. So that left the question as to just what this was all about.

Chapter 10 — A Discovery

Lucian was soon to discover the answer. He went to various, but specific stalls to purchase items. Octavos had strongly recommended them to him before he'd left the house. He had no sooner finished buying wheat grain, a fresh stock out of which the cook and his helper would make bread, then the proprietor of the stall handed him a small sack with coins in it. Lucian raised his eyebrows questioningly at this.

He looked in the bag, surprised at the amount of money there. "You've given me the incorrect amount," he said, glancing from the contents of the sack to the heavyset proprietor.

Now the man had a distinctly worried look. "It's not enough?" he asked, sounding suddenly anxious. "It always was so with Didius, and our arrangement has worked well for a long time this way. Isn't this the arrangement you wish to continue with me?"

Now Lucian knew what he was dealing with. This was a kickback. Apparently, Didius had arranged for periodic payments in return for trading solely with these particular merchants.

"No, indeed, this is perfectly fine," he assured the merchant. "I was mistaken and just a little surprised at how prompt you were with your payment. I'd assumed, as with so many others that I'd have to pressure you for it, since I'm not Didius."

"No need to worry on that score," the baldheaded merchant told him. "I always try to do promptly and right by them that do right by me, no matter who it is."

Lucian nodded his thanks, accepted the money, and continued on his way. He was less surprised now when the other merchants did the same thing, each one handing him a small bag of coins. Although they only contained a few denarii each and this could well serve as the whole of a quarterly or even annual payment, still, over time, the amount would come to a considerable sum.

But what would a slave like Didius do with so much money? Of course, the answer was more than obvious. He no doubt, wished to eventually purchase his freedom, perhaps even have money in reserve for when this happened. What else was there for a slave to use money for?

But perhaps he hadn't tried to accumulate money after all, but instead had just used it to pay for whores, gambling, and drinking in the various tavernas. After all, Marcus was gone all day. Didius could accomplish much on his own in such constant absences, if he'd a mind to do so.

Much later, Lucian arrived back at the house, but he didn't seek out Didius. Instead, he went to look for Octavos. He found him in the peristylium, tending the little garden in the center of the house. He was busily picking faded blooms off the rose bush there and stuffing them into a cloth satchel that he'd slung over his shoulder for the purpose. He looked up at the sound of Lucian's approach.

"Welcome back," he said, standing up. He brushed his hands on his tunic as he spoke, leaving a smear of dirt there.

Lucian stopped at the edge of the garden, and smiled a greeting, before saying, "Hail Octavos. I see you help with the plants. Is the garden so out of control, then?"

"Oh, no. It's just that I like to help. I enjoy being with the plants and feeling the sun on me while I work. I hope that's all right?" he asked, sounding abruptly worried. The expression on his face mirrored his tone.

Lucian waved his right hand in a casually dismissive gesture. "I have no concerns as to how you keep busy, Octavos. I'm just glad to see that you do. And I want to thank you for your advice this morning. It turns out it was invaluable. It has taught me much. And I would like to give you something for your efforts." He approached Octavos, holding out one of the small bags of money for the man to take.

Octavos shook his head. "Thank you, Lucian, but I have no use for such, being only a slave."

"You are no more or any less a slave than the rest of us here, including me," Lucian reminded him. "I intend you should have some every time I collect it. By the way, how often is that?"

"Every month at this time," Octavos said.

Lucian whistled. "That often?" he said, knowing he must look surprised. "That much? I'd no idea such practices were so lucrative in nature."

"Didius is masterful in his negotiations," Octavos said, and then he grinned, before saying. "I imagine it bothers him greatly he could not do his rounds today."

This thought concerned Lucian. "Do you think he suspects I've taken the money in his place?"

Octavos gave a shrug of his shoulders, before saying, "He may suspect, but what can he do about it? He's between two dangerous gladiators in that respect. To say anything to you would be admitting to what he's been doing, which is practically stealing from the master. And if he's wrong, and it turns out you know nothing about it at all, he must then assume you would report him to Marcus for doing such a thing."

Lucian shook his head. "No, please don't tell him, but I wouldn't betray another slave. Never would I, unless it was under extreme conditions, only if he committed some truly heinous crime. I would put a stop to such a thing, but never would I get another one of us in trouble if I could help it."

"No, you wouldn't, Lucian. I know that. But Didius would not know this, and he would assume otherwise, because it's something he, himself, would do, especially if he thought it would win him favor with the master. That's his nature. Didius wants to get ahead. And sometimes, I think at any cost."

Now Lucian slowly nodded his agreement. "I suspect you may be right," he told Octavos. "Are you sure you won't take the money. It's a reasonable payment and one the master would surely consider just, for you will be saving him much money, now and in the future, because of this. You could even eventually buy your freedom with what you save up, perhaps?"

Now Octavos shook his head, very firmly. "I've no wish to buy freedom. Where would I go? What would I do? I'm a small man in a big man's world, and I'm physically no match for most. I doubt if I would survive out there. In any case, I don't want to try. I'm happy here with Marcus, as my master and sometimes lover."

Lucian thought about this a moment. "Does my being here bother you?" he asked. "I think you know Marcus desires me."

"I do. But that doesn't bother me. Why should it? For one thing, Lucian, you're a good man and a most handsome one. The master deserves such as you, someone equal to him in these respects. And I want only what the master wants. I would have his every desire fulfilled, to see him happy."

A realization struck Lucian like a thunderbolt. "You truly love him," he said practically as an accusation. "Don't you?"

Octavos gave a small nod and then just stared down at his feet, as if inspecting the condition of his toes there.

"I do," he said, finally, and in a small voice. "And as such, I'm grateful for his favors to me. More importantly, it's my desire he has everything he wants, and more, if he chooses. You believe me?" Now he looked up at Lucian again.

Lucian considered this for only a second, before saying "I do. I do, Octavos. And if it would be all right, I would like to count you as a friend. Would this be to your liking?"

Octavos gave him another broad smile. "I would," he said,

simply. "I would like that very much."

"Then consider us friends," Lucian said, and then he, too, grinned. He was about to leave when a thought struck him. "Octavos, would you do me a favor?" he asked.

"Most certainly, Lucian. How may I help you?"

"Will you not mention my having gone to do the shopping today to Didius? I think it might be better to leave him in the dark on such matters in the future. Let him wonder. Will you do this for me?"

Octavos pursed his lips, and there was a slight squint to his eyes, as if he were thinking, but he did this only for a fraction of a second, before saying, "You wish to keep Didius off balance? Is that it? If so, it's a good thing, I think. For a long time now, he has been far too sure in himself, too complacent in his power. Yes, let him wonder. Of course, I will do as you ask and say nothing, not now and not ever, unless you tell me to do otherwise. I'll put away the supplies before he sees them."

Another thought occurred to Lucian. "You haven't asked what I intend to do with the money."

"It's none of my concern. I know how you feel about Marcos. It shows well enough in your eyes. You will do what's best with the money."

Lucian only nodded to this, said nothing. He was too overcome by the man's trust in him to say more. Lifting one hand in a casual farewell, he left the garden. Just before entering the house proper again, he passed the limping Capito. When the man gave him a small smile and said hello, Lucian politely responded to the crippled man, but he didn't stop to converse with him, as he usually made a point of doing, for he'd other matters on his mind.

Later, with the white-hazy heat of the mid-summer Roman afternoon beating down upon the tiled roof of the house and heating all within it, including the occupants, Lucian retired to the relative coolness of Marcus' cubiculum, there to recline upon his couch for a while, to think.

Soon, in the early evening, he would take exercise, as he always did. To stay in shape was important to him. This was not just out of vanity, so much as necessity. The slave's life was a hard one. One was at their best when they were young and in good physical form. Lucian knew he wouldn't always be young, but he did do his best to stay in shape.

Nevertheless, for now, with the drowsy warmth filling the confines of Marcus' house, it was time for the afternoon siesta, for those allowed. It was the Roman way to retire from the worst heat of the day. Nevertheless, Lucian didn't sleep. Instead, he lay on his side, supported by his elbow, occasionally reaching for his cup of wine. As he held the piece of pottery in his hand, felt its coolness, he considered all that had taken place during the last twenty-four hours.

First had been the meeting with Sejanus and all that this had entailed. Thoughts of this alone were enough to fill any person's day. Then, there had been the open declaration of love for him by Marcus. That had come as a great shock, as well, a terrific surprise, but a good one, in truth. Lucian knew the man had lusted for him, but he hadn't suspected him of loving him, as well.

Still, there was even more to think about. Later on, he'd also seen how when Marcus was thwarted, how he could so cruelly behave when he was made angry. Suddenly, he'd been no longer the tender, caring lover anymore, but rather the stern, and yes, even furious master. How quickly he'd reminded Lucian he was just a slave and nothing more.

Of course, Lucian knew this behavior had been out of intense pain, out of Marcus having felt rejected. Lucian hadn't handled the last night very well, teasing him like that by kissing Octavos so, and so may have deserved some of what he'd gotten in return this morning. However, he also hadn't taken Marcus' words too much to heart either. One often said things they didn't mean when angry.

Nevertheless, this did remind him of his true status, did press home Lucian's position in the household. He was a slave. That was true enough, still. He should never allow himself to forget this. And if Marcus should ever marry, then Lucian's future would very much be in doubt in this household. That was also true enough.

And there was one other thing for him to consider as well; he also had to figure out what to do with the money, the sum which he'd acquired today, as well as the money he'd be acquiring more of for every month from now on. This was a real quandary for Lucian, because if he brought it to Marcus, then there was no way Didius would avoid getting into terrible trouble. Marcus would want to know where the money came from, and when he learned how, Marcus might very well have Didius badly flogged, auctioned off, or even both.

That Didius had committed a major crime by persistently stealing from his master by such underhanded means was obvious. Even if it wasn't an unusual thing in Rome, it was a dangerous practice for the perpetrator. No, telling Marcus, at least at this point, was not an option, not unless Lucian wished to see the probable end of Didius. This he didn't want for a variety of reasons. Lucian wanted the loyalty here of his fellow slaves. As the nominal head of the household and so of them, Lucian also needed to protect them as best he could.

He also was aware now of how Marcus could be capricious. The man was capable of cruel acts, although he probably genuinely would regret any such behavior later on, but by then it would be too late. Didius would be gone or dead. The other slaves' trust in him would be ruined for having been the informer.

There was another thing. Lucian didn't yet know who the spy in the household was, whom it was who reported to Sejanus. Any major upset in the household would undoubtedly force the spy into hiding and so it would be all the harder to find him. No, it was definitely best if things just stayed on an even keel, stayed as they were for a while more yet.

So what was he, Lucian, to do with the money? The question remained. There was really nothing he could do, he knew, other than to hide the money for safekeeping, at least for the present. At some future date, under a different set of circumstances, he could return the money to Marcus, its rightful owner.

It never even crossed Lucian's mind to keep the money for himself. Such was not in his nature. Even though the money might've meant he someday would be able to purchase his freedom, Lucian would simply never consider such a thing.

He owed a debt to Marcus. He fully intended to pay it in kind, and not in coin. He reflected this probably made him a poor slave, as far as other slaves were concerned, because he didn't put his own freedom above that of his loyalty to his master. Yet, he knew this was a common phenomenon, more so than one might have thought. Many slaves maintained a fierce loyalty for the houses they served.

So a slave he was, and probably a slave he was destined to remain for the time being, at least. Now all that remained was to find a safe place to hide the money. His relationship with Marcus he could deal with later. But where? Where in the house could he secrete the coins? Marcus' home was a place where slaves were free to roam about all the time. Where was there a secure spot to conceal the coins without chance of their discovery by accident, or by someone suspecting their existence and actively searching for them?

He would have to think hard on this matter, and quickly, for he wanted the coins well hidden before Marcus came home. He didn't want any untimely discoveries by him, and certainly didn't want to be responsible for the whipping of Didius, should Marcus find the money, although he suspected Didius richly deserved any such fate and not only for this, but much else, as well.

Marcus came home in the evening in a subdued mood. Gone was the anger and coldness of the morning, and of the previous night. Now, he just seemed…deflated was the only way Lucian could think of to describe it.

"I wish you to eat with me again tonight," Marcus told him, without any preamble. "I wish you to do this every night from now on. Do you have any objections? Again, this isn't meant as a command but as a personal request."

Lucian didn't hesitate, before saying, "I would be most honored to do so, master." Then, because Marcus was in such a subdued mood, he dared to ask, "May I ask, master, are you still angry with me?"

Marcus' dark brown eyes regarded him with a serious look for a moment. Then he gave the slightest shake of his head. "No," he said, and then sighed. "I'm not, Lucian. I'm angry with myself, if anything. I'm angry for losing control, for being jealous after I ordered you to fuck Octavos. I'm also angry for making you do something you wouldn't have ordinarily done. I'm annoyed, of course, you chose so lovingly to kiss the man afterwards, as if it were true lovemaking, but I guess I had that coming. Although," he added, "my purpose wasn't so much to humiliate you, as it was just to be able to be near you in that particular way, and without breaking my word to you.

"Still," he added, "my behavior was base. It was unworthy of me and grossly unfair to you. I swear to you I will not behave in such a way again. Oh, I might fly into a rage, I might throw things about, but I promise you, I will never treat you as a common slave again. Do you believe me in this?"

Lucian smiled. "Oh, yes, master, I do. And I believe you will throw things about, too. Yesterday, I felt certain you were going to aim a vase, a statuette, or something else at me."

"So you were ready to duck?" Marcus asked, and then he smiled. "I would not harm you in such a way, Lucian," he said, more softly. "Not ever. I hope you know that."

Lucian bowed his head in a sign of acquiescence. "I do," was all he said by way of a response, but his tone was a sincere one.

"And Octavos, you harbor no ill will towards him for last night?" Marcus looked concerned now. "You understand he'd no say in the matter."

Lucian shook his head, a casual gesture. "On the contrary, master. Octavos and I are now fast friends. We have decided this, just this morning."

Marcus gave a little frown. "Well, I'm not sure I quite like that. I hope you're not very close. I mean, I know the day has not yet come for the two of us to be together in the way you were with Octavos last night, but I hope you'll try to save yourself for that time, when it finally does come, even as I would hope to do so, as well. I want it to be special."

"You seem very certain the day will come," Lucian said. Then he smiled to take the sting out of his words. "But if it pleases you, I have no problem with repeating last night's events. I enjoyed it. I particularly enjoyed you watching me, and cumming all over me. You were perilously close to breaking the letter of your word at that point." Again, he grinned.

Marcus smiled back. Then he said, "I'll leave you for now. I think I'll lie down in my cubiculum for a short while. It's been a long and especially tiring day."

"And a hot one. Are you unwell from the heat, master?"

Marcus shook his head, an abrupt gesture. "Not unwell, just a bit tired. I will see you in a little while?"

Lucian wasn't going to leave it at this. Instead, he reached for and gently pulled several scrolls out of Marcus' grasp. "I will see you made comfortable, first," he said, softly, as he laid the documents on the table.

He led the way to Marcus' bedchamber. And there in the cubiculum, he helped Marcus to undress. He was wearing the ceremonial toga of his Office of Magistrate, and Lucian removed the item with care. After Lucian has carefully disposed of this, he helped Marcus out of his subligar, the small white loincloth most Romans wore as an undergarment.

He offered the now-naked Marcus a cup of water-diluted wine. Although Roman water was clean by the standards of the day, most people took the added precaution of adding some wine to it, to help sterilize it better. No one wanted a case of dysentery, fever, or some other waterborne malaise that could result in severe illness, or even death. The only other alternative was to drink ale, but this was not a favorite of Marcus' for he found it too bitter.

Now having been refreshed, and lying down in a shady and reasonably cool room, Marcus seemed content. Lucian quietly withdrew to leave him in peace. He, too, was content. Marcus was over his anger. Lucian had managed to hide the money, and in a place, he hoped no one would ever think to look.

He had chosen a loose tile under Marcus' bed. It had required shifting that piece of furniture. By himself, it was no small task for it was a heavy item. However, he managed the task well enough. And having discovering a floor tile not very well set, he'd used a kitchen knife to chisel about it more. Lifting the piece of stone out, he laid the bag of silver in the little hole he'd made there in the substrate of mortar. Then he carefully replaced the floor tile and moved the bed back into position. He hoped this would suffice. It really had to, because Lucian could think of no other location to put the money. Really, the garden wasn't a reliable choice, since Capito might accidentally dig it up at any time. Their meal together that evening was a quiet one. Marcus definitely seemed subdued. Lucian wanted to know what the problem might be, but since Marcus seemed so intent on not speaking of it, Lucian didn't wish to pry. Marcus did seem happy, at least, to be with him again. This was the same for Lucian with regard to his master. He enjoyed just being near him.

If there were other pressing problems, they could wait at least a bit. So they spoke only of unimportant matters as they ate. Marcus didn't seem particularly hungry, though. He barely sampled the roast lamb, and ate only a small portion of the vegetables, ones treated with cloves of garlic, and olives baked into them. The whole meal had been seasoned with a spicy herb, one brought all the way from India, the spice merchant had told Lucian. It was a bit on the fiery side, so had been used sparingly.

Lucian fared better with his meal. Although not ravenous, he'd been busy all day. Between his long hike around the streets of Rome, doing the shopping, and shifting the bed about, along with his other usual household tasks, he'd worked up something of an appetite.

Marcus watched him eat, openly smiling at times. "Your hunger seems unaffected by my behavior," he said.

Lucian nodded, hurriedly swallowed a mouthful of lamb, sipped from his glass of sweet red wine to clear his throat, and then said, "My appetite is seldom affected. It takes more than my lover throwing a tantrum to reduce it." He grinned after saying this.

Marcus smiled back, showing even white teeth, not a common thing in the Roman world. "Ah, I wish it could always be like this, Lucian. How good it is to come home to this house, to you, and the comforts you so carefully provide me. It's a haven in an uncertain world."

This statement concerned Lucian. It reminded him of why Marcus had been late. "How did your afternoon go with the Lady Flavia?" he asked, trying to make it sound as just a casual question.

Apparently, his attempt at nonchalance didn't work, for

Marcus gave a small and rueful shake of his head. "I expect better of you, Lucian. Surely, you can be more subtle than that? And I'm betting you know full well I would not really have gone to see the Lady Flavia. In my anger, yes, I did send Octavos there with a message early this morning, saying I would like to see her this afternoon. But I sent another message by courier, begged off shortly afterwards, pleading the press of an unusual amount of work."

"You sent Octavos to do this today?" Lucian frowned at this. "I met him in the garden early this morning. He said nothing of having already gone out."

Marcus gave a shrug of his shoulders. "Octavos is very loyal to me. I think he actually loves me, for he is excessively faithful. He wouldn't divulge such to you under the circumstances."

"And how do you feel about Octavos?" What Marcus had just said had done nothing to make Lucian's frown go away. "Do you...love him?" he asked, ingenuously.

Marcus gave a small laugh. "Now who is the jealous one? Yes, I'm very fond of Octavos, and I suppose I do love him, but not in that way. He makes for a loyal bed partner and friend, and does everything he can to please me in both regards. For that, I'm grateful. But love, as in the sense that I have it for you, as in with wanting to be with you solely and no other, and to spend my life with just you, no, I don't love him that way."

"You wish to spend your life with me?" Lucian was taken aback. Was this just the first rush of love talking? Or did Marcus really care for him in such a deep way? At this stage of things, Lucian had no way of really knowing. He could only hope it wasn't just Marcus' lust talking, but actually his heart.

He decided to change the subject. "Will not the Lady Flavia be annoyed at you for not keeping your own appointment?"

Again, Marcus shrugged, and then he smiled, before saying, "You know, I really don't care. Although I'm no patrician, there has been no shortage of young women thrust at me for my inspection and approval as possible marriage partners. Being a magistrate, apparently makes me much wanted. It is either that, or perhaps my connection with Sejanus they see as so attractive. You think?" he gave Lucian a mischievous wink.

"Perhaps, master, you underestimate yourself. I don't think your connection with Sejanus is what they look to in this matter. You are an exceedingly handsome man. That alone would be enough to make them want you. It did me. You certainly have won my heart easily enough."

"Have I? Have I, my Lucian? Have I truly won your heart?" His question seemed deadly serious.

Lucian gave a vigorous nod of his head, before saying, "You have, indeed, Marcus. You had it the very first time I laid eyes upon you. Oh, yes, I was very grateful you saved my life, of course. Who wouldn't be? But when I saw you standing there as some golden Apollo and my savior, the combination was irresistible. I not only wanted to fuck you, but I immediately fell in love with you, too."

"You claim the possibility of love at first sight?" Marcus sounded unconvinced.

"I wouldn't have thought it possible before," Lucian admitted. He meant that. Nothing in his life had prepared him for the idea of falling in love at first sight, that such was a real possibility, and not just a silly woman's fantasy notion. "Now I think it's entirely possible, because it's happened to me."

"And yet, you still will not bed with me?"

Lucian gave a slight shake of his head. "Not yet, if still allowed the choice," he said, in a small voice. "But I think the time may not be too far off."

Marcus gave an impatient sigh. "Well, if you love me as you say you do, then I don't understand why we must wait any longer. Why can't we be together now, completely, just the two of us?"

Again, Lucian shook his head. "I can't explain it, but somehow, it seems as if the time is not yet right, as if everything is not yet in place, not as it should be entirely."

Marcus rolled his eyes in exasperation. "Now you speak as if you're an Oracle at Delphi. Are you now a prophet, too, then?"

Lucian gave him a grin, before saying, "Nothing of the sort. But I want to come to you with nothing left unresolved between us. Can you understand that?"

"Are we speaking of choices again, now?" Marcus said in an annoyed voice.

"No, not in that way, but I want to come to you unhindered. And this means, yes, I must exercise the right to choose, the freedom of choice you have given me, for a little while longer."

Again, Marcus rolled his eyes. Then he sighed. "Well, it's of no matter what the reason is, if you're still choosing not to be with me. But I suppose I will have to live with it, since I do love you so much, and like the asshole of a politician that I am, I was stupid enough to give you the right to choose in the first place. So I deserve what I get, I suppose."

"You're most generous, master."

"By Jupiter's big balls, Lucian, you're lucky I did give you a choice, or I'd have you right here and now, on this couch." Marcus said this last in almost a growl, but there was no anger in the sound.

However, his expression took on a more somber note, as he said, "There is something I've been avoiding telling you this evening. But I suppose the time is now…" He didn't continue, but let his last sentence hang there, unsupported by any further explanation.

Chapter 11 — A Serious Matter

Immediately, Lucian was on his guard. Whatever this was about, it didn't sound at all good. "What is it?" he asked him. "I know something is disturbing you, and has, ever since you arrived home."

"I'm surprised you didn't ask me about it then," Marcus said. He arched his eyebrows at Lucian, giving him a speculative look. "Didn't you care enough to bother to?"

"Of course, I did. But you're my master, and it isn't my place to inquire of such things. But more importantly for me, I didn't want to press you. You seemed so tired and disturbed when you arrived home. I thought maybe it was about the Lady Flavia, and so personal. I felt it best to let you rest, to wait until you decided to confide in me, if you so chose."

"Ah, you wanted me to come to you, to share with you my burden, is that it?"

"Was I wrong in wanting this?" Lucian asked, giving Marcus a defiant look.

Marcus hesitated a moment, and then he shook his head, if a little tiredly. "No. I would expect the same thing of you. If you have a burden ever, I want you to bring it to me, share it with me, and for me to try to help you with it. You will do this, Lucian?"

"I will. I promise. Now, what is it that troubles you so, master?"

"I now understand why Sejanus called me to him yesterday. I thought I would have time before I had to face this whole Praetorian Guard issue. I thought he was just warning me the problem might arise sometime in the future. I didn't realize he was playing tricks with me, that fucking bastard spawn of Pluto."

Lucian sat upright. "How so?"

"You were there yesterday. You know already he extended my district clear down to the Tiber waterfront and the new barracks built near there, yes?"

"I did. And I also heard him say you might have to misuse your authority to protect the Praetorian Guard soldiers, if they should come up for trial when it came to any problems with the local merchants and shopkeepers."

"Yes, well, rather than this being a theoretical proposition just to alert me of a supposed future circumstance, it turns out it's already occurred. That's why he immediately had my district extended, so that I would have to handle it and not the original magistrate, who he hadn't placed in his position, so he wasn't Sejanus' man, if you know I mean. In other words, he couldn't be relied upon to do Sejanus' bidding."

Marcus shook his head in disgust. "He knew I would have to face this immediately, even when he spoke with me yesterday. He didn't bother to tell me then, but left it as an unpleasant surprise for me. So now, I don't know what to do, Lucian. I know one thing, I'm his creature, and he feels I must do his bidding"

Lucian didn't answer. Instead, he just sat there and thought. Marcus didn't attempt to bother him in this. It seemed he, too, was lost in his own musings.

At last, Lucian asked, "Is the case much as Sejanus outlined it might be?

"It's almost exactly like that." Marcus said this in a defeated tone of voice, "Just as he outlined it yesterday. I have been ill used in this matter," he added, resentfully.

"Indeed, you have. It seems Sejanus is no true friend of yours. This puts you in an awkward position. If you don't do as he asked, he will strip you of your title as magistrate."

"At the very least," Marcus acknowledged, glumly. "I'm sure this house would go, as well, and without any income, other than my small pension from the army, I would have to sell off all the slaves. Oh, Didius would be no real loss. He does his job well enough, I suppose, but he's a surly slave at best. I would not greatly miss him. As for the others, excepting Octavos and yourself, I would not really feel their loss."

"I'm glad I'm in there somewhere," Lucian said, dryly.

Marcus sat forward. "Oh, I didn't mean—"

"I know you didn't mean it that way. It was just my feeble attempt at humor, to lighten the mood of the situation."

"Ah, so that's what you call humor? It seems you're not so perfect after all."

Lucian laughed, but then he became serious again, as he said, "We must find a way out of this for you."

"And how do we do that?" Marcus, too, now sounded very grave. "How do we manage to satisfy the dictates of Sejanus and still satisfy the dictates of my conscience?"

"Have you sought the counsel of the Commander of the Barracks, as Sejanus suggested you should?"

"I've arranged to meet with him tomorrow. I could easily have passed sentence on the man today, but I gave the soldier a choice—I could find him guilty and sentence him immediately, or I could have a night to think it over first and then do it tomorrow. Wisely, the cretin chose the delay."

"Then I think the only approach is to try to convince the commander that finding the man guilty would be in the best interests of everyone. Oh," he hastily added, when it seemed as if Marcus was about to interrupt him, "Don't let him think you'll always decide this way. But just in this instance, try to convince him it might be better for the soldier to be found guilty. This would then serve as an object lesson to his other men not to engage in such extortion methods. Stress the fact it will help him to control his troops in the future, enforce discipline amongst them better. Having once been a soldier yourself, he may listen to you in this."

Marcus stood up abruptly. "Lucian, you're gifted by the Gods with genius. I know the commander, and I believe he's an honorable man. If approached correctly, he'll indeed see this as an opportunity to instill discipline in his men. It's perfect as a case to set a precedent. I'm sure he will go for it. At least, I think he may," he added, just a little uncertainly.

Lucian also stood up. "I'm glad to be of help, master," he said, "but what of Sejanus? Will he think you've betrayed his trust in you if you do this?"

"No, I'll see to it that he doesn't. I'll send a full report to him on the matter. I'll tell him I took his good advice and sought out the counsel of the commander, and it was his wish to have it this way, as well. That should remove any problems in the making."

Marcus paused and then continued, by saying, "You've lifted a great weight from my shoulders, Lucian. You deserve a reward. What shall it be? Remember now," he warned him, "I'm not a rich man, so please keep your demands within sight of this fact."

"If I may have my demand, then it's that I can give you a ball massage now. I think you're much in need of one. And I can think of nothing I would rather do."

"So you, too, have your own ways of getting around this matter of choice and still being close." Marcus gave him an evil grin and added, "Again, I must tell you, Lucian, that the Gods have not only gifted you with a handsome face, a wonderfully hard body, but a mind that is to be reckoned with, as well. I would grieve for poor Sejanus if he had to do mental battle with you."

Lucian shook his head. "Oh, I would not win there. A good mind, I hope I may have, but it's not a devious one, as is his."

"Say you," Marcus said. "You're so devious, you even frighten me. I would never have thought of this approach to the problem. It is a marvelous solution. I thank you for it. Now, shall we retire to the cubiculum? I find I'm in need of a deep ball massage."

"Allow me to remove these trays, master and to get the oils, and I will meet you there."

"No, leave those. One of the others can take them away. As for oil, I need nothing of the sort. Your firm hands and a little of your spit will do nicely enough." He winked at Lucian.

Chapter 12 — Boundaries

In Marcus' bedroom, after having lighted the lamps, Lucian helped his master to undress. Carefully, he removed the ubiquitous toga, so much a part of Marcus' work as a magistrate, the embodiment, and badge of his office. Next, kneeling down before the man, Lucian pulled his subligar down to his ankles. Marcus casually stepped out of the undergarment and Lucian laid it upon the wooden chest at the end of the bed.

Now he said to the naked man standing before him, "Master, will you lie upon your bed?"

"Would you have me face up, or face down?" Marcus asked. "Which would please you more?" He regarded Lucian with a dirty smirk.

"Ah…" Lucian hesitated. "I think…perhaps, if you would lie on your back?"

Marcus shrugged. "As you wish, but remember Lucian, with you, I'm willing to play the devoted wife, if you would want this, though I've never really done so before."

Lucian swallowed. The sound of his gulping echoed loudly in the stillness of the bedroom.

Marcus moved to the bed and leisurely lay down upon it, and rolling over onto his back, he stretched his legs slightly apart, his cock and balls blatantly obvious. Already, his cock was swelling with anticipation

"Like this?" he asked, sounding and looking as innocent as a boy did.

Lucian managed a nod. "Indeed, that's perfect," he said, as he eyed Marcus' trim, naked form, the magnificent male body displayed before him, being all masculine angles and hard planes, from the triangle of his muscular chest formed, to his bare feet. There was something about seeing Marcus naked and barefoot that excited Lucian, for he could just imagine those toes curling in response to him fucking Marcus, pummeling his ass with his own big prick. He felt his cock twitch beneath his tunic in response to this thought.

He hurried over to the side of the bed and knelt there to perform his ministrations, and thus effectively concealed his growing erection below the level of the bed. He began massaging Marcus' right upper arm, firmly kneading the muscles there, running his hands over the smooth tanned skin, so unmarred, so nicely muscled, as with the bulging biceps, yet the skin feeling like silk to his touch.

"Leave that," Marcus said, and his voice was almost a growl, low and feral. "I would have you work on another part of me, first. It causes me the most tension."

Lucian looked up, made eye contact, and continued to gaze at his master. Marcus stared back with those large, dark, liquid-brown eyes of his. There was a look of raw hunger in them, of a naked desire.

"What part would that be?" Lucian finally asked, ingenuously, as he trailed a forefinger lightly down the length of Marcus' left arm.

"I would have you massage my root of life," Marcus said, softly now. "Will you do this for me, my Lucian?"

"I must do as my master bids me always," he said, equally quietly. "And it pleases me to help relax my master."

So saying, he stood, climbed onto the bed, and knelt between Marcus' thighs. First placing his hands on both knees, he lightly moved them up those beautifully muscled legs, until he reached the thighs, then the area of his master's genitals.

There he paused, even as he heard a sharp intake of breath from Marcus, saw the man's cock begin to rise even straighter from the tight bush of golden pubic hair surrounding it. Lucian watched, as Marcus' balls shifted in their low-hanging sac. Unconsciously, his licked his lips at the sight.

"Perhaps," he said, "a simple massage to relieve your tension is not enough. I think I must resort to something a little more effective." He lowered his head between his master's thighs, opened his mouth, extended his tongue, and with just the tip of it, licked tentatively at those magnificent balls. As he tongued the sac, chased the twin spheres about there, Marcus gave an involuntary groan of pleasure in response. He spread his thighs even wider to allow Lucian better access to his testicles.

So encouraged, Lucian began tonguing the nut sac in earnest. He used the flat of his tongue now to gain the most contact with as much of the sac at one time as possible, and using his lips gently to grab at the skin there, he softly worked it, kneading the flesh carefully. He could easily feel the outline of his master's tender balls inside the sac now, as he pressed a little harder with his tongue, tried to engulf the bag of balls entirely into his mouth. Slowly, Lucian moved his mouth on upward, gradually making his way to the base of Marcus' now fully erect prick. Now his nose was near the base of Marcus' cock, nudging it gently. The male smell of it was enticing.

The thing stood proudly, straight up, rising like a might tree out of the miniature forest of Marcus' blond pubic hair. Like some marvelous and living battering ram, it seemed to wait for its chance to penetrate, a thing so inherently male that worshipping it seemed not enough to Lucian. The head stuck up so proudly, the glans flared out like a bulky shield of flesh, protecting the thick shaft below it. Already, the head was well clear of the generous foreskin encircling it.

Lucian didn't rush things. Slowly, ever so slowly, he continued to lick with his tongue, and nuzzle those big balls with his nose, breathing in the essence of maleness. He lathed those twin globes containing the reservoir, the source of Marcus' sperm. Lucian so wanted to feel the hot fluid of his master jetting down his throat. He wanted to taste the peppery-lemon flavor of it, suck it in, feel jets of it explode against the back of his mouth. He hoped Marcus had a large amount of cum saved up, because he couldn't wait to swallow it all.

Now, at last, and with Marcus moaning loudly and beginning to thrash about, Lucian lifted his head. He teased the very tip of his master's cock, licked at the head there, forcing his tongue to penetrate slightly into the piss hole, parting those tiny lips there. Again, Marcus groaned, even more loudly this time. He was a man in the thrall of full sexual heat.

Then, in one fell swoop, Lucian lowered his mouth completely over Marcus' cock, engulfing first the head, then the top part of the shaft, and finally, with a momentous effort on his part, he managed to encompass the entire shaft, his nose burying into the golden bush at the base of the prick. This meant letting Marcus' dick slide down his throat. His throat muscles spasmed around this huge intruder, clenching at this fleshy invader, and Lucian had to fight a strong gagging sensation.

Yet again, Marcus groaned, a low, guttural-sounding moan, and he actually twisted about on the bed, lifted his hips, tried to drive his cock even deeper into Lucian's mouth, balls, and all. Lucian slowly backed off the swollen cock, that turgid prick. He let it slowly slip back out of his throat, but his lips gripped the mighty shaft still, slowly sliding up it again. When only the engorged head of the prick was still in his mouth, he stopped there, and continued to grip it with his lips, as he ran his tongue around the underside of it, wetting the glans, stroking them with his tongue.

By Jupiter! How Lucian loved doing this, tasting Marcus' massive cock, sucking on it until his jaws ached, making love to it, worshipping that wonderful appendage containing the very essence of his master. Marcus must have liked it, too, for he squirmed and writhed, every part of his body shifting and twisting all but his cock. That he kept right where it was, firmly inside of Lucian's mouth.

- 111 -

Now Lucian began to suck the fat member in earnest. He plunged down it's now glistening length, so wet with his own saliva. He buried his nostrils in Marcus' pubic hair, smelling the masculine mustiness there. Then he would raise his head again, almost, but not quite releasing the prick from his efforts, for he always kept the head just inside his mouth, worked it with his tongue unceasingly, teasing the sensitive glans.

He used his right hand now, grasping the prick firmly by the shaft, fingers barely able to encircle it, squeezing the thing in his hand, and pumping it hard, for all he was worth. Marcus began to gasp. His breath came in shallow, hoarse pants. He strained, arched his back, lifting his hips ever higher, smooth ass now off the bed, as he tried to drive more of himself into Lucian's hot, wet mouth.

Lucian pumped harder, slamming his fist down to the very base of Marcus' dick, banging lightly at his master's balls, as he did so, and then jerking his hand up the length of it again. Marcus seemed to like this added slight pain; for he groaned softly, spread his thighs as far apart as he could.

Seeing this response, Lucian continued to pump the prick, but with his free hand, he ever so lightly and rapidly slapped Marcus' ball sac. If Marcus enjoyed a little pain, a little extra stimulation, Lucian was determined to give it to him. Meanwhile, he also sucked on the immense, swollen head of the cock, his tongue never stopping, never slowing down, as he raced the tip of it back and forth around the glans, tonguing them, tasting them, exciting the nerves in them.

With his right hand acting like a piston, rocketing up and down the hard shaft, slamming into the underside of the head, Lucian worked Marcus' dick as if he were trying to pump water from a well, and force those large balls squirming in their sac to give up their entire supply of hot cum.

Now Marcus began fucking his mouth with ferocity, slamming his hips up to meet Lucian's downward plunges of his mouth on cock. All the while, Lucian kept up a rapid pumping of fist on prick. As Marcus approached his climax, Lucian trailed the forefinger of his left hand along the length of that monstrous engine of penetration, wetting it with the spit that ran from his mouth in streamlets down the shaft, pricking at it slightly as he went with his fingernails. Each time he did this, Marcus winced with the almost unbearable effects of this stimulation, and squirmed more. After reaching the base of the cock, Lucian reached further down, under Marcus' flopping sac, still tickling, still pricking the flesh with his fingernail. He kept this up until he found the tightly closed sphincter muscle of his master's asshole. There, he rubbed around that sacred spot with his finger, then pressed hard against the center of Marcus' asshole.

"Oh, by Apollo's balls! I'm going to cum!" shouted Marcus, and he reared upward, arching his back as far as he could, driving his cock deep into Lucian's mouth.

At that exact moment, Lucian waited no longer. Brutally, he shoved his finger deep into that puckered hole, rudely forcing open the sphincter muscle, thrusting his finger roughly up inside of Marcus as far as it would go, until buried there down to his knuckle.

Marcus howled, followed this by an enormous groan. Lucian, his mouth still on Marcus' cock, felt the thing suddenly swell even more, felt the shaft of Marcus' cock expand with the coming eruption of cum that was even now forcing its way up to the flared head.

Then it happened. Marcus, panting heavily, groaning as if a man in pain, his asshole muscle clenching, and unclenching around Lucian's invading finger, came. His hot, sticky load of cum spurted out of the head of his cock. Like a geyser, the sperm exploded from him. The first wad of it struck the back of Lucian's throat. He swallowed, determined to take it all, not lose a single drop of his master's precious man juice.

Then another shot jetted, and another. Lucian realized

Marcus hadn't lied, that he'd been saving himself for Lucian, and it showed in the copious amounts of cum burbling into his mouth. He could barely contain it all. He swallowed repeatedly, trying to keep up with the flood of sperm, enjoying the sensation of it sliding down his throat as he did so.

Some leaked from the corners of his lips, even as he continued to swallow convulsively, tasted the marvelous and slightly peppery flavor of the man's thick, pearly essence. Repeatedly, Marcus spurted. Jet after jet of white cum burst from his cock. No doubt, this was due in some part to the violent plunging of Lucian's finger in and out of the man's asshole, finger fucking that hole for all it was worth.

At last, Marcus, whimpering now with sheer physical pleasure and a profound relief, subsided. He lay there, quietly quivering, shivering with delight. Lucian immediately stopped moving his finger about inside his master's ass, just let it rest there, instead. Now, he took his mouth from off his cock, so as not to irritate the now-so-sensitive head and glans there. Instead, using his tongue, he lightly licked the sides of that fuck shaft, lapping up the few drops of pearly cum he'd earlier let slip from his mouth earlier.

Marcus, stirred, reached down with his right hand, and placed it on Lucian's mop of dark hair. "Oh, by the Gods," he murmured in a satisfied voice, "I feel so much better now, Lucian.

Lucian lifted his head, a drop of Marcus' cum still hanging from his chin. Using a finger, he brushed it from there, and then putting his finger to his mouth, he pointedly and slowly licked at that last droplet of sperm. Marcus watched him as he did this.

"You are satisfied with the massage, master?' Lucian asked him, at last and in a quiet voice.

Marcus nodded. Then he said, "And you, my handsome slave, do you not need satisfying? I will gladly do the same for you, or roll over and let you have my ass. By Hades, I would consider it a treat."

"Fucking you now would only hurt, since you've already cum."

"I wouldn't mind. It would be a pain well worth bearing to see you happy, as well, to feel you inside of me."

Lucian gently shook his head. "This was just to relax you. I felt it my duty to relieve your tension. But when the time comes for us to fuck, we will fuck each other, the both of us inside each other in turn. Then, I will rape your ass, rip your virginity from you, and it will be no easy thing for you. I will impale you, as if you had been speared."

"Bold words," Marcus said, and then he chuckled. "Bold words, indeed. I look forward to it...slave. I look forward to when you make yourself my master and me your slave in such a way. Are you sure, you won't do this now? I'm willing, you know, and more than willing."

Lucian gave another mild shake of his head. "Not yet, not until we can be with each other on equal terms, for I would not have you any other way, than as my partner in life."

Now Marcus shook his head from side to side. "Very well. Let it be as you wish," he said. "But you know, Lucian, that such isn't fully possible. Our customs don't permit such. Sejanus wouldn't permit such. Rome wouldn't permit such.

Lucian nodded from where he still knelt between Marcus' legs. "I know," he said, quietly. "But who knows? Maybe, there will come a day when Sejanus will no longer be with us, and the customs of Rome will no longer matter."

Again, Marcus shook his head, seemingly regretfully. "That day is very far from now, I fear," he said. "They refer to Rome as the Eternal City, and I'm afraid it will always be so."

"Rome, perhaps," agreed Lucian, "but perhaps not the empire."

Chapter 13 — Love Grows As Storm Clouds Gather

The next few weeks were a marvelous time for Lucian. He was generally in high spirits. The good summer weather held and everything seemed to run smoothly in the household. Even better, the solution he'd found for Marcus and his troubles with Sejanus had worked perfectly. Drusus, the Commander of the Barracks, had agreed completely with the idea and even felt it had great merit. Marcus, true to his word, had sent a full report of the affair to Sejanus. In return, he received high praise from the man…luckily.

So the days seemed to fall into a mostly uneventful and peaceful routine, with Lucian running the house and taking care of everything as best he could. He must have done well, for the household did run smoothly. The slave's all did their work. Complaints were at a minimum. Everything seemed, as it should be.

However, Lucian was no closer to finding out who the potential spy might be supposedly hiding in their midst. His favorite candidate, Didius, had no legitimate means of leaving the house now, so Lucian didn't see how he could be the culprit. Yet, Lucian knew that even so, Didius might be passing messages through some nefarious way with the various tradesmen who came to the door, or through some other equally reprehensible means, as was often the case with the way slaves of different households managed to gossip with each other, and without their masters knowing. Not allowed to leave the premises of a home, they had to find other and more creative ways to stay in communication. The slaves of Rome were truly adept.

Besides Didius, Lucian had no other obvious candidates for the role of household traitor. Marcus' comment about having sent Octavos to the Lady Flavia's house, and Octavos not subsequently telling Lucian he'd gone there that day, did bother him some. But he knew, above all, Octavos was loyal to Marcus, and although he knew the little man liked him, as well, this still was no match for his love for Marcus.

Lucian gave a mental shrug at this thought. This, in itself, could account for why he hadn't given Lucian notice he'd gone on an errand. It was a private mission given to him by his beloved master and thus a confidential one.

So who did that leave? Capito was crippled and so couldn't walk any distance very easily and then only with great effort. Moreover, he, too, never left the confines of the house and its immediate environs. Yes, he could possibly pass messages to the various tradesmen who came around to the house on a regular basis, but Lucian didn't think the man was really the type of person to do this.

Why would he? Where was the motive? Why would he betray the trust of Marcus, the man who had taken him in hand and given him a relatively easy job to do, because of his difficult handicap? Who else would bother to treat a slave so well, and so kindly?

No, Capito was very lucky to be where he was, even still to be alive in the harsh world that was Rome. Certainly, the man must know this. In addition, he just didn't seem the type to gossip, so quiet was he, and so where would he get the information he would be passing along? He kept his distance from the other slaves, did his job, and minded his own business. No, again, he just didn't seem too likely as a spy.

In reality, Lucian couldn't imagine anyone other than Didius being the culprit. And even with Didius, it seemed unlikely. So his progress in trying to uncover the spy went nowhere.

Luckily, his relationship with Marcus did. So happy, so enthused was Marcus with the way Lucian had helped him out of the quandary he'd been in with Sejanus that Lucian could seem to do no wrong. Also, Lucian suspected that Marcus loved his cock sucking abilities, which he praised as a fine art, and which Lucian now did for him nightly. Lucian enjoyed it, too. He loved swallowing every drop of Marcus' prized cum. To service his master in this way was the true highlight of his day. He so looked forward to Marcus coming home of an evening, he could hardly wait as the hour approached.

Marcus always seemed more than happy to see him. He always ate the evening meal with Lucian now. They were on intimate terms, as lovers in most respects. Whenever Marcus had spare time, he spent it with Lucian. Often, this was in the form of casual walks about the city of Rome, fun shopping excursions, visits to the public baths, or simply taking Lucian along with him for company on his missions as a magistrate.

Yet, even spending so much time together, they had no serious quarrels. Although Marcus was constantly trying to get Lucian to surrender his body completely to him, using the ready availability of his own virgin ass as an added inducement, he never pushed this to extremes. It was as if he had a respect for Lucian now, and his self-imposed limits.

Oh, Lucian had no illusions they were now equals. He knew he was still a slave and Marcus was his master. Even so, their relationship flowered, grew deeper, and surprisingly, it was without the act of making complete physical love. Although, Lucian had to admit he would get quite involved in his "massages" of Marcus.

During this time, they did have a tryst with Octavos twice more. Again, Marcos and Lucian didn't touch each other, except to squirt their cum onto each other's bodies. They used Octavos as their intermediary. Both of them lavished attention, kindness, and even a form of love, upon Octavos. The little man responded in kind. He became as a puppy to Lucian, always following him about, always there to see if Lucian needed anything at all, as if he were another master. It became inconceivable to Lucian that Octavos could be the spy. Such was simply not the nature of the man.

Of the Lady Flavia, Lucian heard no more. Marcus never raised the subject. Neither did Lucian. Each was content to forget the matter in its entirety, as if it had never happened. Yet, Lucian knew, someday, Marcus must marry. It was expected. No, in Rome, it they demanded it.

Romans were strict with themselves in many ways, often aggressively so. Status was all-important. Even Roman clothing reflected this, and the difference in styles between patricians, senators, magistrates, matrons, slaves, plebeians, were quite distinct. The lower classes often wore colorless, rather shapeless tunic. Free Roman citizens attired themselves in a combination of the tunic and toga, ones often dyed with various colors.

Magistrates wore a full toga. But the distinctiveness even went beyond this. The color of the stripe on the hemline of tunics denoted one's status, as well. In addition, only the top echelon of society, the true aristocrats, had the privilege of wearing the color Tyrian purple. "To be born to the purple," meant one was virtually royalty.

So, Lucian knew that in Rome, Marcus would have little choice but to eventually marry. Society didn't care if he liked men, not as long as he was the one who did the penetrating and was not the penetrated. After all, even the great Julius Caesar had the reputation of being "every woman's husband, and every man's wife."

However, the last part of this remark had been a disparaging comment, for the statement implied he was the one who was penetrated. And in a male-dominated society such as Rome, that sort of thing the citizens frowned upon, as was using one's mouth in the act of sex. Romans viewed the mouth as a very public thing; one kissed one's loved ones with it, so supposedly they didn't use it for oral sex, the rimming of a slave's tight asshole, the licking of a woman's vagina, or any such similar thing.

Even so, a public moral was not the same thing as private action. What Romans professed to adhere to in public, was often not what they actually practiced in private. Mouths were often in play during sex and in a big way.

The following month, Lucian again did his rounds of all the shops with which his household did business and he collected another bag of money from each. Already, the amount was becoming significant. This made Lucian wonder again, what Didius had done with his wealth while he'd been collecting it.

If the man had been accumulating coin for any length of time at all, as he apparently had been, surely he would have had enough by now to purchase his freedom, if he so chose, from Marcus. The fact he hadn't yet done this, meant he must have spent it some other way, or for some obscure reasons was hoarding it. Judging by his increasingly taciturn and angry nature of late, Lucian suspected the coin had gone for prostitutes. Now, his supply of them, along with the cash to pay for them, had ended.

Poor Didius, Lucian thought one day. He must be becoming terribly frustrated sexually. As it happened, this turned out to be true, for one day, Lucian caught him forcibly mounting Octavos from the rear. It was in the peristylium that he'd chanced upon them.

Octavos had seemed to be in distress, seemed demonstrably upset at what Didius was doing to him. Lucian had stopped this rape, much to Didius' anger. The man was in a real rage. Later, when Lucian was alone with Octavos, the little man told him he hadn't wanted such a thing, but Didius had directly commanded him to do it.

Lucian then sought out Didius and told him to leave Octavos alone in the future. He was to take no one by force. And if Lucian heard he had, he told Didius he would persuade Marcus to get rid of him. Didius knew how great was Lucian's influence with Marcus was now, so he was well aware this was no empty threat.

Although furious at this, Didius had no choice but to obey. But it was with reluctance and an obvious new hatred and resentment for Lucian that he obeyed. Lucian knew how he felt, for the man made no secret of it. Nor was Lucian blind to the snide remarks, the half-whispered lewd comments made about him and his relationship with Marcus, or even between the two of them and Octavos. He ignored these as best he could, not wanting to worsen the situation more by attempting to stop such remarks.

Another day, passing through the peristylium, he found Didius fucking Libo as hard as he could. The young man was naked, bent over a bench, and Didius was plowing his ass furrow for all he was worth.

"What's the meaning of this?" Lucian demanded to know, when he saw them. "What have I told you about this, about using someone without their permission, Didius?"

Didius, bare-assed naked, paused only long enough in his humping to say, "Libo has agreed to let me fuck him. Now go away!" And with that, he began seriously thrusting his cock into the slave's asshole, as if trying to ream it out. His pale ass rose and fell with the effort.

"Is this true?" Lucian asked uncertainly. "Libo, is this with your approval?"

Libo grunted, as Didius shoved his cock particularly hard and deep inside of his gut. "Yes, Lucian," he managed to say. "He promised me extra meat for dinner tonight."

"That would be the master's meat you're promising," Lucian said sharply to Didius. "Who are you to give it away without his approval?"

"Fuck you, Lucian!" Didius shouted. "The master permits me extra once in a while. Who I choose to give it to, and why, is my business. Now, get out of here. I have my own meat to worry about."

Lucian eyed the two men, both fucking like dogs in the street. Libo, pimply-faced, with mouth hanging open and body bucking from the savaging of his ass he was receiving, seemed completely unaware he was even getting fucked. For him, it seemed, it was just a means to an end. But Lucian had to admire Didius to some degree. Although his cock wasn't spectacular, his nut bag was bigger than average, hung lower, and swung beautifully back and forth, slapping Libo's ass, and even banging into his balls, too. Didius had a firm ass, if a little on the hairy side.

"Ahhh…" Didius groaned, as he approached his climax. He was fucking furiously away now, the crude noise of his cock suctioning in and out of Libo's bowels was loud.

"Squeeze your asshole around my cock, Libo," he groaned. "Milk me! Make me cum! "Ahh…that's better," he moaned, as apparently Libo did as asked, for Lucian could see he was now flexing his ass muscles, clenching his butt cheeks, causing his sphincter muscle to spasm tightly around Didius' cock.

Again, for Libo, it appeared to be just a thing to do, not something he received any particular pleasure from, or pain, for that matter, because he didn't wince from Didius' plundering of his asshole. He just seemed to approach the whole business rather mechanically, as if like a prostitute, he was merely servicing his better, in order to reap some reward.

"Gods!" shouted Didius, as he slammed hard into Libo, rutting furiously again and again into his gut, making his own balls swing frantically back and forth. "I'm cumming!" he shouted, and with that, he shoved one more time, thrust himself as deep as possible into Libo, who was pushed forward by the power of Didius' final fuck.

"Ah! Ah! Ah!" Didius kept exclaiming, as spurt after spurt of his cum flooded the young man's backside. Suddenly, he collapsed, flung himself forward, his whole weight coming down heavily upon the back of Libo, who sagged noticeably under the burden.

Lucian, who now had a full erection at this erotic sight, hurried from the room, before Didius recovered enough to realize he'd remained there, watched the two of them rutting as he had. Lucian didn't like Didius, but it was hard to resist watching any two men fuck. For Lucian, it was always such a provocative sight to see balls swinging, cock invading someone's ass like that. It made him so randy.

So life, if it wasn't perfect, definitely had its moments for Lucian. Most of all, he was happy just to be able to go on living with the man he loved. Even so, Lucian knew that someday, Didius would have to go, despite the fine display of ass fucking with Libo he'd seen Didius perform (and which, if Lucian was honest with himself, he'd like to see more of), but Didius' attitude wasn't getting any better.

If anything, it steadily deteriorated. Still, Lucian was determined it wasn't going to be because of him that the slave left. He just couldn't bring himself to exercise such power over another human being, especially one who was a slave. Influence was power, but that power had to be used wisely, and according to the dictates of one's conscience.

Lucian simply decided to put up with Didius' behavior, if only for the time being, but although a relatively easy decision, it was difficult to put into practice. Didius was a daily trial, a constant thorn in his side. So even though those following summer weeks, overall, were good ones, for Lucian, it seemed nothing was perfect, at least, not where Didius was concerned.

There was another shadow hanging over them, as well. Although between them, Marcus and Lucian had come up with a solution for the problem of the Roman soldier charged with extortion against a merchant, they both knew this was bound to happen again. Despite this as such a strong example to other soldiers not to behave so, despite the danger now clearly shown inherent in trying such extortions in future, eventually, someone else was bound to attempt the crime again.

Furthermore, given such an outcome in favor of merchants in the first trial, more merchants were likely to come forward and complain of such events if they did occur, which only made it more likely Marcus would soon deal with the issue again.

Both Lucian and Marcus knew it was only a matter of time before such did happen. This time, Marcus would almost certainly have to let the soldier or soldiers go free, or otherwise risk enraging the Commander of the Barracks, and of course, and much more importantly, the all-powerful Sejanus.

However, even the commander could be dangerous just by himself. It would be easy enough for him, if he felt he had sufficient reason, to arrange for an ambush somewhere in the narrow, twisted, and crowded city streets of Rome, to have Marcus waylaid there. It would be just so simple a task to do. He had the men, his soldiers. All he had to do was have a couple of them dress in nondescript street clothes, approach Marcus, and kill him.

Trained soldiers would make short work of him in such an unexpected attack, even though Marcus, too, once had been a soldier. Still, no one could be on his guard all the time. And although the death of a magistrate would be a notable event and cause something of an outcry, such things were hardly unheard of in the city.

Despite the steady patrols of the Praetorian Guard, the problem of footpads, thieves, and to a lesser extent, cutthroats, was still there. Rome was a large metropolis. Its population was the better part of one million, and still growing. Security was always a problem under such circumstances.

Even the Emperor Tiberius and Sejanus had considerable respect for the threat the mobs of the city presented, the uncontrolled power they could wield. Moreover, these groups were composed of supposedly law-abiding citizens. They didn't even include the professional criminal class. So the death of Marcus as a magistrate would pass with some outcry, but sadly, not much.

There was one bright note less than a week after Lucian's witnessing of Didius and Libo's coupling. A personal messenger came from Sejanus. He carried a gift of 200 denarii for Marcus. Marcus readily accepted the present. Not to do so would have offended Sejanus. And such payments were a normal thing way in Rome. Payments such as these, even nominal bribe, were not usually considered a corrupt thing to do. Rather, they were just another way of doing business.

There was one other gift, as well. Sejanus also had sent along a formal letter, which granted Marcus the right to have a percent of the taxes taken on the transport of tallow. Although this didn't amount to a huge fortune, it did make for a nice stipend. The bad news was one received this stipend only once a year. The good news was the first annual installment was due in just under two weeks' time.

"At this rate," Marcus happily had told Lucian one day, "I shall lose all track of my finances very quickly. I think it best if you take complete charge in all these matters."

"You would trust me so much in this?" Lucian was astounded.

Marcus had merely shrugged, saying, "I would trust you with my life, so why not my money. And as far as that goes, you may as well have the key to the strongbox in the cubiculum. Since you're taking charge of the household finances and all this, as well, it would be best if you kept the key on your person."

So saying, Marcus reached under the collar of his tunic and lifted a chain with a small iron key attached to it from around his neck. He handed this over to Lucian.

Lucian didn't know what to say, as he grasped hold of the iron key. "Are you sure of this?" was all he could think to ask.

"Indeed, it's a relief to me," Marcus admitted. He sounded as if he meant it. Then he gave Lucian a rueful smile, before saying, "I'm not very good in matters of finances. It just isn't something I manage well."

"Still, if things continue as they are," Marcus added, "we can expect more of this sort of thing. It's common for magistrates to get stipends as these, besides the normal income for their services. The theory seems to be that if we have such income, we are less likely to surrender to the temptation of bribes by participants involved in a case. Of course, there are others who say this sort of thing is precisely a bribe, and so puts us firmly in the hands of those who pay the stipends." Again, Marcus had shrugged at this point. "Either way, I think it puts us magistrates in a compromising position."

To this statement, Lucian had readily, if silently agreed, but he was happy about the money. He didn't know why, but he'd a presentment things might soon come to a head. He didn't know how, or what nature events might take, but he just felt a strong sense things were going to change radically sometime in the near future. Perhaps, he reflected, it was his Celtic blood causing this feeling. His people lay steeped in the lore of superstition, prophecy, and all things mystic.

When a few days later he opened the strongbox, he saw the silvery gleam of a good many denarii mirroring back at him. Along with those shining coins, were a goodly number of yellow-glittering, gold ones, too. Lucian realized that despite Marcus' almost cavalier attitude towards money, he was good at saving it.

Upon some further reflection, Lucian felt he knew why. Despite his stunning good looks, his youthfulness, and his position as a magistrate, Marcus just didn't seem to mix well in Roman society. He never seemed to go to dinners at the houses of others, never went out to banquets or orgies.

Perhaps, this in part was because of his strong preference for lying with men. This didn't fit well with other men wanting to go wenching. Marcus didn't frequent prostitutes, or at least, Lucian didn't believe he did. Lucian had no evidence to support such a contention.

Marcus, with his negative views on gambling, never seemed to indulge in the many popular games of dice, nor did he ever haunt the tavernas. So other than the normal household expenses, Marcus had no appreciable debt or outgo to worry about. With his rent taken care of by Sejanus, the extra money he made simply went into the strongbox.

Lucian felt relieved, as he stared down at the money filling the coffer. Whatever tempest was to come, whatever dark storm approached from beyond the horizon, it looked as if they would have enough money to act as a cushion in any such emergency. Still, Lucian was determined to increase this amount as much as possible. It never hurt to have more. That way, they would be safer yet.

Even so, Lucian, and try as he might, could not shrug off the lurking feeling of impending doom. Repeatedly, he assured himself there wasn't any reason for such a negative sentiment. Life was good. Things were going well. Money seemed to be flowing in from every quarter. Yet, still there was the nagging worry, always mentally irritating him at the back of his mind, acting like a low cloud causing shadow on an otherwise sunny day.

Therefore, although it was that Lucian was happy, he knew any of a number of things might come along that could sabotage his joy. In this, he was right, and it came just towards the end of summer. This time, the problem arrived in the form of a marriage proposal.

Lucian had been at home the day the messenger came to deliver the missive. With what Lucian thought was simply too much formal fanfare and flourish, the courier demanded only Marcus should receive the communication directly into his hands, and his hands alone. The bumptious little man wouldn't leave it with anyone else.

Immediately, this tripped Lucian's mental alarms. At first, he thought it might be a summons from Sejanus. But this, he realized quickly, was not probably the case. Sejanus would not have used a courier. He would have used soldiers to enforce his summons. In addition, he undoubtedly knew where Marcus was pretty much at any given moment. Sejanus' network of spies was infamous. So he wouldn't have sent a courier to the house, but rather to the administrative complex, where Marcus was.

This thought of Sejanus reminded Lucian he hadn't been able to discover the spy residing within the household yet, if there actually was one, which Lucian was beginning to seriously doubt. Anyway, it seemed a foregone conclusion Sejanus would have known enough to send soldiers to wherever Marcus actually was.

Lucian had little choice. He ushered the courier in and let him wait in the coolness of the peristylium. Although summer was close to its end, the constant heat and humidity hadn't yet relented. Lucian was sure this was one of the hottest summers ever. At least, it certainly seemed that way to him. Worse, there had been little rain to alleviate the dust, which all the street traffic raised.

Banned during the daytime to allow for the free movement of pedestrians, all the carts laden with freight and supplies for various merchants, shops, restaurants, tavernas, warehouses, and sundry other types of businesses, came to the city at night when the streets were supposedly empty of all foot traffic. This was a practice enforced by imperial law.

However, the constant rumble of these vehicles all night long, combined with the often sticky and oppressive heat, the mostly complete absence of even the slightest of breezes, made sleeping almost impossible at times.

When this happened to Lucian, he would simply lie there on his couch with eyes wide open, staring into the darkness, and listening to the steady breathing of Marcus, asleep in the bed nearby. How the man could manage to go on sleeping under such conditions defied any explanations of which Lucian could think. They had told him as a boy that the innocent slept well.

Perhaps, this was true in Marcus' case. He certainly looked innocent enough, lying there naked, with the covers thrown back because of the heat, and with his boyish face, those chiseled features relaxed in sleep, clean of all signs of tension and worry. Often, it was all Lucian could do not to get up, go over to where Marcus lay, and caress that perfect face, run his fingers through the curly blond hair framing the smooth forehead.

When Marcus came home that afternoon, Lucian was loath to destroy his obvious joy at just being there with him again, by having to tell him of the arrival of the pompous and prune-faced messenger. Still, he had no choice. Not knowing who had sent the messenger (the man would not tell him, Lucian being a mere slave and he a citizen), made the matter all the more urgent to Lucian. Uncertainty was not something Lucian enjoyed.

Marcus, noticing Lucian's pronounced anxiety, also immediately became tense. It showed in the tautness around his mouth, the sudden appearance of frown lines on his forehead. In Rome, surprises most often were not pleasant things. The arrival of this messenger had come from out of the blue, and so was certainly a surprise, always something of which to be wary.

It was with real trepidation Lucian watched as Marcus approached the courier with an obvious circumspection and distinct unease. His body language breathed tension.

When Marcus entered the room, the man immediately stood up from where he'd been sitting on a stone bench. With his right hand, he clutched tight to a rolled scroll, one with a large and impressive red seal of wax securing the contents from prying eyes.

"Greetings to you, Marcus Darius Macro," the man unctuously said, bowing. "I bring a message to you from the noble Vitruvius Maro Nimachis, titular head of the House of

Nimachis." Here, he proffered the scroll to Marcus with both hands. "He asks I wait while you read it, and that perhaps you may have an answer for me to take back to him."

Although taken somewhat aback by the man's flowery words, for Lucian could clearly see the surprise in Marcus' eyes, his lover still managed nicely to recover.

"I will do as your master suggests," he said, calmly enough, considering the · circumstances. He took the scroll from the courier.

"You may wait in the kitchen while I read this and then consider the matter. Ask one of the slaves there to give you something cool to drink. I'm sure after your long walk in this heat you could use something to quench your thirst?"

The man nodded his ready assent. "Indeed, sir, I could. A cup of cool wine would make for nice refreshment."

"Good." Marcus turned to Lucian. "Would you take this man to the cucina?" he asked of him.

Lucian immediately bowed his head. "As you wish, master."

"Return immediately afterward." Marcus gave Lucian a significant look as he said this, which told Lucian what he needed to know. Marcus wanted him there with him while he read the message.

So as soon as Lucian had accomplished his task, he hurried back to Marcus. He'd already opened the papyrus scroll. Marcus held the document in both his hands as he read it. There was a look of consternation upon his handsome features, if one judged by the severe frown he wore.

"I have read the gist of it," he said. "It's a proposal for marriage to the Lady Flavia. Although Vitruvius is not specific about the dowry, he clearly hints it will be most generous. More, he hopes for an answer very quickly. He implies strongly that time is of the essence in the matter. No doubt, he wishes to ask some favor of Sejanus and needs me to ask it for him. I'm betting that's the reason for this rush."

Lucian was silent a moment, digesting this news. Finally, he said, "What do you intend to do?"

Marcus gave a disgusted shake of his head. "I'm not certain. The man certainly knows I have no other attachments in this particular regard, that I'm unmarried. I'm sure his spies have been working overtime to learn everything they could in this way. So I can't plead entanglement with someone else. He simply wouldn't believe me. He'd take it as an insult. Therefore, if I reject his offer, it'll only anger him, and he is a very powerful man. Such would be an unwise thing to do, for he is of the patrician class, and of course, I'm not. So not only is this considered a great offer to me, but to reject it would constitute a grave personal offense on my part. And as a patrician, he has the means to seek revenge in such matters of honor—one way or the other."

Again, Lucian was quiet for several minutes, as was Marcus.

"Then what will you do?" Lucian finally asked again and in a low voice.

Marcus sighed, as he simultaneously tossed the open scroll onto the nearest couch. "I don't know," he said. "I was hoping you might have some suggestions on this matter. You did well the last time I had a problem."

"Do you want to marry her?"

Marcus shot him a sidelong look, one that could have withered roses in the garden. "Of course, I don't! I want things to continue just the way they are. I want to be with you."

"Then we need to find some way around this." Lucian tried to sound confident.

"Really?" The sarcasm was more than evident in Marcus' voice. "And just how do you propose I do that, my lover?"

"Perhaps, we need to think about why he is making this offer to you. As you've said, it's most generous. And being of the aristocracy, surely the Lady Flavia could do better than you."

When Marcus gave him a reproachful look, Lucian hastily added, "I don't mean that the way it sounded. You know, I don't."

Again, Marcus sighed. Then he collapsed onto the nearest couch, flopping down next to the discarded scroll. "Yes, I know. But what can I do about this?" He tapped the scroll with the forefinger of his right hand. "I don't wish to marry Flavia. The thought of bedding that overly buxom female with her big floppy breasts, disgusts me. I would much rather fuck you." He gave Lucian a telling look as he said this last.

The message was not lost on Lucian. "Perhaps, I have handled things badly when it comes to that," he admitted, more to himself than to Marcus.

"Oh, do you think so?" Again, although his tone was light, sarcasm was strongly evident in Marcus' words.

Lucian didn't answer right away. What could he say? He knew well enough life could be harsh, short, and terribly uncertain. And even he wasn't quite sure why he hadn't already coupled with Marcus.

Why not take such pleasure where one could and while one could? A tiny voice in his head whispered to him.

Marcus was regarding him closely. "Well? Have you nothing to say? What should I do about this?"

"I do have one thought," Lucian said. "You can delay in committing by telling him that the honor is so great, the offer so generous, you feel most unworthy of it. Tell him, you must consult the Gods in this matter, seek their guidance. You intend to make sacrifice tomorrow at the Temple of Juno and consult with the priests there. Then, you will have an answer for him after you have had such consultation. After all, to make offer to the Goddess of Marriage under such conditions is what any upright Roman citizen would be expected to do and should do, yes?"

Marcus nodded. "Yes," he said, although many don't bother these days."

"Still, by doing so, you might even please Vitruvius in this matter. You will have followed the appropriate forms, shown you have observed all the niceties, as a proper Roman should, and are showing the utmost respect for such a grand offer, from one so powerful."

Marcus stood. "Yes. I would, wouldn't I?" He looked marginally happier now. "This will buy us a little time, I suppose. Certainly, the man can't object to my making a consultation like this on so momentous a matter. Good. I'll give his messenger this answer."

"And this should hold off Vitruvius for the moment, at least," Lucian said.

Yes, but Lucian, it only gives us about another day or so before I must answer him in one way or the other. Vitruvius will fully expect that answer to be in the affirmative, too. The Gods notwithstanding, he is a very powerful man, and he will not like to be thwarted in something he so desires. And he must really desire this, to imply such a large dowry is in the offing."

Lucian shrugged his shoulders. "I'm sure size of the dowry is meant to be large just so you can give a portion of it to Sejanus, to smooth the path for whatever favor it is Vitruvius really wants out of all this from him. Still, time wise, this is the best we can do for the moment, given how unexpected this all is.

"Then what?"

"Well, at least, we have some time to think of something else this way, hopefully something better and more permanent to avoid you marrying Flavia. By the way, have you been encouraging the lady in any way in this matter of late?" He gave Marcus a penetrating look.

Marcus didn't quail before his gaze, but rather responded by giving him an exasperated look of his own.

"How can you ask such a stupid thing?" He sounded hurt. "You know full well how I feel about you. It's your ass I want fuck, certainly not hers! That aspect of things hasn't changed. So why would I jeopardize what we have by doing something so idiotic?"

"Besides," he added in a softer and lighter tone of voice, "My Lucian, you're difficult enough as it is for me. Why should I want to have an unpredictable female enter into the equation, as well? Give me some credit for not being quite so stupid."

"You don't wish to be married any time soon, then?"

"I don't wish to be married at all, ever, unless some way could be found to do it with you. Since that's not possible, I would rather things continue just as they are."

"As would I, but you know such a relationship between us is truly impossible, don't you?" Lucian had to be sure of this.

One more time Marcus heaved a sigh, before saying, "Oh, yes, I know that more than well enough. By the Gods!" he exclaimed in a louder voice, "I'm so tired of duty and customs. Why can't I just live my life as I choose? In so uncertain a world, is it so very much to ask, to snatch a little happiness while one can, while one is still young enough to enjoy it?"

"Oh, Marcus, I have wronged you."

Marcus looked up at him now. "What do you mean?"

Lucian shook his head. "I see now I've been playing games. They were stupid games and a pointless waste of our allowed time together."

Marcus raised twin, questioning eyebrows. "You've decided your exercising of your choice not to be with me was now a wrong decision?"

Lucian nodded. "I have. It was dull-witted of me."

Marcus flashed him a brief smile, and then said, "Well, there is something we can both certainly agree upon there."

Rather than being offended, this just made Lucian chuckle. "Shall we use our ploy of you having to consult the Gods to get rid of the tiresome man sitting in our kitchen and so be left alone, to attend to our own affairs?" he asked, suggestively.

"Oh, yes! I'm more than happy to do so. Then, perhaps, we can do something about correcting this 'big' mistake you claim to have made." He winked and then gave Lucian a lewd grin.

Lucian said, "I'll go and bring the man to you. The sooner we are rid of him, the better." And having said this, he fled the room to accomplish his mission, to get rid of the man just as quickly, as he could.

Chapter 14 — The Storm Breaks

U nfortunately, Lucian discovered his desires thwarted for the time being, at least. For even as he led the man back to Marcus, Didius, admitted yet another messenger. This time, it was a soldier in full uniform, including helmet. Lucian came across them just as Didius admitted him into the atrium. The soldier was from none other than Sejanus and so was far more important than the other messenger had been.

Only after some difficulty and a great deal of persuasion, did Lucian manage to have the man be willing to wait in the atrium. He accomplished this by ordering Didius to bring the soldier a pitcher of their mulsum, a honeyed wine, and by making the promise his wait would only be for a few minutes, at most. Having placated the solider, Lucian rushed to bring the other waiting messenger back to Marcus.

Marcus gave the man the sealed missive he and Lucian had worked out only moments earlier. As the man departed, he glanced at the solider sitting on a bench in the atrium, busy guzzling his wine. The man went out the door with a slightly sour expression upon his face, as if he strongly disliked soldiers. Then, judging by his shriveled, prune-faced features, Lucian wasn't sure if this wasn't the messenger's permanent appearance and so marked nothing out of the ordinary.

Lucian rushed to inform Marcus of the soldier. His master immediately went to him in the atrium. Lucian didn't go with him, feeling it might be better for Marcus if he wasn't always in such close attendance with him. He was sure Sejanus knew all about them already, but there was no sense in driving home the point of his close relationship with Marcus, should Sejanus later question the solider about what he might have seen. The less Sejanus knew about such things, probably the better for them.

Shortly later, Marcus came back into the room. He wore a worried expression. "I must leave right away," he told Lucian, and there was an edge to his voice as he spoke. "Sejanus needs to speak with me immediately."

Lucian was silent a beat, before asking, "Is everything all right, Marcus? You're in no danger?"

Marcus rolled his eyes upward, as if beseeching the help of the Gods. Then he said, "I think no more than usual. But something of some importance has come up, or he wouldn't demand to see me this late in the evening. He dotes on his family and guards his evenings with them jealously. But enough, I must leave. It doesn't do to keep Sejanus waiting. The longer he waits the angrier and more ill-tempered he becomes."

Lucian handed him a dark cloak, and Marcus drew it about his shoulders, letting Lucian secure the tiny brass chain at his throat meant to hold the cloak in place. It wasn't cold out, but it was incumbent upon Marcus to appear dressed in full formal attire." Cloaks were the usual form of outer nightwear.

Lucian trailed him and the soldier to the outer gate. Marcus gave him a quick wink, and before Lucian could even think of a way to respond to it, he and the soldier were gone, walking off up the street leading up to the Palatine Hill. Soon they were lost in the evening's gathering gloom, just shifting shadows in the light of the street torches.

Lucian still stood there, gazed forlornly after them for several long minutes, although he could no longer see them. Then finally, quietly, he closed the gate, walked the length of the narrow vestibulum, and returned to the atrium.

He knew his plans for the evening were no more. Even if Marcus weren't long at his task, whatever Sejanus wanted, undoubtedly would result in Marcus being too mentally preoccupied to want to bed Lucian. And Lucian couldn't blame him. He was no longer in the mood, either. Life and death matters had a way of interfering with sexual desires.

As it turned out, it was quite late when Marcus returned. Lucian had been lightly dozing on a couch on the bench in the atrium, the same one the solider had used earlier. Lucian had been determined to wait for Marcus there; no matter what hour he came home. The sound of the gate opening and slamming shut, and the hollow footsteps of Marcus' sandaled feet on stone tiles in the vestibulum, awakened him.

He sat upright, just as Marcus strode into the room. Without even bothering to remove his cloak, he slumped onto the bench next to Lucian. Marcus gave a great heave of a sigh, but said nothing. He just gazed with a soulful look down at the floor tiles.

"You need refreshment," Lucian told him. "You're tired and no doubt hungry. I've kept the cook up. I'll have him prepare you something."

"I want no food," Marcus said, dismissing the idea with a desultory wave of one hand. "I'm too tired to eat. I could use some wine, though."

"Of course." Lucian fled the room to do his master's bidding. He returned as quickly as he could with a fresh pitcher of wine, but only one earthenware goblet. Ever mindful he was still only a slave, Lucian hadn't presumed Marcus wanted to have him join him in having a drink.

He filled the cup with the typical red wine Marcus seemed to like so much and then added some honey to sweeten it in order to create a mulsum. After stirring this mixture with a small wooden spoon, Lucian then handed the goblet to Marcus.

His master accepted it, and took a great swig from the cup. Setting the now only have-filled vessel onto the surface of the marble table standing before the bench, he said, "The worst thing that could happen has happened."

"Sejanus knows of us and wants you to be rid of me?" Lucian darkly guessed. "He summoned you to tell you he wanted you to marry the Lady Flavia."

Marcus shook his head. "Well, when you put it that way," he said, "perhaps it's not the worst thing that could happen, because that isn't it. I don't believe Sejanus cares who I fuck, unless he can somehow use it to his advantage over me. And since we don't fuck, he really has no advantage in that regard, although he might mistakenly think he has. Besides, I'm not even sure if he knows about the offer of marriage to Flavia. Although, upon consideration, I suspect he might. There isn't much Sejanus doesn't know."

Lucian moved closer to Marcus on the bench, uninvited. "Then I'm at a loss," he said. "What's this great problem of which you speak?"

"By all the Gods, it's those damnable soldiers of the Praetorian Guard again. This time, it was three of them. They demanded money from a fabric merchant and when he refused, they killed him, ran him through with their swords."

This news stunned Lucian. "They killed him? Why would they do such a stupid thing?"

Instead of answering, Marcus gave a small groan, before saying, "And that's not all of it. The merchant is related, if only slightly, to the noble house of Quidius Carrudus, the head of which, Claudius, is known as something of a friend to the Emperor Tiberius himself, no less."

"The Gods save us," Lucian whispered in soft dismay. Then more loudly, he asked, "What is it Sejanus wants you to do?"

Marcus shook his head, raised both his hands in an open-palmed gesture of despair. "It's complicated. On the one hand, he is furious at the soldiers for committing such an act. They were drunk, of course, when they did it, although I understand they sobered up quickly enough afterwards when the commander confronted them with what they'd done."

"And the commander, what does he want to happen? Did Sejanus tell you this?"

Now Marcus nodded. "Indeed, he did. He told me much else. The commander doesn't mind a flogging, but it must be at his command, under his jurisdiction, and upon the barracks grounds. He doesn't want them to face justice from the civilian court. However, the merchant's relatives want exactly that. They want the soldiers tried and summarily executed. They'll be satisfied with nothing less, or so they say.

"And if they don't get this?"

Marcus shook his head. "If they don't get it, then it's highly likely Claudius Clavius will seek justice from the emperor. He'll do this, even if it means his going all the way to the Isle of Capri to talk with the emperor in person, or again, so he insists. This was made clear to Sejanus by Claudius in no uncertain terms."

"And so what is it Sejanus wants you to do about all this? Make the men stand trial?"

Again, Marcus shook his head, it was an exasperated gesture this time, but just whom he was exasperated at, Lucian for asking the question or the situation itself, Lucian couldn't tell.

"Jupiter only knows," Marcus said, heavily, at last. "He was so upset himself about this matter, he wasn't very clear in his wishes, other than the whole thing should just go away. He raged at everybody, the dead merchant, the three soldiers, the commander, and the entire family of Claudius Clavius. The only one he exempted was the Emperor Tiberius."

"But he must have said something to you about what he wanted," Lucian pressed him.

"Oh, yes. He did. He wants me to find some solution, as I did before, something to save the day," and here he glanced pointedly at Lucian, "to resolve this situation and quickly. He said he was relying on me to do so."

This news stunned Lucian. He was silent for several

moments, mentally digesting it all, before saying, "Marcus, I honestly don't think there is a solution to this, not one that will satisfy everyone."

"Oh, you think?" There was Marcus' sarcasm again. "It seems that I, really meaning you, was too good at fixing the last problem. Now Sejanus thinks I'm a magician, or a student of real magic, perhaps, because he thinks I can find something that will please everyone in this matter. Gods!" he exclaimed, "How they must be laughing at me right now."

Lucian shook his head, before saying, "I don't know what to tell you. How long do you have before this must be settled?"

"Just a matter of a few days at most, and then all parties must be satisfied. Oh, Gods," he moaned. "What am I to fucking do?"

"And then there is also the matter of the Lady Flavia, we must still contend with, as well. That, too, must be decided very soon."

Again, Marcus groaned, but he'd no more definitive response than that.

Lucian stood up. "I think it's best if you retire now, Marcus. You're too tired to think clearly at this late hour and too much has happened today to deal with it all right now. You prepare for bed, and I will bring you some more wine. It will help you to sleep better. Perhaps, a massage might help, as well."

"If you don't mind, Lucian, I'll settle for just the wine tonight. I'm exhausted and just wish to go to sleep and forget it all. It's difficult dealing with Sejanus at any time, but when he is in such a fury, it's almost impossible. I felt as if one wrong word and he would throw me into prison. The whole thing was like walking across a pit of hot coals, and without sandals, at that. It's a wonder my feet aren't blistered." He gazed with a mock-soulful expression down at his sandaled feet, as if they'd really encountered such a fiery trial.

Lucian couldn't help but smile at this. No matter how depressed Marcus might be, he always, somehow, seemed to manage to retain some sense of humor. This ability to laugh in such situations was one of the things he loved about Marcus.

Even so, Lucian knew it would take more than a sense of humor to get them out of this particular conundrum. No matter which way Marcus decided the matter, someone was going to be very angry and want vengeance. Moreover, by squarely dumping the problem onto Marcus' shoulders, Sejanus had seen to it Marcus would take the brunt of that anger and resulting desire for vengeance, and not himself.

Sejanus might be many things, but one thing he was not was a fool, it seemed. He knew how to shift blame onto others. For that, Lucian hated him with a cold and implacable hate, for the man threatened his Marcus' well-being, and Lucian wouldn't countenance anyone doing this. He knew it was up to him to find another solution. This wouldn't be easy to do. Marcus had already made clear enough that there were a number of factors involved this time, ones complicating the situation.

Certainly, the commander of the soldiers didn't want to see the men executed. It would not show well with regard to how he protected his men, and loyalty to them must be foremost in his decision making, for otherwise, he could face mutinies. Oh, yes, he could have them executed, perhaps, but to have a civil authority order this was entirely another matter. Then he could lay the blame safely at the feet of the magistrate and not himself.

Lucian sighed. Of late, it seemed the Praetorian Guard was almost outside the law, or rather a law unto itself. Sejanus, under Tiberius, had been expanding their numbers from a mere elite guard to a full-fledged army, one that now thoroughly controlled Rome, but in the process had created a powerful force, one difficult to control.

But to murder an innocent citizen so callously would not sit well with the merchant's family, of course, but even more importantly, it would anger the average citizen of Rome. Lucian could even see them rioting as a result, if the soldiers escaped conviction and proper punishment for their crime. So, what was Marcus to do? How could Lucian help him through this?

Chapter 15 — A Temporary Solution

Next morning, the two spoke little prior to breaking their fast. It wasn't they were angry at each other, but rather they just seemed both to be lost deep in thought. Lucian knew he was. He had lain on his couch, fully awake most of the night, tossing, and turning, racking his brain, trying to come up with some resolution to Marcus' predicament. He'd thought of none.

Now, in the harsh light of morning, he picked at his rapidly cooling porridge. He had never particularly liked this meal, not being a big fan of tasting garlic or smelling its strong odor first thing in the morning. Besides, his thoughts were elsewhere, rather than being concerned with eating.

The same seemed to hold true for Marcus. Although he'd greeted Lucian warmly enough earlier, upon first arising, now he was uncommunicative and seemingly mentally far away.

Lucian couldn't blame him. This matter was a grave one, and none of Marcus' doing. Sejanus was entirely at fault for this. The man had thrown Marcus to the wolves once more, in order to keep his own reputation pristine. If he wished to stay in power, despite his enemies, he had to have the Praetorian Guard completely on his side.

At the same time, he couldn't risk angering the aristocracy too much, or the general mob either, for that matter. He'd built enough resentment in these last two groups as it was, what with his often heavy-handed manipulations, and constant cries of treason against his enemies in order to destroy them.

And Sejanus had to tread carefully for another reason. Emperor Tiberius was a capricious ruler. He could take offense at the smallest things. Therefore, Lucian could readily see why Sejanus wished to walk warily on his path to power. Not to do so could easily result in his immediate execution. No doubt, only his prowess at administering the affairs of the Empire kept him from such a fate.

On great matters, those who knew said he always referred to Tiberius, by sending a messenger to him and then waiting for an answer before proceeding on any course of action. This was to make sure the emperor wasn't dissatisfied with Sejanus' decisions, and made it seem more as if Tiberius were still in direct control. The fact it was really a matter of dumping the truly serious problems into the emperor's lap didn't seem to occur to the aging Tiberius.

Thinking this, an idea occurred to Lucian. "I think I may have a solution," he said loudly and suddenly. Without realizing it, he dropped his wooden spoon and with a resulting loud clatter onto the table's surface, he was so excited.

"Eh?" Marcus looked up at him from stirring his porridge, blankly. "What's that? What are you saying, Lucian?"

"I said, I think I may have an answer, at least a temporary one, and perhaps a more permanent one. We'll have to wait and see."

Now Marcus' eyes widened. "Lucian, do you? Do you really?

Lucian nodded. "I think so," he said.

"Well then, don't keep me in suspense, man. Tell me!"

"I was just thinking how Sejanus was always so careful never to allow blame to come upon himself or anything of that sort, like with his behavior toward you, making you the scapegoat in this whole Praetorian Guard issue each time. If there had been a good answer, he would have seized upon it himself, you can be sure of that, and thus receive the attendant praise for resolving the matter well. But obviously, he sees no ready answer to this issue. No matter which way he decides, someone is going to be angry with him.

"So, it's better for him if everyone is angry at me, as the magistrate in charge of the case, instead of him." Marcus' tone was an acerbic one and so his expression was equally sour as he said this. "But this we already know, Lucian, so what is your solution to all this?"

"We can do exactly as Sejanus usually does in such matters when he can't find a safe answer to something, or the consequences of taking any action may be too great to risk undertaking them."

Now Marcus' eyes grew even wider, if that were possible. "You don't mean..."

Lucian nodded vigorously. "Oh, yes. That's exactly what I do mean. Have the matter referred directly to the Emperor Tiberius. A courier could be sent outlining the particulars of the case."

Marcus seemed to think about this, but then he said, "I don't think it would work. Sejanus would never go for it. He wouldn't want to bother the emperor on something like this. It isn't important enough, and he knows Tiberius doesn't like to be bothered with relatively insignificant problems, such trivial matters."

"But it is an important matter! The Praetorian Guard is the personal guard of the emperor. A matter as great as this is, concerning three of his soldiers, and possibly the resulting anger of the entire army of the Praetorian Guard or the mob would certainly concern him personally."

"I tell you, Sejanus will not go for it. His predicates his whole position on his not bothering the emperor, doing all the dirty work for him, and on a day-to-day basis. He's Tiberius' drudge. Everybody knows that."

"You must make him see this otherwise," Lucian gently persisted. "Stress the emperor could be furious if this doesn't work out right. Make it clear to him what he already really knows.

That is, on the one hand, the Praetorian Guard's soldiers could rebel if a civilian magistrate executes three of their own. Yet, on the other hand, make it also equally clear to him there could be massive riots in the streets if justice is not seen to be properly done. You must make him see the safest solution all round is to refer the matter to the emperor, that in this case, as a civilian magistrate, you don't have the authority or jurisdiction to resolve such matters on such a scale concerning the Praetorian Guard. The emperor alone has this right."

Marcus was silent a long moment, and then said, "You have a mind with a legal bent to it, Lucian. I wonder how you ever came by it, not having been trained in Roman law, or even having lived in Rome all that long."

Lucian grinned, before saying, "Does this mean you will do what I ask? You'll go to Sejanus, and try to persuade him to contact the emperor on this matter?"

Now Marcus smiled. "I'll do it," he then said. "The truth is you're right. This matter really is out of my jurisdiction. As you say, the Praetorian Guard is the emperor's personal army, his bodyguard. They don't really answer to the likes of me. And my just consulting with the commander isn't enough in this case. I'll let Sejanus know it's far better for the emperor to talk directly to the commander, to let Tiberius tell him what to do. And as you point out, this relieves both Sejanus and me of the burden of having made the wrong decision."

"Do you think he'll go for this approach?"

Marcus nodded. "Yes," he said. "I hope he will. Whenever he can safely sidestep an issue, he will. It's his nature, I'm finding out. And in this matter, it's far better to let the emperor make the decision concerning his own bodyguards."

"Yes, but just in case, I think you must have one weapon in reserve," Lucian told him. "After all, he can equally sidestep reaping the blame by still leaving this matter in your hands. So we must have some method of convincing him otherwise."

"And just what is that, my crafty lover? How can anyone at my low level of society have any sort of weapon against such as Sejanus?"

"If he resists you on this matter, if he says he won't do it, then and only then, you could tell him you have already done so."

"What? What do you mean, Lucian?"

"I mean, as a last resort, you can tell him you've already sent a courier to the emperor, that he left last night and you're now awaiting his reply. This way, he'll think it's too late for him to try to intercept the messenger, and the emperor is bound to hear your request for him to handle the matter."

"Oh, by the Gods, Lucian! I can't do that! He would be livid. He would throw me into the arena immediately and let the gladiators have their way with me. I wouldn't last ten minutes after saying something like that to him."

"Oh, but I think you would, Marcus. After all, the emperor supposedly would be responding to you in particular, wouldn't he? And he would want further reports from you on the matter, yes?"

Marcus shook his head. "No, Lucian. If I did such a thing, Sejanus would have it in for me. Oh, he wouldn't move right away against me, because he wouldn't dare, not in matters where the emperor is directly concerned. But you can bet after this matter has died down, has been mostly forgotten, he would then go after me for real. I'm sure I would be the victim of some footpad coming home some night. I'd have my throat slit in short order, or be arrested on a trumped up charge of treason or something."

"Yes," Lucian agreed. "But that trouble would lie much farther down the road. You're in big trouble right now. And it's what we need for now, not something much later on. Besides, I'd only use this approach as a last resort, if nothing else worked with Sejanus. You could then immediately send a courier after meeting with him if this turns out to be the case, if this became necessary. He wouldn't be looking for you to send one now, since he'd already believe you to have sent the messenger last night. Yes? The plan works perfectly in that regard."

"But he keeps tabs on me. He knows what I'm about always. I'm sure. He'd know I didn't send a courier. Wouldn't he?"

"My guess is he probably wouldn't. He has a spy in this household, or so we believe. But the spy can't see everything that happens here all the time. As a slave, they're restricted to their quarters at night. So they couldn't know what was going on then, not without a great deal of risk of someone catching them. More, I've checked. There's no one on the streets watching the house. So I think you're safe enough in lying about having sent a courier already, but I repeat, only if necessary."

"Very well, then, I'd do it, but as you say, as a last resort only. If I have to go to such an extreme, you and I would have to flee Rome, and sooner than later, before he had a chance to move against us. But I've no idea in the world where we could go to be safe, for Rome is everywhere and thus so is Sejanus. His reach goes to the very ends of the empire."

"But not beyond," Lucian said, disagreeing. "Believe it or not, Marcus, there is more to the world, far more, than just the Roman Empire."

"So you say." Marcus' tone was a derisive one. "But the current maps of the world seem to disagree with you."

Lucian smiled at him, but it was a mirthless one, because he hadn't been joking. He didn't bother to argue that the maps of the world, as Marcus referred to them, were maps made by Romans, and they were only of the world known to them. Whether Rome liked it or not, the world did continue well beyond its borders, despite their conceit it didn't.

Chapter 16 — Strange Happenings

Luckily for Marcus, Sejanus gave in, if a little petulantly, to the idea of referring the matter directly to the emperor. Although clearly not pleased with Marcus wanting to proceed in this way, he couldn't seem to refute the validity of Marcus' arguments, not after a long and silent period of considering the situation. Therefore, obviously grudgingly, Sejanus referred the matter on to the emperor, and this, without Marcus having to pull his trump card, of lying about having already sent a messenger to Tiberius.

That Sejanus was displeased with Marcus now there was no doubt. His surly manner and irritable behavior didn't leave this to the imagination. Marcus realized the man would have preferred him just calmly to accept his fate as the man to fall on his sword for Sejanus in this matter.

However, Marcus felt this was more a momentary displeasure than anything else and not a permanent state of affairs. This annoyance was not of the fatal variety with regard to Sejanus maybe wanting to seek vengeance. Marcus and Lucian even dared to hope Sejanus, in the future, might be a little more circumspect about trying such a maneuver, knowing now Marcus had successfully fended off two such attempts of using him as a scapegoat already.

So Sejanus duly remanded the whole thing for judgment to the emperor himself. Marcus was relieved and released of responsibility. What's more, on his own initiative, and following Lucian's example of how to deal with such issues, Marcus had mentioned the possibility of a marriage contract between himself and the Lady Flavia. He went on to stress to Sejanus how unworthy he felt because of his low status in society, having been born to the lower class. He also mentioned how he felt he would never quite fit in with the aristocracy through such a close marriage to them, and he would always feel uncomfortable. Marcus also casually mentioned what a good connection a marriage to Lady Flavia would make for someone else.

Sejanus was quick to absorb this last fact. Always on the lookout for ways to secure his connections with the upper classes, to ingratiate himself with the aristocracy of Rome, being born only of the equestrian class, himself, he immediately advised Marcus against such an ill-suited marriage.

Marcus readily agreed. He further suggested Sejanus might find a more suitable substitute, a more worthy candidate in his stead. Sejanus was more than happy to arrange such a thing, He told Marcus he would be in immediate contact with Flavia's father on the subject.

Marcus smiled to himself as he walked home that day. He had resolved the matter, and without Lucian's help. True, his approach had borrowed heavily from Lucian's abilities at such diplomacy. Marcus had followed his example. But so what? The method had worked.

Marcus realized then that not only was Lucian benefiting from his relationship with Marcus, but the reverse was true, as well. Marcus was learning the fine art of diplomacy, as well as the ability of subterfuge such often involved. He had Lucian to thank for this, although where the young man had learned to do such, Marcus simply couldn't fathom. Perhaps, it was just a natural gift. Nevertheless, Marcus was grateful.

So their lives once more settled into a relatively happy routine. A tempest had come and gone, and if anything, the two of them were the stronger for it all. There was only one problem; where once Lucian hadn't wanted sex with Marcus, now Marcus felt this way about Lucian.

Oh, Marcus wanted to fuck all right, but after the uproar over almost being forced into a marriage with the Lady Flavia, now Marcus fully understood what it meant, truly meant, not to have a choice in such a matter. He understood all too well.

As a result, he simply couldn't take advantage of Lucian's weak moment, by taking him to bed, although he still availed himself of Lucian's "massages." Marcus realized now that to do more was simply wrong, not to treat someone who should rightly be his equal in such a way.

He explained this feeling to Lucian. Lucian, despite still being ready to please Marcus in any way, agreed with him. He was glad Marcus now really comprehended how he had felt about the situation, but also, he was dismayed at yet another delay in their finally making love fully and completely.

But, as Lucian joked with him one day, they always had Octavos. Increasingly, they used that hairy little man on a regular basis, much to his joy and their own. Neither one stopped to think of how this was really a rather hypocritical substitute for the real thing, since they were both present at the same time, so closely involved in the act, but then they were both young, and when it came to sex, such subtleties were lost on them. As long as they didn't fuck each other, they were observing their promise.

It was one such evening Lucian finally had his way in the matter, and maneuvered Marcus into fucking Octavos again, while he watched. He simply sat there on his couch, hand pumping his cock, as Marcus fucked Octavos for all he was worth. In and out his cock went, reaming that little asshole, stretching it. Lucian always marveled at how wonderfully perfect Marcus' balls seemed, as they slapped against that hairy ass, smacked up against Octavos' own dangling nuts. Marcus was a master at fucking, an expert at such erotica.

Well, Lucian thought, with that huge cock, who wouldn't be?

He continued to stare, flailing away at his own hard meat, as Marcus fucked ever faster. Lucian fixated his gaze on Marcus' tight ass, the brief glimpses he caught of his puckered asshole when he flexed those firm butt cheeks. He fantasized about thrusting his prick deep into that hole, forcing it open, and then sticking his cock far into Marcus, possessing him. He masturbated faster now, fist wrapped around dick, thumb flicking the glans each time his hand moved up his shaft.

Marcus, too, was fucking away for all he was worth. Octavos, lying on his belly, face pressed into the mattress, took the pummeling without complaint. Quite the opposite; he moaned and groaned with pleasure. Repeatedly, he murmured the words: "Fuck me," over and over again.

And Marcus did. So aggressive was the assault that Lucian wondered if Octavos truly wouldn't walk "funny" the next day, so sore might he be from this ass-ripping fuck. Now, all such thoughts fled Lucian. He was about to cum, as was Marcus.

Lucian stood, and still stroking his cock for all he was worth, moved the few steps to the base of the bed. There, he stared down at the naked figures writhing in such sexual ecstasy.

"Oh, Gods!" Marcus exclaimed. He raised his ass, so close to Lucian he could have reached out and caressed it, touched the big balls swinging below the twin cheeks. "I'm cumming!" And with that, he lunged forward, shoving his big member all the way into Octavos, forcing the man's asshole to widen even more to accept this assault.

At the same moment, Lucian trembled with his own climax. He furiously pumped his meat, felt his ball sac tighten, as his sperm surged up the length of his shaft. The cum exploded from him.

"Ahhhh!" he moaned loudly, as the hot liquid jetted from his cock, arced through the air, and sprayed in thick white spatters over Marcus' perfect ass. Another eruption of cum shook him, caused him to weaken at the knees. He leaned forward, supporting himself with one hand on the bed, even as he fucked his own cock with his fist, made it spurt yet again, and then once more.

Marcus relaxed, sprawling onto the now quiet Octavos.

"You've cum all over me," he told the still trembling Lucian. "What a flood! What a mess back there," he added, and then laughed heartily, even as he lay there.

"I can take care of that," Octavos said in a muffled voice from below Marcus. "I'll be glad to lick you clean, master."

"You don't have to do that," Lucian said, still breathing heavily, watching the very last of his cum drip from the head of his fat dick onto Marcus' right buttock cheek. "I'll wash him clean."

"I want to," Octavos said, still sounding muffled. "It would be my pleasure, I promise you."

"Then get to it," Marcus told him, and he rolled off the little man, although careful not to disturb the sperm dripping down his ass, as he did so. "But hurry," he said, "or it will make a mess of my bed."

"Oh," Lucian heard Octavos say in a suddenly worried tone of voice. I'm afraid I may have already done that myself, master."

At this, both Lucian and Marcus burst out laughing.

And so things went. Marcus continued to be a worthwhile magistrate. He was earning a reputation for being a very fair one. Reelection for him seemed a foregone conclusion.

When the Emperor Tiberius ordered the soldiers, who had killed the merchant to be flogged to within an inch of their lives, and that their own commander had to see to it, and the merchant's family was given a large settlement from the emperor himself, as well, to expiate their grief and loss, Marcus' image was further improved. Everyone now seemed reasonably happy. His image as magistrate remained untarnished. They hailed his decisions in various trials as laudable, much more often than not.

Lucian did the rounds again the follow month, collecting the money from the various merchants and trades people. These proceeds, he always dutifully hid away beneath the loose tile under Marcus' bed. Between the legitimate funds pouring in from

Marcus' efforts as a magistrate, the ones going into the strongbox, and these illicit funds, they were doing financially very well. Although, Lucian didn't tell Marcus just how well they did, for fear of having to explain where the source of the extra funds.

Still, there was the matter of the spy. Neither Lucian nor Marcus had any better idea of who this could be. This situation rankled, because Lucian, in particular, felt he should have made more headway in the problem by now. If he was to serve Marcus faithfully, he needed to find out the spy's identify. If he did, he'd no plans to remove him. But once they knew who it was, both he and Marcus could see to it that whatever information the spy received was at their choosing, and not otherwise.

But as before, all this time, Lucian had a strange presentiment, was haunted with a feeling events would again take a turn for the worse. He wasn't alone in this feeling. Many in Rome seemed to feel the same way of late. The gossip at various market stalls was all about the political situation.

Sejanus had made many enemies over the years. Now, they seem to be getting together to plot against him more openly and more decisively. Rumors even said some of them traveled to Tiberius to let him know how much power Sejanus had acquired for himself, how much he now took upon himself in way of authority over the empire, and behaved as if he were the outright emperor, instead of Tiberius.

Rumors in the form of various letters and missives going back-and-forth from one person to another, all of them filled with accusations and counteraccusations, seemed to be the order of the day. The atmosphere in Rome, as a result, became tenser. It seemed as if everyone was trying to form alliances with everyone else. Accusations of disloyalty flew about the place. The fact that some of these accusations were about people being disloyal to Sejanus, while others were made against persons being traitors to Tiberius, seemed to make no difference. Everyone, according to gossip, was being disloyal to someone.

In the middle of it all, as a magistrate, Marcus tried to sail a neutral course. This was becoming increasingly hard to do. Sejanus, finding the situation more unstable, wanted to know who his real friends were. Apparently, he now had his doubts about Marcus, at least, some of Marcus' friends so informed him.

That Marcus didn't trust Sejanus was true enough. After his two attempts to throw Marcus to the wolves, he didn't consider Sejanus any sort of a friend, or indeed even a friendly colleague, but rather a dark force with which he had to reckon.

As summer faded and the blessed relief of fall's cooler air finally came upon the city, matters only seemed to worsen. One day, Marcus came home with a face like thunder.

"What is it?" Lucian asked, the minute he saw him, for he knew well now his moods. "What's wrong, Marcus?"

Marcus gave his habitual sigh, before saying, "Something isn't right, Lucian. There are strange rumors about all of Rome."

This news didn't surprise Lucian in the least. He already knew this much. "Rome is always full of rumors," he said, dismissively, "and has been. Why should things be any different now?"

Marcus accepted the cup of wine Lucian handed him, then moved to the nearest couch, and slumped onto it. He didn't even bother to adjust his toga to do this. Despite this, as always, to Lucian, Marcus looked as a God to him, although perhaps a slightly disheveled one right now. And even with a troubled expression on his face, Marcus was like some beautiful Adonis.

"You don't take me seriously in this matter," Marcus accused him. His forehead wrinkled into a frown. "I mean what I say, Lucian. There is some very strange gossip circulating lately in Rome."

"Who does it concern?" Lucian asked, striving now to appear more serious. Marcus' expression had shown that he, too, was deadly serious, that this was no small annoyance for him after all.

Marcus shrugged slouched shoulders. "Who else, but Sejanus and Tiberius? There are reports from all over of letters having been sent by Tiberius to various senators and friends of his."

Lucian moved over and sat down on the couch nearest to Marcus' own. "And what does the content of these letters concern? Is it good news or bad?"

Again, Marcus shrugged broad shoulders. "That's the strange part. It all seems to be very conflicting. Some say the letters castigate Sejanus, even have Tiberius call him an outright traitor. Other letters, also from the emperor, purportedly praise him and to a high degree. No one seems to know what to think, or more importantly, what the emperor thinks. Everything is mass confusion."

Lucian thought about this for a moment. "And what do you think?" he then asked. "What do you think it all means?"

For the third time, Marcus shrugged, and this time it seemed a desolate sort of gesture. "I have no idea. It depends on what version of events is true, I suppose. If Tiberius is really attacking Sejanus through these letters, then it means he's about to move against him. If, however, he is really praising Sejanus, then the rumors that he plans to give Sejanus even another high office to add to his credit, may be true. But I really don't know."

Lucian was the one who sighed this time, a heartfelt one. Then he said, "And as always in these things, somehow this must affect you, personally?"

"As the Gods would seem to have it, yes. Either I'm about to ride on the back of Sejanus' chariot to greater heights, or I may be headed for a terrible fall along with him. I have no idea which," he said, in a very low voice.

"But you're no longer that close to Sejanus, not since you forced him to go to the emperor on that matter about the

Praetorian Guard. Hasn't he been cold and rather distant toward you of late? You've said so."

"He was for a while, but in the last two weeks, he's been warming towards me again, it would seem, at least, judging by his missives praising my work he's sent me. Of course, he may have had early warning of this other matter, the letters, and so wants anyone around him he thinks may prove a useful ally, even a relative nobody, like me. So how genuine his feelings toward me are, I don't really know, but then I've never been sure of them. Anyway, I don't know what to do."

Lucian spread his hands in a gesture of futility. "What can one do? All we can do is to wait and see which way the political wind in Rome blows."

"And if it's an ill wind that then blows?" Marcus raised his eyebrows, an inquisitive gesture, as he asked this. "What then?"

"Then we had better be prepared," Lucian said. He stood and moved to Marcus' side, sat down next to him on the couch there. He put one arm around Marcus' right shoulder, and gave him a quick squeeze.

"You have me, Marcus," he told his lover. "I'll do everything I can to help. Starting tomorrow, I'll see what I can find out about all of this."

Marcus turned to him, a surprised look on his face. "You? What can you find out? You're just a—"

"Slave?" Lucian grimly finished for him. "Yes, but sometimes being a slave can be very useful. People stop seeing their slaves after a while, don't even notice them being there. So they talk freely in front of them, not realizing they're still being overheard. But slaves do listen, because their very lives and futures can depend on what they hear. They always try to be one step ahead of whatever is coming."

"And so what are you going to do, my little slave boy, knock on every door in Rome, bat those long, dark eyelashes of yours, and ask after any news?"

"I don't need to go quite so far as that," Lucian told him. Then he gave Marcus a slight smile, before adding, "I have but to go to the marketplace. News passes about through the vendors and hawkers of wares there. They love to gossip and the slaves readily enough supply them with such, knowing full well it will be passed on to others."

"By Jupiter's great cock, I'd no idea slaves were so organized. It's a wonder we Romans are still in control."

"Isn't it?" Lucian archly raised one eyebrow, a quizzical expression, but then he smiled, to soften what he'd said. Marcus could be so touchy about such matters, get so defensive.

"So you think you can really find something out?" Marcus' expression was not a humorous one, but rather eager.

This sobered Lucian. This was a life or death matter for Marcus, at least so he seemed to feel. He should take the matter more seriously, too. He nodded his head. "Yes, I think I can find out which way the wind is blowing for sure, whether it be ill news or otherwise. If it's as bad as you seem to think, then every major household in Rome must be talking about it and the slaves will have overheard something of substance somewhere. The marketplace will be buzzing with news about it all."

So it was the next day, although not the usual day for this, that Lucian headed to the forum. Normally, he would just seek out the smaller marketplaces and cheaper ones, those on the twisting side streets. But today, he felt he had to go to the main source of such news. It was there first, any rumors would be disseminated, and still be in their purest form. Often, by the time such gossip made it to the side streets, it was corrupted, exaggerated by repetition, and so less reliable as a result.

He made his way through the colorful throng of people, being jostled in the process and often pushing other people out of the way, as was the nature of Romans when in a thick crowd.

The place was incredibly noisy, with people talking, vendors shouting their wares, and various entertainment acts performed in the hope onlookers might contribute some coin if they liked what they saw. Monkeys chattered, parrots squawked, chickens cackled, and pigs squealed. In short, it was a veritable cacophony of noises, ones so loud, one could hardly think, let alone hear.

Lucian made his purchases, but also made it a point to chat a little longer than usual with the sellers occupying the various stalls there. He also tended to over tip, but this was on purpose. A few coppers for a cup of ale to salute a merchant's health, as Lucian would put it, helped to grease the skids when it came to those men repeating anything they've heard of interest.

What Lucian did hear didn't sound good. Marcus had been on the mark with his worries this time. So it was with heavily laden baskets and an equally heavy heart he trudged his way home through the crowded streets of downtown Rome, and headed up the hill towards Marcus' house.

When his master arrived home, it didn't take long for him to see the state of Lucian's spirits. His glum expression, no doubt gave it away.

"You've had bad news," Marcus said, coming straight to the point.

"It would seem so," Lucian acknowledged in a low voice. "As for the wind we were talking about blowing through Rome of late, I tell you this, it's a strong wind, and I think a very dangerous one. You were right to be worried."

"Exactly what have you learned?" Marcus asked, and he sounded a little impatient now.

"That many figures of importance, senators mostly, have indeed received letters from Tiberius. And some do seem to speak the praise of Sejanus, while others seem to want him buried. It's a very strange matter, just as you claimed. There seems to be no accounting for it. And all it seems to have done is to have sown mass confusion throughout the city."

"This can't be by accident," Marcus said, pensively, seemingly more to himself than to Lucian. "If the emperor is intentionally creating confusion, it's for a reason, but what reason?"

"I'm not sure, but I fear no good can come of this. It would seem events are reaching a crisis level."

"Yes," Marcus said, in a still-thoughtful tone of voice. "And I'm guessing this is also the emperor's direct doing and I'm betting he is doing all this quite on purpose."

Lucian sat forward. "But to what purpose, exactly," he wanted to know. "If he intends to move against Sejanus, if he believes Sejanus' enemies and what they say about him, then why not simply make his move outright?"

"And therein, lays the problem. Why not do as you say, Lucian, and simply marshal his forces and go after Sejanus? Why bother with all the confusion, the contradictory letters?"

"Could it be to throw Sejanus off his guard?" Lucian asked. "If he doesn't know what's true, whether he's to be elevated by Tiberius, or condemned by him, doesn't that make it easier for Tiberius to strike? After all, Sejanus controls the Praetorian Guard here in Rome. If Tiberius tips his hand too soon, or too clearly, he'll have to deal with Sejanus being in total control of Rome."

Marcus seemed to think about this a moment, as well, for he was very quiet, and then he said "It may well be you're right, Lucian. Really, it seems to explain all of this. It is either that, or old Tiberius is losing his mind at last, and I very much doubt that. He's a cunning devil. And this would be something right out of his conniving sort of style."

"Do you think Sejanus is aware of this possibility?"

Marcus shook his head at this question. "No, I don't, not really. He may have considered it, but such is his power, so long has he possessed it, and so many are his connections, I just don't think he would take Tiberius as being about to attack him too seriously, because despite the negative letters, so many other people are claiming they've received letters praising him. I fear he might just put it down to the usual gossip-mill grinding away again, just so much more negative grist for the mill, as it were."

Lucian said in a soft voice, "Do you think we should try to warn him?"

"Warn him of what?" Marcus turned to regard Lucian full on now. "This is only our conjecture, Lucian," he said. "We've no real proof. And I think we would only anger him, because I don't think he even wants to believe this might be true. I know I don't. And he's an arrogant son of Pluto, and he doesn't' like to listen to bad news. He's not kind to the bearers of such, especially when it's more mere conjecture than fact. He may not quite resort to killing the messenger, as some have done, but he might come close."

"So you won't warn him?"

Marcus shook his head. "I repeat; there is nothing to warn him about other than our own idle suppositions, which could be very wrong. And I might very well end up in prison for my efforts. Again, in such uncertain times, the powerful like to seek out scapegoats, those they once lied to and called friends. Besides, I'm not in the greatest of favor with Sejanus right now, as you know. What little warming there has been of late in my regard could easily turn cold again under such conditions. Very cold!"

"Very well, then," Lucian said, decisively, as he stood up. "Then we must make plans to protect ourselves."

Marcus also climbed to his feet. "And just how do you plan to go about doing that?" he asked.

"I'm not sure," Lucian freely admitted, "I'll have to think on it."

"Then you had better think swiftly," Marcus told him, "or you may find your master has already been sent to the arena as fodder for the gladiators."

Chapter 17 — Lucian Makes Plans

Lucian wasted no time the next day preparing for any eventuality. Marcus, as was usual, set off to do his daily duties as a magistrate. Lucian had to push him a little to do this, because Marcus wanted to stay near him and protect him, as he put it. However, Lucian had argued his absence from his normal routine would only be a cause for curiosity. Right now, it was very important to make everything seem as usual, to keep a low profile. Marcus reluctantly agreed, and so set off to work.

"Will you be going to the marketplace soon?" Didius asked him just shortly after Marcus had gone.

"Why do you ask?" Lucas was suspicious of the slave's motives.

"It's just we are low on supplies for making bread," Didius said, sounding innocent enough, but now his expression seemed a suspicious one to Lucian.

Lucian realized he might be overreacting. He was telegraphing his nerves to this man, and worse, stabbing at shadows, inferring things that probably weren't there. He shouldn't do that. Everything must seem as nearly normal as possible, he knew.

Lucian didn't know how long such a state of affairs would last, or even if it could last. He was hoping, despite his gathering dark presentiments, nothing bad was going to take place after all, that all would calm down again, as it had several times before.

Nevertheless, like the chill wind blowing this day, sweeping dust up the streets of Rome and heralding summer's end, Lucian felt the relative period of peace they'd enjoyed was also over. He could feel it in his bones, as it were. Trouble was coming and this time it was not of the minor variety.

"No," Lucian now said to Didius, with a forced nonchalance. "Not today, for I have a few other household chores to attend to first. One of the master's togas has a tear and he wishes to wear it tomorrow," he lied. "So I must repair the thing. If I have time afterwards, I may go shopping. I presume you have enough bread to last us for today and tomorrow?"

"Just enough," Didius said, now in his usual surly tone of voice. This type of response actually relaxed Lucian. When Didius was being surly, then everything in the house was going as usual. It was only when the slave deviated from his constantly spiteful behavior, Lucian worried something might be wrong.

Having dismissed Didius, Lucian hurried to Marcus' cubiculum. Here, he quickly grabbed a fresh tunic of his master's, and one of his own, His was the only clean spare he had right now. For unlike his master, Lucian had few belongings. Marcus had seen to it he'd several changes of clothing, all of decent quality, and Lucian felt grateful for this. But when Marcus wanted to get him more, Lucian had demurred, for he wasn't one to enjoy many material possessions.

Having selected the appropriate tunics, he found some spare material, good strong linen, and using his sewing abilities (learned from working with the skins of animals while still amongst his own people), he quickly sewed several hidden pouches inside each of the two garments.

When he'd completed this, Lucian went to the strongbox and opened it. He sorted through the coins and took out all the silver and gold ones, but included just a few lower denominated ones, as well, for good measure. He put equal amounts of these in the pouches he'd sewn into both tunics.

Then, he filled two extra money pouches with the remaining coins hidden under the floor tile, as well as a few of the leftover denarii, and a lot of the yellow brass coin, the sestertius, from the strongbox. He ignored the half-value cousins, the dupondius, as not being worth enough to worry about.

Having done this, he drew the drawstrings tight together. Then he placed the pouches back in the strongbox. The tunics, he hid in a cedar chest, but at the very bottom, under a pile of other items. It was the best he could do, because he couldn't lock the chest.

Next, armed with sheets of parchment, a quill, and pot of ink, he sat at a small table in the atrium. Lucian's writing skills were certainly rudimentary, never having had formal lessons, but his task was a relatively easy one. He wrote several short letters, ones freeing the household slaves. Each letter had the name of a slave in it, including even the detestable Didius. Of course, he could not sign for Marcus. This didn't matter. Marcus, even if they were in a hurry, could make short work of signing a few such letters. Such would only take seconds.

Finally, he went to the kitchen. He sent the cook there off on an unnecessary task to collect some herbs in the garden. While he was gone, Lucian filled a cloth sack he'd brought with cured meats, various sausages, large chunks of three types of the drier cheeses, and two flagons of wine. As an afterthought, he also tossed in some raisins and dried figs.

Not waiting for the cook to return, he left the cucina, and went back to the cubiculum. There, he stored his sack of food in the same chest as he had the money-filled tunics. Next, he sent Libo, one of the two young slaves to find Octavos.

Octavos arrived within minutes of his summons. "You needed me, Lucian?" he asked, deferentially.

"I do." Lucian gave Octavos a faint smile before saying, "Octavos, if for any reason Marcus and I had suddenly to leave here, never to return, what is it you would most like to have or do? Is it your freedom, you would want?"

Octavos just stood there with his mouth hanging open, apparently too surprised to answer.

"Come, come," Lucian ordered him, impatiently. "I haven't

much time and I need to know your answer. What is it you would want under such circumstances, Octavos?"

Octavos gulped. "I...I...I would want to go with you," he said in a stammering voice.

Lucian firmly shook his head. "No, my friend, Octavos. That's not an option. I think it best if you have your freedom under such circumstances, and perhaps some money to help you make a new start in life. Don't you think so?"

Now it was Octavos' turn to shake his head. It was a vehement gesture, an outright negation. "No. I desire that least of all. What would I do with my freedom?"

Lucian shrugged, not having expected this particular question. "I don't know," he said, knowing he sounded uncertain now, and he was. "What does anyone do with their freedom? They do what they like. You could start a small business, or perhaps buy a small farm. I'm sure Marcus could see his way to giving you enough money as a down payment for such, and then you could pay what you still owed from a portion of your harvest each year until you had cleared the debt."

"I'm no farmer!" Octavos exclaimed, sounding stressed.

Lucian thought for a moment, and then he said, "Well then, perhaps you could just buy a small apartment here in Rome, or even rent one. Many of those are available and that way you could save the greater portion of the money Marcus would give you. There are many choices open to you as a freed man. Perhaps, you could even leave Rome, and go back to your people."

Octavos looked downcast, as he said, "I have no people. I was born a slave here in Rome, and so were my parents, I presume they are dead now, for they had hard lives, and served a terrible master. I haven't seen or heard from them in a very long time. Besides, they aren't here in Rome the last I heard. Where they are, I've no idea. I've tried to find out on occasion and have heard nothing."

"I'm sorry to hear about your mother and father," Lucian said, meaning it. "But their tragedy isn't yours. You're still young. You could enjoy the rest of your years in freedom. Why don't you want to do this? Freedom is a wonderful thing."

Now Octavos looked up at him, gazed at Lucian squarely on. He exuded a look of stubbornness too obvious for Lucian to miss.

"I want to go wherever you and Marcus go. I want to serve the two of you. It's all that matters to me, and all that ever will. I've no need of freedom or money, if I can stay with you two."

Lucian shook his head. "As I've said, that would be impossible under the circumstances we envision. If Marcus and I leave, we don't even know where we'll be going ourselves, and our travels will be uncertain, perhaps far-reaching. Surely, someone as used as you are to a peaceful life here in Rome wouldn't want to have to go through the trials of such an ordeal."

Octavos fell to his knees. Clasping his hands together in front of him, he looked up at Lucian. "Please," he begged of him, "don't leave me behind. The only love I have known in my life is that for Marcus, and now for you, as well, Lucian. You're the only people who've treated me with kindness, you, and Marcus. You alone have shown me care, consideration, and compassion. There's no one else. There's no point to my life if I can't be with the two of you, serve you. Please, in the name of all the Gods, take me with you, for if you don't, I'll kill myself."

This last statement of Octavos' took Lucian aback. He knew the little man cared for Marcus, and yes, himself, if perhaps to a slightly lesser extent, but he'd no idea how strongly he felt about it all, just how loyal he really was. Truly, Octavos wasn't the spy, for there was no faking his emotional involvement in what he'd just said to him.

"Very well," he told Octavos. "I'll speak to Marcus about

this. Perhaps, there's room for you to travel with us after all. But I warn you, it won't be an easy trip, and you'll have to do your part. There could be many hardships. At times, you may have to sleep out in the rain, or in fields under the cold stars. There will be times when we may have to hide in unsavory places, go without food for long periods. Can you do this? Do you want to? Think carefully before you answer me."

Octavos didn't hesitate. He nodded eagerly, and said, "I can do all these things, if I can just be with the two of you. So you will take me?"

"I must speak with Marcus first, of course, but I think it may be possible, but I can't promise yet. But be sure this is what you really want, Octavos, because once committed, it will be too late for you to turn back. There'll be no place for you to come back to. This house will belong to others."

Octavos gave him a little smile, and then said, "Rome holds no special place in my heart, if you two are not here. There is nothing of importance I would be leaving behind. In truth, I look forward to such a journey, such an adventure with you two. It sounds exciting."

"Well, in all likelihood, it probably won't even be necessary. But be on your guard, Octavos. If I come to you and say we are leaving, you must be ready to go at once, and I mean at once, without a minute's delay. So keep your possessions together, Take only what is important to you, and have it near you, ready to go."

"It will be just as you say," Octavos assured him. "Again, I leave nothing here of any importance to me, or that I need to take with me, other than some clothing."

"Very well, then. I'll speak to Marcus. Let's hope he and the Gods favor your decision. Now," he added in a tired voice, "please leave me. I have other things I must attend to and they can't wait any longer. Oh, and speak to no one of what we've talked about here, please. That's imperative, Octavos."

Of a sudden, Octavos grabbed at Lucian's right hand. He leaned forward and kissed it. "Thank you...my friend" he said, and then, he hurried from the room.

Lucian just gazed after him, wondering at how someone could be so loyal and care so much for people who really hadn't shown him very much kindness to warrant it. After all, true kindness would have been to set him free, help him to learn to live a life of his own as a free man.

But Lucian suspected this option was already too late for little Octavos. Whatever other burdens they might carry with them out of Rome, he suspected he and Marcus would be carrying a living one, as well. He was sure Octavos would be trudging along just behind them, through whatever kind of weather and other conditions they were going to have to face along the way.

Lucian could only hope all his elaborate plans turned out to be unnecessary. How much more pleasing it would be if they could all just go on with their lives as they were, comfortable here in Marcus' little house, living together without any major problems, and with no more political crises to interfere with their lives.

Small chance of that happening, Lucian thought, morosely. For better or for worse, the die had been cast and whatever Sejanus' fate was going to be, so too, would it intimately affect everyone's in this household, and throughout Rome, as well, no doubt.

Damn, the power-hungry fool, Lucian thought, him and his need to make the Castra Praetoria and thus himself so damned powerful! This is what comes of such greed.

Then Lucian's mind turned to other, more immediate and practical problems. One of which, was to determine some quick way out of Rome, without running into the Praetorian Guard, or the vigiles, who served as Rome's corrupt police force, and occasionally as rather ineffective firemen. Then, of course, there were just the standard soldiers of the Roman Legions to worry about, as well, those on leave, or stationed just outside of Rome and most of whom were usually drunk, and so on their worst behavior. Accosting innocent citizens was often a common thing for them to do.

Yes, to get out of Rome and well away from it was not going to be easy, especially not if Octavos was with them. Lucian fretted about this. Three seeking refuge would naturally be harder than two, or even just one. However, he had promised the little man could come (assuming Marcus agreed). His unquestioning loyalty to them demanded this much. Yet, it made things that much harder for them to be able to get away unnoticed.

Still, Lucian couldn't do much about it. He was too fond of Octavos to leave the little man behind. Again, it would still be up to Marcus to make the final decision on the matter. It would also be up to Marcus to make the final judgments on which slaves he freed, all, or any.

There were several ways in which they might be able to spirit themselves out of Rome, Lucian knew. The first was to boldly go out the city gates, and hope nobody had alerted the guards about Marcus. However, if Sejanus were to fall, his enemies would go after any of those they considered to have been Sejanus' friends in any way. And Marcus was too prominent as a magistrate not to be on that particular list. So that idea was risky in the extreme.

The second way was to try the same thing, but to use a disguise, bribery, or both, as a means of passing on through the gates. Lucian didn't much favor the bribery part of the idea. After all, what was to stop the soldiers from taking the money offered, and then arresting them anyway, if one of them recognized Marcus?

Such practices were hardly unheard of. Such a tactic might even make the soldiers decide to arrest them, so they could search them for any more money they might have.

And to be honest, Lucian knew well that Roman soldiers were usually, despite everything said about them, loyal. For the most part, they obeyed commands well. They were not terribly subject to bribery on important matters from all accounts, although Lucian had no direct experience of this one way or the other, never having attempted such bribery. Still, disguising themselves was a distinct possibility, and Lucian would have to think on that more.

The third way was to sneak out of the city unnoticed, hidden in some way, as in a cart or something. This, they could do by either day or night. Both times had their advantages, and disadvantages. If they chose to go by day, and paid someone to hide in their cart, so busy were the gates of Rome, they might just slip by without the guards checking the vehicle too closely. The throngs of pedestrians, those on horseback, and all the rest would force the guards to be quick about their tasks, and so less thorough. Romans made for a restless and therefore often dangerous crowd. They didn't like to wait long without getting noisy, hostile, and violent into the bargain.

By night, it was much more just a matter of freight-laden carts crossing back-and-forth, in and out of Rome, carrying supplies or exports. This was a much more homogenous traffic, and the negative was the soldiers had set procedures for examining each cart going through. Again, however, they had to be quick about it to avoid traffic backups, so they weren't necessarily very thorough. Moreover, being late night, often they weren't very alert.

Lucian decided he would have to discuss this with Marcus when he arrived home that evening. Any of these possible ways of escape could be fraught with danger and ultimately, the possible loss of their lives.

It never occurred to Lucian his Marcus wouldn't be willing to go. Now that he thought about it more, that, too, was a distinct possibility. Marcus loved him. Lucian had no doubt of that. But he was a Roman, and one with a Roman office. And

Romans were invariably proud, even arrogant. Marcus was no exception to this, being a loyal son of the city.

As much as Lucian loved him, he had no illusions on that score. Marcus might just decide to stay and fight, or even fall on his sword. Many Romans before him had done this in just such similar situations. And judging by his discussion with Marcus earlier, the man had no idea there could be a life beyond the boundaries of the Roman Empire. It was as if the world stopped for him at the very borders.

With these bleak thoughts, Lucian became even more worried; what if all his carefully laid plans for their escape were for naught? What if Marcus simply refused to leave Rome?

Well, there was no help for it. All Lucian could hope was that he could convince Marcus to go with him and to bring Octavos, too. And failing this, his only other recourse was to hope there would be no crisis.

So with all this in mind, now Lucian prayed to the Gods at the little household altar that Sejanus would not fall, that the rumors circulating about the Senate of Rome were just that, and nothing more. However, Lucian knew in his heart, this probably just wasn't so. Something definitely was up. One could feel it. Something was coming…he just knew it.

Chapter 18 — The Situation Worsens

The following days brought no relief from the tension. If anything, it only seemed to worsen, to build. Gossips still insisted the letters from Tiberius to his friends in the Senate said very different things. Some said Tiberius was on the verge of death, while others said he was returning to Rome and was in rudely good health. Rumors spread it was Antonia, mother of Livila, Sejanus' betrothed, who had actually traveled to the Isle of Capri, and had personally alerted the emperor to the ever-increasing power of Sejanus. The gossip had it the woman couldn't stand the thought of her daughter marrying into a lower class upstart, as people said she thought of him.

A few days later, more news arrived. This said the Emperor Tiberius had given up his consulship. This seemed a real fact, for this news was by official public decree. Since Sejanus shared this office with the emperor, in the emperor's absence, he'd no choice but also to give up the position, as well, and it was a powerful one. This did not bode well for him.

It was now the Ides of October and Rome was in a veritable uproar. Lucian and Marcus' concerns were climbing, because there was no official word from Sejanus. He said nothing, seemed oblivious to anything, but continued to occupy his offices, those now remaining to him. Apparently, he chose to pin his hopes on those letters of Tiberius that had praised him, instead of those condemning him.

Was he living in a fool's paradise? Lucian had no way of knowing. He was not a politically minded person, although he'd become more so since living in Rome. When the lives of so many rested upon the daily whims of those in power, it was incumbent upon anyone in Rome, aristocrat, plebeian, and slave, alike, to be at least somewhat aware of what was happening.

The problem, Lucian soon realized, was one couldn't be sure which news item was the correct one and which was just a product of the rumor mill. He'd gone to the market almost every day in a row, for an entire week now, trying to ascertain what exactly was really happening. All he could be sure of was something was happening. It concerned Sejanus and the Emperor Tiberius, and really, little more of substance.

He decided to broach the subject of perhaps leaving Rome to his master. Marcus merely stared at him, when he told him his idea.

"Are you insane?" he asked of Lucian. He sounded angry. "I know you're an intelligent man, but you have this all wrong. Those close to Sejanus assure me the emperor still holds him in high regard. He has read copies of various letters sent to some senators saying this very thing. Why, it seems the emperor even may soon honor him in some way."

"Has Sejanus, himself, told you this?" It was a pointed question.

Marcus frowned darkly. "Do you doubt my word, Lucian?" he asked in a suddenly cold tone of voice.

Now it was Lucian's turned to frown. "Don't be absurd, Marcus. I believe you in all things. Anything you tell me I take as if the Gods themselves had spoken the words to me."

Marcus' features visibly relaxed at this statement. "Then why do you argue with me?"

"Because it's obvious you have not met with Sejanus, not in many weeks. This is true, isn't it?"

Marcus glanced down at his tanned feet, as he said, "and what if it is?" He sounded for all the world like an irritable child. "It doesn't mean what his close friends tell me isn't true."

"Oh, I believe it's true enough, as far as it goes," Lucian said, carefully. "But I believe it's just as true the emperor sent letters to other senators, saying he hated Sejanus and that he's a traitor and he wants him removed."

Marcus gave a great sigh, before saying, "Really, Lucian, you can't have it both ways. Either one is true or the other, that both are true just cannot be. Surely, you must know this much?"

The comment exasperated Lucian. "How can you say such a thing?" he asked, annoyed. "Haven't I demonstrated my abilities to you already with regard to political matters? Didn't I advise you both times in your dealings with the Praetorian Guard when the soldiers committed those crimes?"

"Yes, yes, I admit, you most certainly did, Lucian. I meant to cast no aspersions upon your abilities, but you seem so blind in this matter. You insist upon stabbing at shadows. I don't think Sejanus is in any great danger. Even if he is about to fall, why should it affect me? I'm not a close ally of his. I'm a veritable nobody. Surely, I see no reason to leave Rome. Where would we go? What would we do? How would we survive? We would have nothing and no place to go."

"We would have each other," Lucian pointedly reminded him, still annoyed. "And we would be alive together. I should think that would be better than nothing." He knew he sounded angry now, but couldn't help it. Marcus really was going too far in his stubbornness.

Marcus shook his head and slumped onto the nearest couch. "I'm sorry, Lucian. I don't know what I'm saying half the time, lately. All this exhausts me, the worry of it all. I don't think I was ever meant to be a magistrate. I can do it, but I don't like doing it."

Lucian sat down next to him, and placed one hand on Marcus' bare right thigh. "I know you're tired," he said in a low and soothing voice. "You're still my master, Marcus. I must care for and watch out for you. It's my duty as a slave, and my sworn duty as your friend and lover. And I tell you, Rome is unsafe for you, if Sejanus should fall."

He paused before trying to explain by saying, "Purges always follow these things. Do you really think Tiberius would be content with simply removing Sejanus, but allowing all of his minions, the network and organization, he's had years to build, to stay intact? No, he will seek them all out, consider them his enemies, and kill them all. He will want to find out anyone who had anything to do with Sejanus and tear them out of the government, root, and branch. He will not stop until they're all dead."

Marcus turned to look at them. His expression was one of real worry now. "You really think this could happen?"

Lucian patted his thigh again, a gesture of affection and reassurance, but he nodded his head at the same time. Then he said, "Yes, I do. I have no doubt of it. The world has worked this way now for some time here in Rome. Think about Sejanus, himself. Has he not done much the same thing? Didn't you, yourself, tell me he regularly trumped up charges of treason against senators he felt were his enemies, had them arrested, tried, and executed, and then seized their estates? Didn't he also seek to gain more power by engaging himself to a member of the imperial family with his betrothing himself to Livia?

"And," he continued in a slightly softer tone, "Wasn't it you who also told me he may have been culpable in the death of Germanicus? And all of Rome knows of his network of spies. Tiberius has been complicit in much of this surely, if not in the death of his beloved Germanicus, so overall, he's been no better in this regard. What makes you think, then, that the same thing won't happen to Sejanus when he falls from power? He must have many powerful enemies by now, at least, those he hasn't managed to have executed already."

"Oh, enough!" Marcus exclaimed. He abruptly stood up. "I can't think anymore right now. I can't argue with what you say, Lucian, for you say it too well and I'm too tired. Yes, all you say may very well be true, perhaps even likely, but to leave Rome? Surely, you can see how impossible that would be. I mean, perhaps we could leave Rome itself, but the empire? There is no other place to go!"

Lucian also stood up, but this was out of respect for his master having risen. "As you say, master," he said in a soft voice. "Since it's your wish, we shall discuss it no further. But all I ask, is we insure our own survival should the very worst happen. Isn't this just a reasonable thing to do?"

"Yes, I suppose it is at that," Marcus conceded. He gave Lucian a tiny smile, then said, "All I really want to do is spend my life with you, Lucian, in peace and quiet, just live out our years of life allotted to us and be together, in work and pleasure. One wouldn't think that would be such a crime, would one?"

"No," Lucian gently told him. "One wouldn't. And, it's all I want, too."

That ended the conversation. Lucian had never even managed to get around to asking if they did flee, could Octavos go with them. That, he supposed, would have to wait for another time. He thought he'd made some headway with Marcus, though. After all, his lover had at least admitted all he wanted was to live his life with Lucian. So maybe, where they lived wouldn't be so important in the final analysis.

Oh, Lucian knew it would take more persuasion, and he resolved to do this in a step-by-step process, to try not to push Marcus all at once on this issue. After all, he constantly reminded himself over the next few days, Marcus was a true Roman. Therefore, for him, Rome was the center of the universe.

So Lucian was determined not to let Marcus' resistance keep him from continuing with his plans. He had come up with one in particular. And if Marcus didn't like the idea of leaving the empire, then Lucian was betting that he wouldn't like this idea any better. But when the time came, if necessary, he would broach it to him. Then, under such dire circumstances as might exist at the time, Marcus might actually be willing to try it.

He had persuaded Marcus the next day of doing one thing; he'd agreed to sign the documents freeing the slaves. But he also insisted that Marcus place them in the strongbox and lock them up there. Marcus didn't want the slaves having their freedom, if there was no necessity for it, if everything quieted down again. And he still maintained everything would work out just fine. As for Lucian, himself, he was far from as sure of this as Marcus was.

The next day, more rumors circulated. Now they were becoming wild, so Lucian had little faith in them. It was late that night, and just after midnight, when Didius answered the door to find a messenger waiting there. The caller asked for Marcus, again, of course. Lucian waited where he was, scared this was it, that Marcus was about to be summoned before Sejanus.

But the messenger was only from another magistrate, a good acquaintance of Marcus', who had promised immediately to send news of anything he heard, just as Marcus had promised this in return. The message said Tiberius was to honor Sejanus. He'd received a letter from Tiberius ordering him to appear in the Senate on the morning of the 18th, to have the Tribunician powers bestowed upon him.

This was a great honor, indeed. More, it was a sure sign of the emperor's favor, and more importantly, his faith in Sejanus. All would be well after all, it seemed.

"You see," Marcus practically crowed to Lucian shortly after he'd dismissed the messenger with his thanks and some coins clutched in his fist. "I was right. Sejanus has not fallen out of favor. Those letters you spoke of must have been wrong or simple forgeries."

Lucian wasn't so easily persuaded in the matter. "Why would the emperor send a letter to Sejanus to summon him to the Senate? Since when has the emperor ever worried about what the Senate thought or felt? Why wouldn't he just summon him to appear personally before him, and then grant him these powers, or declare them by public edict?"

"Oh, Lucian, my handsome man, you worry too much. You see a problem where none lies. It's a bad habit of yours. Things are going well, after all. Can't you just accept the fact and be happy?"

"I would better accept it when I actually see such happen."

"Well, you shall see it happen soon then, for early tomorrow morning, Sejanus appears before the Senate to accept his new power. So your wait will not be a long one."

Lucian had merely nodded at this statement. Privately, his concerns had only worsened, grown in stature. Something was wrong here, very wrong. He knew it, could feel it. This made him wonder if Sejanus did. Then, Lucian really didn't care one way or the other what the man thought. The only thing important to him now was the safety of Marcus. And despite Marcus' reassuring words, more than ever now, Lucian felt their personal safety was in real jeopardy.

Despite this, he knew he couldn't convince Marcus of this fact, not yet. His master still clung to hope, the idea the news they'd just heard was good news. Events would have to prove otherwise before he'd change his opinions. As Marcus had said, they could only wait and see and that was an unnerving proposition for Lucian, at best. It would be better for them to leave Rome now, before anything happened, while exiting the gates was no problem, and when it was still easily permissible.

All that night, Lucian lay on his couch and listened to the deep breathing of Marcus. Why did the man have such an ability to sleep like such an innocent, while he, Lucian, lay on his couch, tossing and turning, and with worrisome thoughts crowding his mind? It just didn't seem fair. Then, nobody had ever told him life was supposed to be fair. Moreover, in Rome, it certainly wasn't.

Even his love for Marcus came at a high price. Everything

in Rome seemed to come at a high price, Lucian felt, if all it meant was constant worry and concern for his loved ones. When he started thinking of Octavos and considering his future, too, Lucian had had enough.

He rose, naked, from his couch, and padded on bare feet out of the cubiculum. He went in search of a cup of wine. Perhaps, he needed more than one, because he desperately wanted just to go to sleep and not even to dream. Especially, he didn't want to dream about the Prefect Lucius Aelius Seianus, otherwise known simply to all and sundry as Sejanus, that "tyrant of Rome."

Chapter 19 — The End Of Sejanus

The next morning started well enough. Marcus was in a good humor. Lucian, although still worried, began to relax some. The day was a bright sunny one. The sky was a deep and peerless blue. How could anything awful happen on such a beautiful day? Perhaps things were going to be all right after all.

But at the gate to the house, where Lucian said his usual goodbyes to Marcus, both realized something strange was going on in the street. Several people were running. Oddly, they ran in both directions, so they weren't running away from something or to something in particular. But that they were in a hurry and had panicked expressions upon their faces was all too obvious. Immediately, Lucian's mental warning flags went up.

"What is this?" Marcus shouted at one of the men racing up the street past the two of them. He was dressed in the clothing of a freed man, and headed in the general direction of the Palatine Hill. "What's happening?"

The man barely paused in his mad dash, but almost breathless, he did shout, "Sejanus has been arrested. He went to the Senate this morning at dawn, and there Naevius Sutorius seized him. He's now in complete charge of the Guard. They say it's at Emperor Tiberius's direct command."

Lucian knew both he and Marcus would've liked to learn more, but the man was too far up the street now, running for all he was worth again, as if a horde of the Praetorian Guard were after him already.

Which just might be the case, Lucian thought with a sudden new fear. Who knew to whom they owed allegiance now? Who was truly in charge of Rome today—anyone?

Turning to Marcus, he said, "I think it's best if you don't go today. If what that man said is true, then it could be very dangerous for you."

"I'm a magistrate, Lucian," Marcus told him flatly and just a shade arrogantly. "I must do my duty, even in such troubled times as these."

"And who appointed you to that duty?" Lucian reminded him, almost brutally. "It was good Sejanus, wasn't it? And does his authority still count now they have arrested him? Or, are you under the law no longer a magistrate now?"

Marcus didn't answer right away. He remained where he stood, immobile, as if he were a statue. "I don't know the answer to that, exactly," he said, at last, sounding uncertain for once. To Lucian's eyes, he looked it, too, for his face was a mask of worry.

"Then in such an event, I think you should stay home today. The city will be in an uproar. Nobody will know who is really in charge for some time. It's best if we don't venture abroad under such conditions; no need to make ourselves unnecessary targets for the soldiers when we don't have to yet. After all, there is the mob to consider, as well, and even the vigiles. With no one clearly in charge, who knows how they will go about their so-called duties? They may just arrest anyone they feel like, just to be on the safe side."

Marcus nodded at these words. "Even so, Lucian, if I don't go, how will we know what's going on? Staying shut up in the house won't tell us which way the wind now blows in Rome."

Lucian gave him a dour look, before saying, "No matter which way it blows, master, it blows ill for Sejanus and all his friends. This much we do know; people are going to die, one way, or the other, and perhaps many of them. I don't like to think this will be so, but I fear it is."

Marcus gave a sigh. "You're probably right," he said. "I suppose we could always send Didius down to the market later. He should be safe enough. No one ever notices slaves, especially when such matters are going on as now."

Lucian nodded his agreement. "And that label fits me, just as well, being a slave, too. I don't trust Didius to ask the right questions, to bring us all the news we need, or even to tell us what he really knows, what he may find out. He is a shifty one. So with your permission, master, I will be the one who goes to the market later."

"No!" Marcus exclaimed. "Not you. I won't have you risk your life like that."

"But you said slaves would be safe under such circumstances."

Marcus vehemently shook his head. "I meant they would be relatively safe, Lucian. I didn't mean for you to risk your life in going there. You mean too much to me. I can't lose you. Do you understand that?"

"I understand only that I can't tell one of the others to do something I'm too afraid to do myself. It must be me. Marcus, with your sense of Roman duty, you of all people should know this and understand. I can't ask others to endanger themselves, while not being willing to do so myself. I'm no coward in that regard."

"Are you then no coward in any regard at all?" Marcus softly asked of him.

Lucian immediately nodded. "Yes. In one way I can think of," he said. "When it comes to your safety, Marcus, your well-being and life, there I'm a coward. I would willingly sacrifice others in order to save you. I would try not to, but I fear in the end, I would. I would even willingly sacrifice myself under such circumstances."

"I don't know where you managed to come by your sense of duty, Lucian, for you're not a Roman. But I know this; you do have a strong feeling for such. Yet, I still don't want you to go. Send Didius. Despite his faults, he'll do well enough for this purpose, won't he?"

"I repeat that I don't trust the man." Lucian knew he sounded stubborn. "And worse, it's because I dislike him that I can't bring myself to send him. I would always wonder afterwards if anything happened to him, if I wanted it to happen. No, I want no such burden on my conscience."

"Very well, you go to your market," Marcus said, but in a grim voice. "But so help me, Lucian, if anything happens to you, I swear I'll punish you with the lash." Then he smiled, before adding, "Please the Gods, you remain safe. Take no chances when you go. Accost nobody who looks the least bit dangerous. Stay away from the authorities. Avoid them. You understand me? And don't tarry long!"

Lucian nodded. "Believe me, master, I'm no hero, even if I don't think of myself as a coward. I'll do just as you say. Now let's go back indoors, if it pleases you to do so, for I think it might be dangerous even out here. Who knows what the street rabble might get up to given the chance? It's better by far to be off the streets as much as possible, I think. In the meantime, for my sake if no other, please stay inside the house, and by Mercury's swift balls, please take off that magistrate's toga!"

Lucian was uneasy from the outset of the trip. He'd left Marcus and home just a little after that talk, before too many were up and about the streets of Rome. The lanes were still mostly empty of people, an unusual situation in daytime in Rome, even for this early in the day. Even at nighttime, so few people was unusual, for that matter.

And when he did see anyone, they wrapped themselves in their cloaks, often wore hoods, ones that mostly hid their forbidding faces. They scurried and rushed about as if on secret missions, which might have been the case. There was no easy banter or any friendly chatter among them.

This situation didn't do anything to make Lucian feel more comfortable. In reaction to this, he unconsciously increased his pace. He just wanted to get the whole trip over and done with as quickly as possible, find out what he could, and get back to Marcus and home, although he doubted it would be their home very much longer.

At last, he made it to an incredibly narrow street, which was one of his favorites for shopping. Here, the stalls with their brightly colored awnings jostled and crowded each other on each side of the tightly-spaced lane, barely leaving room for pedestrians, let alone a cart or chariot to get through. But today, there were almost no pedestrians and it came as no surprise to Lucian that very few of the stalls were occupied, or displayed their normal panoply of wares for sale.

However, there were a few vendors. These were selling foodstuffs, some hot, some cold. Even in very difficult times, one could usually rely upon a few such stalls being open. People had to eat, after all. When they did, then there was money to be made, even if making it under such conditions could be dangerous.

He stopped at the first open stand he came to. There were no other customers. The vendor was a very fat man, balding, and with a large growth of beard, which was unusual for a Roman. Most Roman men preferred to be clean-shaven. What made him even more unusual was he also wore a slave's collar. Apparently, the owner hadn't wanted to risk his own person, so he'd sent his slave to do his work, instead.

"Can I be of service?" The man rumbled in a solicitous, if low growl of a voice. From his tone, Lucian surmised he didn't know that he, too, was a slave. He decided not to bother to tell him. He might get farther if the man thought he was a free Roman, or even a full citizen.

"I would like to buy eight of those meat pies," he said, as he pointed to a rack of fresh pastries, ones resembling large turnovers. "What kind of meat are they?"

The big man gave a shrug, and said, "I'm told by the owner they're rabbit. However, I wouldn't want to testify to such before a magistrate, for fear of perjuring myself. They are just as likely to be dog as rabbit, I fear, judging by my master's greedy nature, and desire for profit."

"You are bold in your speech about him," Lucian said, intending it as a mild rebuke, as such a slave would expect from someone above his status. He handed the man his empty wicker basket.

"These are bold times," the man said, as he accepted it. Then he shrugged before adding, "They call for bold measures, I would think."

Lucian had a sudden epiphany. "Am I wrong in guessing your master was a supporter of Sejanus?" he asked.

The fat man smiled. Then spreading his hands wide in a disarming gesture, he said, "Indeed, good sir. That he is, or was. He doesn't claim such now, although he used to brag about it greatly to our customers. Now, he is suddenly silent on the subject. One of the reasons he doesn't appear here today is he fears arrest. Some of his friends, also adherents of the now not-so-noble Sejanus, are already in custody, just so much meat for the arena, I expect." As he spoke, the slave filled the basket with the pastries, carefully placing them inside, to avoid breaking them apart. With the basket almost filled now, he handed it over to Lucian, who accepted it without comment. He gave the man some coins as payment.

The fat man glanced down at them. "You have given me too much, sir," he said.

Lucian waved one hand in a dismissive gesture. "Keep it," he told him. "Have you any other news?"

"Besides the arrests, you mean? Yes, they say the Praetorian Guard are angry for the accusations of their being in collusion with Sejanus in a plot to overthrow Tiberius. There's fear they may riot. Those in power fear the mob may riot, as well, for many there are, who hated Sejanus. It's quite likely they will take out their vengeance upon all those who profited by his favors, such as my master. It seems many are convinced such profits came at the cost of their own incomes. In fact, good sir, I wouldn't recommend you being on the street just now. Rome is not safe. Things could grow ugly at any moment."

To this, Lucian nodded. The slave was right. "And you, what will you do if your master is arrested?"

The man gave an elaborate shrug. "The master has no relatives, no one to claim us slaves for their own. Rather than become a prize of the new government, it may just be I shall remove this collar some way and leave the city. After all, who would there be to stop me with all the confusion? Who then do we have to fear, but those who bring about Tiberius' wrath. And the further from Rome one is, the safer one probably is under such circumstances."

At this, Lucian smiled. "There is much merit in what you say. Try to be safe," he told the man, and then he turned to leave.

"And you, good sir, may you fare well, too," The fat man shouted after him.

Although Lucian didn't turn back, he did raise a hand in a brief farewell, as he continued to walk away. Reaching the end of the street, he turned and headed back to Marcus' house.

He'd learned enough, perhaps too much, he felt. Just the fact the roads of Rome were so empty, was somber news in itself. Romans didn't stay indoors for long in good weather, unless they feared for their lives. Moreover, the warning the fat slave had given him now rang true more than ever, as Lucian scuttled alone through the empty streets, heading for home. He didn't care for this state of affairs at all.

When, in the distance, he saw a contingent of soldiers marching down a lane in his direction, Lucian ducked down a side street, and circled around them, taking a longer way. It was just safer to do this. Now, all he had to do was make it the rest of the way to the house without anyone else intercepting him.

This was no easy task. He was unfamiliar with this particular area, the warren of twisting and curving lanes. He hurried on, searching to find a way back to the main road, keeping to the shadowed side of the empty lanes, fearful he might meet with some gang member or other in such a dismal and lonely setting.

Chapter 20 — Convincing Marcus

Arriving at home, Lucian rushed into the atrium to find Marcus standing there in the middle of the room, rigid, as if standing at attention. Lucian immediately wondered if he'd been waiting there like that for him all this time. He quickly told Marcus what he'd heard and seen, or rather worse, hadn't seen concerning the lack of anyone but soldiers being about the streets of Rome. Nothing was normal.

Hearing this news, Marcus slumped down onto the nearest couch, as seemed to be his habit of late. His despair showed clearly in the worry lines etching his handsome face.

"What are we to do?" he asked, sounding thoroughly defeated. "You're right, Lucian. This is a full purge. And as a magistrate, having been so favored by Sejanus, they will come for me soon enough, too. It is only a matter of time before they start a house-to-house search. They will start with the big fish first, no doubt, and then work their way down to me. I would imagine we only have a day or so left at the most, before they come and arrest me. Tiberius' men are not yet organized well enough from what you say, but when they see how little opposition they have, they soon will be. Then their search will become more systematic, more thorough."

"Then we must away at once, this very night," Lucian told him. He placed one reassuring hand on Marcus' right knee. "As soon as we have the cover of dark, we simply need to leave Rome."

Before Marcus could object, he added, "If only for a while, at least, until things settle down once more and we can fully ascertain what the consequences of all this will be. Do this. I beg of you."

Marcus remained stubbornly quiet and Lucian didn't wish

to say more. He knew his lover had to think about things, weigh the alternatives for himself. That took time. And although he was dying to get moving, to get out of there, he knew Marcus had to reach this decision for himself.

Marcus turned to him, and now he placed a hand on Lucian's bare left knee. "I'll do this," he said in a very low voice. "Understand, I do it as much for you as for myself. If they arrest me, they would confiscate you as one of my assets, and that I can't have. I don't know what would happen to you then and I would be in no position to help you, especially if they have me executed. I must keep you safe above all other things, Lucian. So yes, we must leave Rome.

"Although truthfully," he continued, "I have no idea where we could go to be safe, because there are soldiers stationed everywhere, and they will probably already know, or will soon be alerted to what's happening, perhaps already have been. Tiberius has not ruled for this long without learning to be wise in such matters. He wouldn't want his enemies to escape easily, to survive to gather and plot against him later. But again, I say, I don't know where we can go."

"I have a place in mind. We could travel to the most northwestern regions of Gaul. There, we could slip across the waters, to my homeland, Britannia, as you Romans call it. It's not yet occupied, not part of the empire. We would be safe enough there. I speak the local language, and we'll have money, the best kind, Roman coin. Again, we should find refuge there, at least for a while."

"Britannia?" Marcus looked stunned. "But it's so far to travel to, and why would anyone want to live there? It's a place of savages, hordes of blue-painted barbarians rampaging about, they say. Such creatures have no civilization."

"Admittedly, that may be true in the more northern regions, but the southern areas have been trading with Rome for many years. Far to the southwest, a place has tin and copper mines. I understand there is even a small colony of Roman merchants there for this very reason."

"You have been there, Lucian?" Marcus asked of him.

To this, Lucian gave a small shake his head. "No, I've never traveled so far. My people were not traders, were just a small tribe in the area where our parents were born and their parents were born before them. But we weren't violent people, as you seem to think, or barbarians, nor did we keep slaves as you Romans do. And we elected our chief. He didn't inherit the position or have to kill someone to get it."

"How very democratic of you," Marcus said, sarcastically. "But then never having been so far west, you can't really vouch for what you say, or can you?"

Again, Lucian shook his head. "No, but I heard much as a child. The traders who sold us things, told us stories, and those tales were always much the same. They were consistent. In any case, what choice do we have? If we stay here, they'll arrest and imprison you. Possibly, they could even execute you. And as you say, then they will sell me off to someone else, along with the other slaves here, including little Octavos. We will never see each other again and never have a life together. Do you want that, Marcus?"

"Well, when you put it like that...," he said. "Very well, at least it's a destination, a goal, a place to head for. We'll do as you say. I suppose you're right and we should leave as soon as it's dark, you say?"

"That we should, master, but first we must prepare a few things to better make our escape."

"You mean gather together the things we will need for the trip?"

"Yes, that and give the other slaves here their freedom. Oh, there are two other small matters I failed to mention earlier..."

"Oh?" Marcus lifted one suspicious eyebrow. "And what

might those be, my Lucian?"

Now Lucian knew he was actually squirming a bit, as he said, "Well, there is the matter of Octavos. I have spoken with him already. It seems he doesn't want his freedom. He is adamant about this"

"And?" Now Marcus was staring at Lucian full on. Lucian didn't like that look. It was too penetrating, resembled too much a thunderstorm approaching on a summer's day.

"And... and he would like to come with us," he finished in a small voice. "He was most insistent about this. He threatened suicide if he couldn't come."

"Oh, fuck a Vestal Virgin!" Marcus swore. "All of a sudden, all my slaves seem to be dictating to me and threatening me into the bargain, it seems!"

"Now, Marcus," Lucian started, trying to sound soothing, to placate him, "It's only out of his extreme love for you he says this. He truly just wants to be with us. If you consider, he might come in handy at times. If you're in fear of being recognized, perhaps he could run errands or missions for us or...something, instead of you having to do it."

Lucian knew this argument sounded rather weak, so he added, "I'm sure he might turn out to be very useful. He's a good slave. And he does love you," he repeated.

"Yes, yes, I know the little shit loves me. And he seems to love you, too, judging by the way he always kisses you with such fervor when I have you fuck him. He never kisses me."

"That's because he is afraid to. He would like to, I know, but you're his master and as much as he adores you, he never dared to forget the fact. He wouldn't dream of such a familiarity with you."

"I should think when I have my cock all the way up his asshole shooting cum into his bowels I'd be familiar enough then." Marcus sounded disgruntled. "Very well, he may come with us. But it's only because I'm fond of the little rascal, too. You have no objections to this do you, Lucian? You wish to permit this. You don't see him as a possible rival?"

Lucian laughed, before saying, "Of course, I don't. And I'm fond of him, too. But as a rival for your affections, no, I have no fear of that. I'm the one you want. I know."

"Mmmph," grunted Marcus. "You're awfully sure of yourself. That's too bad. It wouldn't hurt you to be a little more insecure about my feelings for you. It might make you a better lover; add a little zest for our lovemaking, if we ever get around to doing that for real. Now, what is this other matter you spoke of?"

"Ah..." Lucian paused, before continuing. He didn't quite know how to approach the subject. "Have you ever wondered what it's like to be a slave?" he asked, hesitantly.

By the look on Marcus' face, he seemed surprised at the question. "Only once or twice," he said, flatly, "but never for long. Why would one? Why do you ask?"

He had asked this so innocently, so naïvely, Lucian found it hard to tell him what he planned. "Well, you see..." he said, and then he had to pause before he could continue.

Marcus' eyes widened. "Oh, no! You don't mean..." Then he, too, fell silent.

Lucian could only nod.

"Oh, no," Marcus protested again. "No! No, Lucian, I won't do that! Not that!"

Chapter 21 — Escape From Rome

"I'm not at all enthused with any of this," Marcus said, as he stared down at his new costume with more than an obvious distaste. "Such dingy rags just don't suit me."

Lucian looked up at Marcus from where he was kneeling at his feet, adjusting the clothing. His expression was a thoughtful one. "It's odd," he said, "But you know, just a few months ago when you bought those for me, you said they were perfectly wearable, items which seemed only slightly used."

Marcus gave him a stony look, as he said, "Yes only slightly used, but by another slave. That's not quite the same thing as the wearing of a toga of a magistrate. Is it?"

"You should learn to end your sentences with the word 'master,' lest we are found out," Lucian said, ignoring Marcus' question.

"You're enjoying this? Aren't you?"

"A little, perhaps," Lucian freely admitted. "But you can hardly blame me, given our past circumstances. However, I'm not joking about your use of the word 'master.' You must be careful, Marcus. You need to use it always. Such a slip-up could be our downfall, for all of us, including little Octavos."

"And we wouldn't want that," Marcus said, and the sarcasm in his words was self-evident. Then he gave a heartfelt sigh, before adding, "But I see your point, master. I'll try to remember, master," he said, overly emphasizing the word "master" both times.

"That's much better," Lucian said. He smiled pleasantly up at Marcus, who only glared stolidly back at him.

"Well." Lucian stood up, in order to better review Marcus'

outfit. All you need now to complete the look is a slave collar.

"Oh, no! I'm not wearing any damned slave collar." Marcus sounded inflexible about this.

"Oh, but you must. Romans don't even look at slaves if they're wearing a collar. They have no need to. They just see, or rather don't see, another slave. No one will look at you twice if you're wearing one. Do you understand? It's all a matter of deception and illusion. We want to focus everyone's attention on me, as your supposed master. Let them look at me, for they won't recognize me, as they might you. You and Octavos must seem as only slaves."

"But Octavos is a slave. I'm not," Marcus hotly protested.

"Don't whine, Marcus. It doesn't become such a man as you. Now, let's go and free the other members of this household. That way, we can help them remove their collars. Then we can use one of them for you." Lucian started walking from the room.

Marcus trailed behind him. "All right," he said, giving in. "I'll do it, but it's under extreme protest."

"That's fine, whatever makes you happy. Oh, and once I've assembled the slaves, let's make sure to give Didius his freedom last."

"You want him to suffer, eh?"

Lucian nodded, but didn't turn around, as he usually would have when dealing with his master, taking his new role as Marcus' owner seriously. Instead, he continued to the cucina. "Yes," he said. I want to see him sweat a little first. I admit that."

"You are evil," Marcus said, still trailing him, "You do know that, don't you, Lucian?"

Again, Lucian nodded, but still without turning around. "I am," he admitted, "but just a little. If I was truly evil, I'd have you sell Didius to the salt mines!"

"Remind me never to make you really angry," Marcus

murmured from behind him. And glancing down at his apparel, he added, "especially when I'm wearing such as this!"

It didn't take long to finish their next task. The two teenagers were practically out of the house before Marcus could hand them their papers, remove their collars, and thank them for their services. They rushed out into the gathering gloom of evening without a backward glance. Nor did they think to thank Marcus, so intent were they upon enjoying their newfound freedom. Silent while he had removed their collars, they acted afraid, as if it weren't really happening. They didn't hesitate once the collars were gone and he had handed them their letters of freedom. They dashed for the door.

The cook took it a little better, having the grace to offer his gratitude to Marcus for all his kindnesses, and now this, his freedom.

"Where is Capito?" Lucian asked him, when he realized the man wasn't there.

Didius just shrugged his shoulders and said, "He's off on his twice weekly errand for the master, as is usual. Why?"

Lucian ignored his question and instead turned to Marcus, who was standing next to him. "Do you send Capito off on errands?" he asked of him "If so, I didn't know this."

Marcus shook his head. "No. I've never sent him anywhere on errands. The man is crippled, for the Gods' sakes. He'd make a damn poor messenger. Why should I choose such as him for a task like that?"

Lucian didn't answer this, but now he had his own strong suspicions as to why Capito went off so regularly. What's more, he could kick himself for not having noticed his absences. Then Capito always seemed so quiet, seldom was seen around, and always acted so withdrawn, that it wasn't surprising Lucian didn't notice when he was missing. It was more surprising to notice him when he was there, so little impact did his presence ever make.

Even so, Lucian should have. He had been remiss in his duties. He should have discovered this.

"Here is your document of freedom," Marcus told Didius. He handed the man the rolled-up scroll.

Didius accepted it without comment.

"Have you nothing to say to your master?" Lucian asked.

Now Didius looked openly belligerent, as if all his pent-up aggression could now have free rein, released at his will, as he said, "Why should I? He's no longer my master. This document says so. Now I'm free and I have to answer to no one. I'm a full citizen of Rome now and unlike Marcus here, not liable soon to be arrested."

"You dare much, Didius," Marcus told him in a stone-cold voice, and the hard expression on his face made Didius quail before him. "I could still kill you where you stand, or forcibly take that document back from you, and then have you sold to the salt mines. Would you like that, Didius? I think you might do better in the mines than you have here. You've been a poor slave at best, and so I doubt you will make a good citizen."

Then he added, "In any case, you're not a full citizen of Rome and never will be. Unless I were to record that document, you have no right to vote, never will have. So free, you are, but little more than that. And I advise you never, ever to compare yourself to a full citizen of Rome. You would regret it, probably at the point of a sword. Now get out of my house!" Marcus roared this last; his face was red with rage.

"Yes, go!" This came from behind Lucian and Marcus. The two of them both turned simultaneously to see Octavos standing there. He held the handle of Marcus' sword awkwardly in his right hand. The weapon was much too big for the little man, but he gripped it as if he would never let it go. In addition, he looked as furious as Marcus did.

"And know this Didius," he added, "if I ever run into you

again, I will kill you without a doubt. My masters have been too good to you. They deserve better and you deserve worse, much worse. If I ever see you, I'll see to it you get just what you deserve, and as the master says, at the point of a sword."

Octavos seemed to unnerve Didius even more than Marcus had. He gulped loudly, and then rushed from the room, clutching his document of freedom in his right hand.

"He will go straight to the authorities," Octavos told them, calmly. "We'd best leave, masters."

"But I'm not your master," Lucian protested.

"Well, you are now," Octavos told him, in a no-nonsense tone of voice.

Lucian, rather wisely, he thought, said nothing. This was a new Octavos, one he hadn't seen before, a man of iron will and purpose, and holding a sword into the bargain.

"Let's leave this place now," Marcus said, calmly enough, although it meant a phase of his life was over forever. "I feel truly as if my stay here is now over for good. I want nothing more to do with this place. Besides, it belongs to Sejanus, or did, and never to me. He turned and began to walk from the room. Octavos led the way. Was there a bit of a new swagger to his walk? Lucian couldn't be quite certain.

Then Lucian remembered something. "Oh," he called to them, "one more thing." he picked up the one remaining scroll from the table, the one meant to give Capito his freedom. Emphatically, he tore it into tiny pieces, as the other two watched him.

"That is what a spy and a traitor gets," he said. "May Capito spend the rest of his life rotting away as a slave somewhere, the traitorous, miserable pig. Now I'm ready to leave here," he told them, after having done this.

They went straight to Marcus' cubiculum. After undressing, Lucian put on the tunic he'd made for himself, the one with the pouches filled with money hidden inside. Marcus already wore his. Lucian placed Didius' slave collar carefully around Marcus' neck.

"There," he said when he'd completed his task of fastening it there. It was a temporary measure, easily pulled apart, but it looked convincing enough if not too closely inspected, what with the two pieces forced back together, and the weak connection hidden from view, just under the neckline of Marcus' tunic.

"Now we can leave," he added. So saying, he slung the heavy sack of food he'd prepared several days earlier over his shoulder. Together, the three of them left the home of Marcus Darius Macro for good, exiting the gate onto an ominously empty street. Torchlights, scattered widely apart down the length of the street, ones attached to the walls of houses as sconces, formed a weak, orange, and flickering illumination for them.

"It seems strange leaving here," Marcus said, as they started walking. "To leave this home forever seems odd to me." He sounded depressed as he said this last.

"Soon enough, it wouldn't be your home any longer, anyway," Lucian reminded him. "You stay there rent free thanks to Sejanus. Without him, that wouldn't last much longer. And I'm afraid your new home might have been a dungeon."

"True enough," Marcus said in a rather philosophical tone of voice, "and still might be if we're caught. Well, onward to new adventures, I suppose." But even as he said this, Lucian noticed he gave one last glance backwards, as if in final farewell to the home and life he'd known there.

They hurried down the avenue, with Lucian in the fore, followed by Marcus, and with Octavos bringing up the rear. The little man was breathing heavily. With the speed they were traveling, he was having trouble keeping up with his more long-legged companions. However, Lucian didn't want to slow down. The sooner they were out of Rome the better, he felt.

"Are you planning to take us right through the downtown," Marcus asked of Lucian at one point.

"No," Lucian said, over his shoulder as he continued to lead the way. "I've studied a map. Although there is safety in numbers under normal circumstances, the streets are probably as empty as this one is now. It's also probably where the soldiers will most likely congregate, along with the vigiles, because I'm betting the crowds will grow later on, as the evening progresses, and I wouldn't want to be caught up in a riot, although I saw no sign of anyone much this morning."

"Neither would I," Marcus admitted. "I mean about the riot. And mobs tend to form quickly, at a moment's notice, it seems. I know. I've witnessed such. The rabble just suddenly boil out onto the streets," he added.

"My main concern is getting you safely out of the city, Marcus. And the quicker we do that, the better I'll feel."

"Have you any idea how we will get past the guards at the gate?"

Lucian shook his head. "Not a firm plan," he said. "But, I'll simply plead a matter of urgent business, and offer them a bribe. I hope the combination will be enough. After all, they aren't looking for me. Now Lucian paused in his walk to turn back to Marcus, who also stopped. Behind them, Octavos came running, using their pause to catch up. He was panting heavily.

"Listen to me," Lucian said to Marcus. "When the guards look at you, make sure you're always looking down at your feet. This won't come easy to you. It isn't natural, but Roman citizens don't like slaves to look right at them. It just isn't done, as I'm sure you already know. Besides, if you're always looking at your feet they can't get a clear view of your face.

"What's more," he continued, "if they do take you for just being another slave, they won't grant you much attention in the first place, won't examine you very closely. So please, Marcus, play the part as well as you can. You must do this for the safety of all of us, and not just yourself. Please don't let your pride get in the way with this."

"Whatever you say, master," Marcus said stressing the last word again. "I'll do your bidding."

Now they continued with their walk. They traveled as quickly as they could, perhaps a little too swiftly to not look suspicious, but following Lucian's lead, they used as many side streets and circuitous routes as they could, staying well away from the main boulevards, sticking to the more shadowed sides of lanes.

As always, poor little Octavos hurried to keep up the rear. Every so often, they would pause to let him. Several times, they saw soldiers or vigiles in the distance. Each time, Lucian's group deviated from their route, detoured to avoid meeting up with them. This added time to their journey. But it was necessary, Lucian felt, to be safe rather than sorry.

At last, after what seemed like a very long time to him, they approached a western gate of the city. Here, Lucian had them turn down a side alley, for ahead of them was an unruly crowd, milling about the exit.

"We all need to catch our breath before we approach the soldiers," he told both Marcus and Octavos. Octavos, who was huffing and puffing, simply nodded his head, too out of breath to speak. "We must appear as calm and casual as one could be under such circumstances as these," Lucian added. "We don't want to arouse their suspicion in any way. When I approach them, I want you two to stand several feet away from me, and again, whatever you do, don't look at them directly. I want their attention focused mainly on me at all times. Try to keep to the shadows as much as possible. Now, are we ready?"

Marcus actually glanced nervously at Octavos. He nodded. Now Marcus turned to look at Lucian again. "It seems we're ready." He gave Lucian a tentative little smile.

"Lucian, if this doesn't work; I want you to know that I love you more than life itself. I'll know you tried your best. If they arrest me, just let me go, for my fate will be sealed then. There won't be anything you can do about it. Just concentrate on your own safety, Lucian, and that of Octavos here. That would provide me a great deal of comfort if you do this, to know you're both well and safe."

Lucian gulped loudly with emotions that seemed caught in his throat, before saying, "That won't be necessary, Marcus. We'll get through. I promise you. We'll all be safe—all of us," he added, as he gave Octavos a significant glance."

The little man nodded and then grinned, as if in reassurance.

They left the alley then, and continued the last block to the arched gateway. It was set in the original walls of the city. Actually, the city had grown past this barrier, but they still used the old gate as the legal entry and exit point for all commerce and traffic. It was here all taxes and tariffs, as well as duties or levies were exacted by the customs official.

Lucian could see five guards through the crowd ahead. There might be more, but if there were, they were inside the guardhouses. They had small rooms built right into the interior of the wall itself, so there was little room for more men to hide there, he figured.

The waiting people were restive. This was good news, for three of the guards seemed busy, occupied with crowd control. The mob, composed of mostly men, seemed alternately loud and then unusually quiet by turns, as if they couldn't quite decide how to behave. Some muttered under their breath, but others boldly spoke out of current events.

"I heard they executed him by strangling, and tossed him down the stairs," one grizzled ruffian said to his companion.

At this comment, Marcus gave Lucian a significant glance.

"And I heard tell the crowd pulled his body to pieces, and now they're rampaging down by the harbor, and over by the villas, as well. One fellow told me they were killing anyone who has been friends with Sejanus. They just drag them out of their houses and tear them limb from limb, then steal everything in sight."

Now it was Lucian's turn to look at Marcus, giving him a look of real concern.

Slowly, they shuffled forward, as one by one; the crowd ahead of them went through the gates. The process was far slower than normal, so Lucian knew the guards were being much more careful, more thorough than usual.

Finally, Lucian, being the first of their group, approached the guards actually standing on duty. He had to wait several more seemingly endless minutes, while the one soldier examined a laden cart just ahead of them. Tension mounted steadily. The atmosphere seemed thick with it. Lucian watched as the driver of the cart finally handed the guard a few coins. Then, finally, and with a shouted command to the horses, and then the loud crack of the whip, the driver was off, trundling past the guardhouse and the grim-faced men who manned it.

So bribery was acceptable. Lucian had thought this was so, but this helped him to be sure. One didn't pay any duties on leaving the city, so surely the exchange of money had been a bribe.

Now it was their turn. Lucian shuffled forward into the full light of the torches burning so glaringly bright in their sconces on the wall next to the great gate.

"Who are you and what's your business beyond these walls?" the soldier demanded to know of him in a loud and uncompromising tone of voice. He only seemed to have eyes for Lucian, having given Marcus and Octavos only the most cursory of glances.

Lucian had already made up a name for himself and despite his limited skills; he'd manage to write up a simple invoice, one with his phony name on it. He handed this scroll to the guard, as he said, "I'm Lucian Artorius Callidius, a merchant, an importer of tin. My home is in northern Gaul and I came here on business. Now, I travel to the southwest coast of Britannia, to make purchases of metals there."

"This document is insufficient for identification purposes."

Lucian nodded. "With respect, sir, it's all I have left. A gang of men attacked and robbed me at a taverna just this day. There were no vigiles about to stop them. And with all the administration offices closed today, I'd no way of procuring the proper documents."

The soldier shrugged. "What's that to me? Wait until tomorrow or whenever they do finally open again."

Now Lucian gave the guard his best pleading look. "Please, sir, but I cannot wait. I have a competitor who left several weeks ago, traveling mostly by land. If I hurry, I can beat him there, for I intend to travel by sea. If I arrive in time, it will mean a big contract for me, and much money. I'm in need of it most desperately after the robbery."

Again, the soldier gave a nonchalant shrug. "I say again, what's that to me? He stared with dark eyes pointedly at Lucian, as he said this.

And Lucian knew a cue when he saw one. "Perhaps, this other document may further prove who I am," he said, as he withdrew a pouch of money from his cloak. He handed it to the guard.

The man loosened the drawstrings and looked inside. Then he tightened the strings once more, and still clutching the pouch, he said, "These do look in order. You may pass."

Lucian nodded, smiled his gratitude, murmured his thanks, and hurried on by the man. He gestured for Marcus and Octavos to follow.

"Wait," the soldier ordered them. He turned to Lucian who stood just past the guardhouse now, quietly waiting. "Are these your slaves?"

Lucian glanced at his two friends. As promised, Marcus had his head down, stared resolutely at his dusty, sandaled feet.

"Yes," Lucian said. "They are, for what little worth they are when it comes to protecting me. They were right there when I was robbed and did practically nothing!"

Now the solider examined Marcus more closely, apparently choosing to ignore Octavos. "This one is tall and rather pretty with his golden hair. You fuck him?"

Lucian nodded. "I do. He's far cheaper than prostitutes are, so I use him on almost a daily basis. Are you interested in purchasing him? He isn't the best slave, being rather lazy, but he serves me well enough as a good fuck, although his hole is getting rather loose of late."

The solider inspected Marcus for another moment. "No, I suppose not," he said, sounding slightly reluctant. "I can't really afford the upkeep of a slave and in any case, if you have him as often as you say, he's probably past his prime when it comes to his ass being tight. And I do like them tight."

Lucian gave an elaborate shrug. "What can I say? I'm partial to blondes, even loose ones."

"And whether male or female, it would seem," the soldier remarked, snidely. "A hole is a hole for you, is it? Then, as they say, 'any port in a storm,' I suppose. Very well, you two can pass." he motioned for Octavos and Marcus to proceed, which was just as well, for a restless group of other travelers was forming into a tight knot behind them, and they were becoming decidedly verbal at the delay.

Lucian watched, and then sighed with relief when both Marcus and Octavos were safely past the guardhouse.

When they had walked several hundred yards farther down the road, Marcus leaned over and whispered harshly into Lucian's ear, "Thank you so much, master, for making me out to be not only your whore, but one with a wide asshole, at that."

"It worked, didn't it?" Lucian innocently asked, and then he paused in his walk to turn and grin at his lover.

Marcus paused as well, held his stern look for a moment longer, and then his mouth relaxed into a smile. "Well, enough, I suppose," he admitted. "But I'll show you soon enough my asshole is as tight as can be. It suffers from lack of stretching, if anything."

"Are we going to Ostia?" Octavos asked at this point. He'd been standing patiently near Marcus, like the perfect little slave he was.

"Indeed, we are," Marcus told him.

"Are we?" Lucian was surprised by this statement." I thought we would travel overland, cross by sea to the north to avoid the pass through the Alps, and so travel on to northern Gaul.

Marcus shook his head. "No, the way you told the guard is much better. Why do that long and difficult route when we can travel so much more easily by sea, and be beyond the reach of soldiers and all their endless checkpoints along the way."

"There will still be some, no matter which way we go," Lucian reminded him. "You Romans are very good at them, and we will be making port at several locations where they will have customs."

"True enough, Marcus said, "but we needn't leave the ship if that's the case, until the final port. Besides, now we've practiced here in Rome at that one," he nodded over his right shoulder toward the distant guardhouse, "we should be in good shape to get through any few others we find ourselves having to deal with."

"I suppose," agreed Lucian. "And the fewer checkpoints, the better, I admit. I was surprised we made it through this one, truthfully, but the plan worked. Still, I'm betting they'll get the order to refuse anyone to pass soon enough, to close down the gates."

Marcus frowned at these words. "Yes, I hadn't thought of that. It's only that events have happened so quickly, the powers-that-be are still disorganized, apparently, which may have allowed them to still be open even this long. We were very lucky, I'm thinking. Another hour or two, and we might not have been able to make it out of the city at all."

"And it may be that once they're organized, they'll search the highways near Rome, too, looking for those like us, ones trying to escape their clutches. It would be well if we stayed away from the main roads as much as possible for that reason. Even so, we can make it to the harbor by tomorrow morning, despite being on foot, if we hurry. So, then it's by way of Ostia and the sea?" Lucian asked.

Marcus glanced at Octavos. "Is this all right with you, my little friend?"

Octavos grinned, but then said, "I'm only a slave. You needn't ask me about such things."

"Where we're going, there are no slaves," Lucian told him, happily. "So you are, indeed, just our friend now, and a very faithful one at that. So what say you, Octavos? On to Ostia?"

Octavos nodded vigorously. "On to Ostia!" he almost shouted it.

Now, both Marcus and Lucian smiled. Then Marcus said, "Let's get going. The farther away from Rome we get, the better I'll feel."

Together, carrying their kit, they headed toward the very outskirts of Rome. Soon, the houses thinned out and then ultimately disappeared. In their place was a seemingly endless line of grand tombs stretching along either side of the paved road. Roman law forbade burials within the city, so the rich had quickly learned to intern their loved ones along the edges of the highway just outside of the metropolis.

That night, after many hard miles of walking, they camped in a vineyard, sleeping between the already-picked vines, huddled together for warmth, for already it was getting colder, as winter drew ever nearer. They didn't dare light a fire for fear of causing an alarm and having someone then discover them. The last thing they needed was a horde of soldiers galloping at them from out of the blackness of the night.

The next morning, well before sunrise, they started their trip again. Still half-asleep, they plodded their weary way along an empty road, for there was no safer route they could take at this point, no shortcut available.

"Who's that coming," Marcus asked after a while. They'd been walking about half an hour.

Lucian squinted, trying to make out what Marcus referred to, but it was difficult in the dim light of the gray dawn.

"Two cavalry soldiers, I think," he said at last, as the figures on horseback neared them.

"Should we take to the fields?" Octavos asked. The little man sounded distinctly nervous.

"Too late. They've already seen us. I'm sure. See how they've increased their speed?" Marcos was silent a moment, and then he added, "We'll just have to brazen it out, I suppose."

With horse hooves making a dull clomping sound on the paving stones of the Roman road, the two cavalrymen galloped up to them. They reigned in their horses. The black creatures seemed offended at being brought up short, because they both reared up on their hind legs. One neighed loudly, the sound splitting the quiet of the misty morning. A cloud of dust rose about them, giving the whole scene an unreal look to Lucian, as if the creatures had sprung from the earth, escaped denizens from Hades.

"Hold!" exclaimed the soldier on the right. "Who are you and what's your business on this road?"

Lucian stepped forward. "Hail to you," he said, dipping his head in an abbreviated bow to the two riders, as he spoke. "I am a merchant, Lucian Artorius Callidius by name. I'm traveling to Ostia to take ship there."

"Those two?" asked the cavalryman on the left. He was the slightly smaller of the two, and what little Lucian could see of his face under the helmet wasn't promising. The man had an uncompromising look about him, a forbidding expression.

"They are my slaves," Lucian said, gesturing casually with one had at Octavos and Marcus. "Unworthy creatures, to be sure, but the best I could afford."

The cavalry officer was silent a moment. He just stared, his eyes glittering hard from under the shadowed brow of his helmet.

"You, there!" he called, "the blond one. Raise you head so I can look at you better."

Lucian's heart beat suddenly faster, as Marcus slowly raised his head to stare directly at the mounted soldier.

"I recognize you," the man snapped out. "You're that magistrate, the one appointed by Sejanus! You were involved in that case where that Praetorian Guard tried to extort money from the merchant."

"You must be mistaken," Lucian said, quickly. "He's just a slave—"

"Silence," said the other soldier. "Nobody is addressing you."

Lucian gave a little nod, and did as told. He felt it best not to aggravate them.

"Answer me," commanded the first officer. "You are that magistrate, aren't you?"

Marcus shook his head. "I'm sorry," he said, "but you've made a mistake. I don't know of whom you speak. I'm just a slave. See?" He gave the slightest tug at his collar, not one hard enough to pull it off him.

"By Venus' two tits, you lie! You are that magistrate. And I'm placing you under arrest, as ordered by Emperor Tiberius for all friends and acquaintances of that traitor, Sejanus." Saying this, the burly soldier dismounted from his horse. He strode toward Marcus.

Lucian, desperate now, and without thinking, dashed the short distance to the soldier. Grabbing the man by his arms, he pleaded, "Please, sir. You have it wrong. You've made a mistake. This is just my unworthy slave."

"Get off!" shouted the soldier, "or I'll arrest—"

He stopped, realizing Lucian had pulled the sword from his scabbard and now brandished it before him."

"What is this?"

"You won't have him," Lucian growled, through clenched teeth. He gripped the short sword for all he was worth, and now he stood between the soldier and Marcus.

"Lower that sword, I'll run you through!" shouted the other man, from where he sat, still mounted on his steed."

"No you won't!" shouted Octavos, and he hurled a handful of dirt at the man. When he'd scooped it up, Lucian couldn't say, but it was a mix of sand and stones. It struck the horse in the face. Whether this was Octavos' intention or not, Lucian didn't know, but the effect was perfect. The horse neighed loudly in alarm and then reared high on its hind legs. The soldier, caught unawares, tumbled backwards. His feet left the stirrups and he fell from the horse onto the road with a thump and clanking of his breastplate and helmet. He lay there, obviously stunned.

Marcus didn't wait. He ran to the man, followed closely by Octavos. Together, they pounced upon him. Marcus grabbed for the sword, jerked it free from the man's scabbard. Meanwhile, the soldier facing Lucian moved toward him, arms spread. He was a picture of the menacing Roman soldier, if without a sword in this case.

"Stand back," Lucian ordered him in a loud voice, "Or I'll run you through! Make no mistake, I'll do it. I swear!"

The soldier didn't respond. He just kept slowly advancing on Lucian. When he was within just a few feet of him, he suddenly pulled a knife from a sheath belted to his waist. Lucian hadn't seen this. Now, he inwardly cursed himself for being so remiss, so unobservant.

The Roman soldier lunged at him and using his right hand, he brought the knife around in a wide arc, a swift, horizontal slicing motion. Lucian danced back from it, his chest just missing the tip of the blade. As soon as the man's knife flashed by him, he took advantage of the opening and lunged forward.

Thrusting his sword upward to avoid the other man's protective breastplate, and without quite knowing how he managed it, he pierced the man's neck. Blood spurt like a geyser, a bright carmine fountain jetting out of the soldier's throat, looking incredibly red in the first rays of the morning sunlight.

The soldier's eyes widened, as if in sheer surprise. Then, without saying a word, he tumbled backward, and lay still, his body sprawled there in the dust of the road. He didn't stir. His horse danced nervously away from the corpse, its eyes rolling whitely in panic. Then, as if reaching a sudden decision, it galloped off, without its rider, on down the road and in the direction of the city of Rome. Its hooves beat a dull cadence on the paving stones as it went, the noise slowly fading with distance.

Lucian, not hesitating, now turned his attention to the others. Marcus was rising from beside the still form of the soldier there. He clutched a sword with a bloodied blade in his right hand. Octavos just stood there by Marcus' side, gazing down at the dead man.

"Are you all right?" Lucian shouted, as he ran toward them.

"Yes," Marcus said, if a little shakily. "The cretin pulled a knife. He almost got me with it, too. Ruined my tunic," he added as he gazed down at a large rent across the front of his garment.

"Are you wounded?" Lucian asked him. He was by Marcus' side now, and he reached out to check for himself, to pull aside the torn fabric, but his lover shook his head.

"No," he said. "He just missed me. I stabbed him with his own sword, right up in the crotch, so he'll never have the balls to do that again!" Now Marcus chuckled, but it was a nervous sort of laugh, the kind that usually came from reaction.

"I helped," Octavos said, sounding proud. "I hit him in the face with that rock." He pointed to a large chunk of paving stone lying next to the fallen soldier.

"Looks like more than once, too," Lucian observed, giving only a quick and covert glance at the dead man's smashed face, before looking away.

"Now what do we do?" Marcus asked, sounding uncertain, and still standing there with the sword dangling from his right hand.

"This," Lucian said. He moved over to the one remaining horse and slapped it as hard as he could on the flank. The animal neighed loudly, and then took off galloping down the road, headed in the same direction as the other horse had. "And now we take care of these two."

"What do we do with them?" Octavos asked, as he stared with a worried expression at the bodies sprawled there on the paving stones.

"We pull them off the road, far enough into that field," he pointed to his right, "where they won't be seen from here. We don't want them discovered too quickly, at least, not until we're well away from here."

"Right," Marcus said, and he began tugging the one dead man by his booted feet.

"I'll help," Octavos said. Together the two of them dragged the soldier's body well out into the overgrown field, being careful to hide the remains in the tall grass and weeds growing there.

Meanwhile, Lucian had been doing his best to haul the man he'd killed, but he was grateful when the other two joined him in the task. The three of them made short work of concealing the body.

"We're lucky nobody chose to come along the road just now," Octavos said, as they set off on their journey once more.

"Yes, these roads usually are heavily traveled," Marcus said, by way of agreement.

"But it's still very early," Lucian pointed out. "And we're nowhere near a way station or inn, so that worked in our favor. Still, the farther we get from here and the sooner, the better I'll feel."

"May the Gods agree with that," Octavos said, fervently, as they all trudged together down the highway.

"I owe you both my life," Marcus said after a period of silence. "The two of you saved me. Lucian, I couldn't believe it when you snatched that soldier's sword from him. It was amazing, just like something one would expect from a legion soldier."

"And Octavos throwing those stones at the other one's horse was sheer brilliance," Lucian said, glancing at the little man as he said this.

Octavos beamed back at him.

"So," Marcus added in a softer tone of voice, "You're debt to me is paid."

"So it is!" Lucian exclaimed, remembering his vow to his master. "Octavos and I just saved your life."

"Now, you're released from your bond to me, aren't you? You're free to go your own way."

Lucian paused in his walk just long enough to turn to Marcus, who also halted, as did Octavos, in turn. "Marcus," he said, "I am going my own way right now. My way happens to be with you, as long as you'll have me, want me. I just want to be with the two of you. For better or worse, the three of us are family now."

Marcus grinned. "Well," he said, looking suddenly happy, "let's all hope it's for the better!" Then he started walking again, one arm around Lucian's right shoulder, and the other slung over Octavos' left one.

They made their way into the port city of Ostia just a few hours later. They entered the busy metropolis by way of the main gate, and fortunately had no trouble with the guards there. Ostia was Rome's most important harbor, for it was where much of the grain and other foodstuffs that fed the city came from Egypt and elsewhere.

The first thing they did was find a place to eat and to ask a few guarded questions, in order to ascertain the lay of the land. Here, everything seemed more normal, as if the troubles that plagued Rome now were farther away than just the few miles they were. Citizens, slaves, merchants, laborers, and various tradesmen, all moved about freely, without seeming to have any great fear or hesitation. Moreover, although there were soldiers about, they didn't seem particularly on the alert, compared to the eagle-eyed ones in Rome.

While munching on a meat and garlic pastry, Lucian (still acting as the nominal master of the other two), asked the attendant at the stall what news he'd heard from Rome.

"If you're talking about Sejanus and all that uproar, they say he was killed last night, executed."

Lucian saw Marcus' eyes widen slightly at this confirmation of the news they'd heard earlier. "Was he, indeed?" Lucian asked in what he hoped sounded like a calm tone of voice.

"And none too soon, I say," said the thin attendant. He was dressed as a free man, but in the simplest of tunics. "That Sejanus was a right monster from all reports and corrupt beyond belief, they say."

"Was he tried first?" Lucian asked, again trying to sound as casual as possible.

"They say the Senate had a lengthy letter from Tiberius read aloud to him, and while that was happening, Graecinius Laco of the Vigiles had the building surrounded. Macro seized control of the Praetorian Guard. Then when the letter openly denounced Sejanus and ordered his arrest, well it was all over for him."

"How did they execute him?" Lucian wanted to know.

The man shrugged, before saying, "Like they usually do when this sort of thing happens. The Senate convened the Temple Of Concord last evening, condemned him to death and so he was strangled right then. They threw the cretin's body down the Gemonian stairs for the crowd there to have. A soldier last night said the mob tore him literally to pieces and then went on a rampage, seeking out and killing anyone even mildly acquainted with him. I heard the Praetorians rioted, as well, because people accused them of siding with Sejanus. It was a real mess, and still is, or so I'm told. It's a wonder the city didn't go up in flames."

Now the attendant looked at Lucian more closely. "Here now," the man said, "Why don't you know more about this? Everyone else does. Where are you from?" His voice sounded harsh, almost accusing, and definitely suspicious.

"Ah, we've traveled up from the south, from Neapolis," Lucian said, thinking quickly. "A hot and dusty trip, I'll tell you, and the roads seemed about deserted. We wondered what was going on to make it so. Except for a few cavalry soldiers thundering down the road on their mounts, driving us all into the ditches in the process, there was practically no one. Now, I understand why."

The attendant's face lost its dubious look. "From the south?" he asked, in a more normal tone of voice.

"Yes," Lucian said. "I'm a trader trying to make my way to Britannia. I have friends who tell me tin is a good investment these days."

The attendant gave a slight shake of his head. "Wouldn't know about such things," he said. "I don't risk my money on speculations. But if it's a ship you're wanting, go down by the harbor. I hear there's one putting out to sea on the turn of the tide this afternoon, bound for around to the west coast of Iberia and then on up. They may have berths for you."

"You've been very helpful," Lucian said. He handed the man a silver denarius.

"Thank you!" exclaimed the man, as he examined the coin in his hand. "That's most generous."

"If you've saved me days of waiting here in Ostia Lido for a ship, that's nothing compared to what these two oafs would then have cost me in food and drink, and a place to stay," Lucian assured the man.

They departed the stall and made their way down to the quayside through twisting and narrow streets. Again, here there was no grid system as the Romans so preferred for their cities, for Ostia predated such modern niceties, being an ancient town in its own right. Tiberius had seen to it a new forum had been built to please the citizens of the burgeoning metropolis. Of course, there was the lighthouse, as well, which was something of a wonder in its own right, Lucian had been told, but they didn't take time to sightsee any of this. They wanted a ship and escape.

Reaching the docks, Lucian searched for the harbormaster's office. There, after giving the attendant a liberal bribe for the information, he told them of the ship they wanted, the one mentioned by the man back at the food stall.

Searching along the docks, they finally found where the vessel lay anchored. It was a sailing ship, but with galley capabilities. The ship's homeport was out of southwestern Gaul, but it plied the waters all around the Iberian Peninsula, supposedly, and well into the bay above there.

Lucian negotiated with the captain for passage for the three of them. It went easier than he'd thought it might. Apparently, there wasn't much trade now to the area. Lucian didn't ask why, but only assumed it was because weather conditions were deteriorating with winter coming. The great sea beyond the strait was a very rough place to be in bad weather—dangerously so.

The same afternoon, on the turn of the tide, they departed from Ostia. The three of them stood on the deck, staring at the harbor town as it diminished into the haze of distance.

"I doubt we will ever see Ostia or Rome again," Marcus said, sounding a little sad.

Lucian turned to him. "No, perhaps not, at least not for many years, I suppose. I, for one, shall not miss Rome, though."

"You wouldn't," Marcus said, simply. "I suppose you can't wait to get to Britannia, to be home again?"

Lucian gave a slight shake of his head. "It isn't my home where we're going. Our destination is many, many miles away from there, a very different place. As it happens, I don't wish to go home, anyway."

"Why not?"

"You never asked me how I became a slave," Lucian said, in a slightly disapproving tone of voice. "Well, times were hard for my tribe. Two summers in a row, the weather had been too wet too often for good crops. We were going hungry and it was getting worse. My brother, Keltor, was the head of our household at the time, my father having died the year before. Keltor always disapproved of me. He knew I preferred men to women, you see, and he didn't like that. He felt it demeaned our family. So when the opportunity came, he tricked me, and then sold me to a slaver. He just came while I was sleeping, placed a sack over my head, tied me up, and sold me. That's the last I ever saw of my family and my home."

"And you don't want to go back?" Marcus said this softly, "if only for revenge?"

"Not ever!" Lucian exclaimed. "Revenge is pointless. We will make a new home, the three of us," and here he glanced at the silent Octavos standing next to Marcus. He'd been listening to everything they had said.

"We will have enough money to buy land, for it's very cheap there, I'm told, perhaps enough even for a vineyard and to build a decent villa. We can sell wine to the Roman merchants and their families who live there, and for much cheaper than they can import it."

"I doubt if it will be as good a quality," Marcus said, sounding dubious. "We know nothing about making wine."

"It doesn't have to be very good. When you're stuck way out there in the middle of nowhere, beyond the empire, as the merchants undoubtedly see the situation, they'll be happy for anything that smacks of the comforts of home. In fact..." and here Lucian trailed off, as he paused in thought.

"Yes," Marcus prompted him. "What?"

"I've heard tell of a place north and a little east of there that has natural hot springs. It could be we could create the first true Roman-style baths in Britannia."

"Truly?"

Lucian shrugged his shoulders. "At least, it's a thought. We'll have to go and see if it's possible. Now, I have a small berth below, but there is only room for one to sleep there. Octavos, would you like the privilege tonight? Marcus and I can sleep up here on deck."

"I could never take such a liberty," Octavos protested.

"Certainly, you can," Marcus warmly told him. "You more than any deserve it for all your help. Tonight, we two shall sleep under the stars, and you can snuggle up in a warm place. Who knows? Perhaps if you try hard enough, you can find a willing mate before it's time to turn in." He glanced suggestively at several nearly naked sailors, those only wearing loincloths as they hoisted the sails, back muscles glistening with perspiration as they strained with the effort.

Octavos' gray eyes widened as he followed the direction of Marcus' gaze. "Do you think so? Is it permitted?" he asked, as he gazed in wonder at the tanned young men.

"You are free, Octavos," Lucian reminded him. "Anything permitted by law is now open to you to do. If I were you, I'd start hunting for that one particular man you might like. Find one that hasn't had a chance to go ashore in Ostia or anywhere else for a long while, and I'm betting you'll find an excellent lover for the night, someone to fill your ass with all the cum you could want." Now he grinned.

Octavos grinned back and then said, "If you two will excuse me for the evening, then?"

"Oh, go away with you," Marcus said, good-naturedly. "But whatever you do, don't end up by falling into the sea. We three must stay together. As Lucian said, we're family now. And we have vineyards to plant and baths to build, as well as a villa. Maybe, we can manage to bring some of the good things of Roman life to Britannia, eh?" And here, he winked at Octavos.

Now Octavos grinned more broadly, a smile so large it looked as if it might split his face. He gave Marcus a mock salute and was off, heading toward the far end of the deck where most of the crew was still busy raising the square sails.

"He's happy," Marcus said, watching him go.

"And you, Marcus, are you happy?"

Marcus turned to him. The late afternoon sun lit his hair, turning it to a fiery golden color, with red-copper tones. "I am," he said, simply.

And when Lucian gave him a penetrating look, he added in a defensive tone, "No, truly, I am. This is an adventure, a chance for a new life and more freedom. And what's more, I get to have it with those I care about most, our friend Octavos, and you, Lucian, my lover."

"Well, I truly will be your lover after tonight. I intend to fuck you all over this decking once it's dark enough to do so. Your ass will be full of splinters before I'm through with you."

"What?" Marcus' face held a mock expression of dismay. "You're choosing to finally let me fuck with you, but you still deny me first privilege to have your beautiful ass, before you take mine? What happened to your need to be equal all of a sudden?"

Lucian gave a wry smile, before saying, "I don't' have to worry about that anymore, Marcus. You forget. Now that I'm the master, I'd say I was more than equal."

"Ah… and you will not then give me the same privilege as a slave that I gave to you, the freedom of choice?"

"Not on your life!" Lucian exclaimed. Then he laughed.

"Shall we pick out a quiet, out-of-the-way spot? Marcus suggested.

"What are you waiting for?" Lucian was already turning, scanning the rear of the ship. "There," he said, pointing. "I see a place between the capstan and locker. We can lie our bedding there. It's very private by the looks of it."

"As you wish, master," Marcus, said, as he stooped to pick

up their belongings, "As you wish."

They moved over to the relatively secluded area, a little space of decking. After spreading their two blankets, they lay down upon them. It was completely dark now. Stars glittered in the night sky, but there was no moon yet to brighten things too much.

Lucian, lying next to Marcus made the first tentative move. He rolled over onto his side to face him. Reaching out with his left hand, he ran his fingers lightly over Marcus' brow. Then moving even closer, he levered himself up with one elbow, and kissed his lover.

Their lips met. At first, it was a gentle kiss, one filled with their love. This quickly changed. All of Lucian's pent-up needs, his aching lust for Marcus, now came to the fore. He kissed hard, passionately. Marcus responded. Now, they locked in a tight embrace, as Lucian climbed on top of Marcus, pressed his body against him. His tongue probed, found its way inside Marcus' mouth. Marcus moaned softly.

Lucian's hands now roamed freely over his master's chest, reaching inside his tunic, tweaking first one, and then the other nipple. Again, Marcus gave a soft moan at this. Encouraged, Lucian let his mouth roam just as freely, kissing Marcus on the chin, then the neck, then his upper chest, where he tasted salt from the man's perspiration.

"Wait!" Marcus exclaimed in a harsh whisper. He pushed Lucian to one side, sat up.

"Is something wrong?" Lucian whispered back.

"No. I just want to get this tunic off," Marcus told him.

Struggling and wriggling his body about, he finally accomplished this task. Now, with only his subligar remaining, Marcus lay back down again on the blankets. His naked flesh, except for the area still covered by the loincloth, now lay exposed, vulnerable, gleaming faintly in the starlight. His arms and legs were sprawled apart, relaxed, as if he waited without worry for what was to come next.

Without prompting, Lucian removed his own garment and his loincloth, as well. Then he straddled Marcus, lay down on top of him, his cock, and balls pressed against the fabric of Marcus' subligar, rubbing against the Roman's still-hidden genitals. They explored each other's bare bodies with their hands. Lucian began kissing him again, while at the same time tweaking his nipples, running his hands over Marcus' pectoral muscles. Lucian was getting very excited now. His cock was fully hard.

Marcus, too, was reacting. He started to move about, lifted his head to watch, as Lucian's mouth worked down his body, lips and tongue following the treasure trail of fine hair along his stomach, until he reached the upper area of his pubic region, the demarcating line of gold hair that showed just above the loincloth he still wore.

"This has to go," Lucian said. And even as Marcus raised his hips, Lucian sat back on his haunches, pulled the item of clothing down over Marcus' thighs, his calves, ankles, and then off his feet. Now Marcus lay complete bare before him. Already, the man's cock was swelling with lust, burgeoning with a sexual need, enlarging to prodigious proportions.

Without waiting, without hesitating, Lucian plunged his mouth on that rapidly growing cock, engulfed the head of it, his tongue licking and probing at the generous foreskin encircling the knob, teasing it.

Marcus groaned for real this time, a deep, low, throaty growl of physical pleasure. "Ahh…" he moaned. "That's it, Lucian, suck me. Taste me, boy. Eat my cock."

Lucian did as commanded. He slowly lowered his mouth to the base of Marcus' massive prick, engulfing it inch by hard-rock inch. The head was now in his throat, trying to push down it. Lucian compressed his lips, tightened them around the shaft, determined to give Marcus the maximum pleasure possible.

At last, with almost super human effort, he made it to the base of the prick, his nose buried now into the fine-spun golden hairs massing so tightly there. He could smell the scent of clean male sweat, the heady aroma of masculine musk. Still, he couldn't hold the position for more than a moment. He couldn't breathe. In a rush, he withdrew his mouth back up the meaty shaft, up to the head; where he managed to gasp for breath, take in some air around that fat knob.

"Suck me, please," Marcus pleaded.

Again, Lucian did as commanded. Holding the enormous phallus with his right hand, he started sucking, bobbing his head up and down the thick cock, licking the sides of the shaft of that swollen dick. Faster and faster, he went. Lucian used his right fist to help jack the rigid prick. Marcus' ball sac bounced up and down in rhythm to his pumping action. Lucian watched this with fascination, as the balls jiggled about in their bag. How long he'd wanted to pump that cock, watch those nuts bang in their sac, and milk them of all Marcus' man juice.

Marcus moaned softly, and his hips rose and fell to meet each pumping stroke of his cock by Lucian's fist. With his free hand now, Lucian gently and rapidly slapped the balls, as if they were impacting his ass, stimulating them in this way. The sac began to tighten, to draw up towards the base of the prick. Still, Lucian didn't stop, but get pumping, kept sucking on the knob, running his tongue around it, tickling and teasing the glans.

"I'm going to cum!" Marcus fiercely whispered, and almost as soon as he said this, he spurted. A great wad of cum jetted to the back of Lucian's mouth. He worked Marcus' prick harder now, determined to extract every drop of sperm still in his nut sac. Lucian was determined to drain it dry.

"Oh, Gods!" Marcus exclaimed, as he shot another squirt of cum. More of the hot liquid sprayed out, filled Lucian's mouth. He swallowed, convulsively, making a loud gulping noise as he did so. He felt the sperm course down his throat, tasted the pungency of it on his tongue, and still he sucked for all he was worth, jacking Marcus' cock without mercy, without letup.

"Ahhhhhhhh! Marcus moaned, lifting his lean hips high off the blankets. He spewed again, and this time, at the last second, Lucian removed his mouth, just in time to see the white cum erupt. The sperm squirted into the air, a thin stream of glistening white in the starlight. It arced across open air, and splattered onto Lucian's face, catching him on the cheeks, nose, lips, and chin.

Now, Lucian was more merciful. He stopped pumping the dick so madly, slowed his pace way down, turning it into just a gentle milking action, as repeated lesser sprays of cum welled up out of the head of the cock, dribbled down over his encircling fingers. Lucian bent forward, licked hungrily at the liquid, lapping up every trace of the man's juice he could find. He tasted Marcus' essence, savored the quintessence taste of his maleness, before swallowing.

At last, he stopped jerking Marcus' prick altogether and gently let it flop onto to his lover's belly. It lay there, only half-erect now, a spent but still wonderful looking thing. Marcus was quiet now, just breathing heavily, his chest rising and falling with deep breaths.

"That was wonderful, Lucian," he murmured. "Wonderful…but what about you? I want you to come, too. Can I suck you now?"

Lucian shook his head, a vague gesture in the darkness. "No. I want you to roll over. I told you I was going to have your ass, and now I will."

Bracing himself on his elbow, Marcus half sat up. His dark eyes, twin pools of shadowed blackness in the dim light stared up at Lucian. "But you said it hurts to much that way," he said, "after one's cum."

Lucian nodded. "Oh, it does," he whispered, "but it will be a good hurt, I promise you. I'll make you cum again, you'll see.

Now roll over."

"But, Lucian…" Marcus began, but he was cut off, as Lucian roughly pushed him onto his side.

"Now," he told Marcus. "I can't wait. I want to fuck you right now, when you'll feel it the most,"

"But the pain…I don't know if I can handle it like this."

"You're a Roman, aren't you? What's a little pain? So your asshole burns a little. You can handle my cock if you really want to."

And so saying, Lucian, now with Marcus' reluctant help, rolled his lover over onto his stomach. Lucian stared down at the twin, white ass cheeks, those two orbs of firm flesh glistening, looking positively virginal in the starlight.

"I'm going to fuck you good," Lucian growled. And without any foreplay, any kissing, licking, or lubrication, he positioned his erect cock between those masculine buttocks, those hard, round, and now quivering cheeks.

"Fuck you!" he exclaimed, as he thrust forward, pushed with all his might.

"Aiii!" Marcus actually shouted, but it was to no avail. Lucian didn't stop. He pushed hard, forcing the head of his cock into Marcus' narrow crevice, banged his cock's knob up against his lover's virginal hole, pressed it there, pushing, shoving, determined to gain entrance. He didn't let up, but kept banging at that sphincter muscle, Marcus' asshole.

"Now, you'll know what it really takes to be a man," his whispered hoarsely, as he drew back ever so slightly, and then having found his target, the bulls-eye of the sphincter muscle, he shoved forward again. This time, pushing with all his might, he made it. The big head of his cock stretched the muscle, forced the asshole to open, and then he was in. The knob of his prick popped inside. He felt a strong burning sensation from the friction, the lack of lubrication on his dick. He knew it was worse, much worse for Marcus.

Marcus raised his head, arched his back, and instinctively clenched his ass muscles together in a primeval effort to force the invading monster back out of his asshole.

"Unnhhh…" he groaned, as Lucian only pushed more, harder, sticking his cock in even deeper, forcing the asshole wider still, to stretch out and surround his thick shaft. "You're ripping me apart," he groaned, as Lucian did this. "I thought you wanted to make love."

"This is how men make love," Lucian responded in a guttural voice, busy still trying to force his way into Marcus' gut. "At least, one of them. And we want you to remember your first time, don't we?" And with this comment, he shoved again, pushing his cock up the other man's crack. He plunged deep into his hole, up into his gut, until he'd buried the stiff thing all the way into Marcus, balls deep. He fell forward onto his lover, his belly pressing into the small of his man's back.

"There," he said, softly, as he just lay still there a moment, feeling his throbbing member all the way up inside of Marcus. "Your ass fits my cock like a glove, Marcus," he whispered into his lover's left ear. Can you feel it? Can you feel me all the way up inside of you? The Gods, but you're tight. You really are a virgin."

"Thanks for noticing," Marcus murmured, and then he chuckled. "I didn't think you were going to rape my ass, though, Lucian."

"I'm always going to rape your ass," Lucian whispered back, knowing his breath was hot on the other man's earlobe, as he did this. "I'm going to take you as if it was the first time, every time like this, as if you were still a virgin. And you'll grow to love it, want it as you want nothing else. I'll make you beg for it."

"It hurts still," Marcus said.

"Yes, it hurts," Lucian agreed. "It even hurts me. But this is skin on skin, Marcus. This is cock in ass, and that's as it should be. I'm part of you now. I'm going to give you the best gift a man can give another." And saying this, he began to fuck, gently, slowly, ever so carefully, at first.

As he pulled his cock out, almost to the limit and then pushed it again, Marcus grunted each time.

"Do you like that?" Lucian asked him softly. "Do you like my cock in your ass?" He shoved in harder as he said this.

"Yes," Marcus whispered back. "Yes. Fuck me."

"Beg me."

"Please, Lucian, fuck me. Fuck me hard."

"Oh, I will, I promise you," Lucian told him, and he began to fuck harder, make his strokes longer, until only the head of his cock barely remained inside Marcus' asshole. He'd pull the shaft out, and then shove it again with all his might, slamming it home up his lover's plundered hole. Marcus reacted by taking the pummeling, but groaning all the while. He clenched and unclenched his butt cheeks as he tightened and loosed his sphincter muscle around Lucian's hard prick, unconsciously trying to milk the thing of all its cum.

Lucian fucked way, doing his best to impale Marcus' ass and gut with his thick thing, ramming it in, pulling it out with an accompanying sucking noise, so tight was the asshole, only to plunge it in again, fucking Marcus for all he worth. He increased his pace. Like a crazed man, he rode Marcus, looted his tight hole of its virginity, determined to spill his seed inside his lover's belly.

Now Marcus started to respond for real. His groaning took on a note of pleasure. "That's it, Lucian," he whispered repeatedly, "fuck me. Mount me you bastard whoreson of Hades. Fuck me!"

Lucian did his level best to comply. With his leg and ass muscles straining, he rammed his dick home. Like a pile driver, he kept pounding away at Marcus' ass, going balls deep on every stroke now, nuts slapping against ass, ripping his cock in and out of Marcus, fucking his gut for all he was worth.

Marcus physically squirmed now, wriggled about like a bug impaled by a sword. He raised his buttocks, the better for Lucian to drive his dick all the way home up it. "Oh, Gods!" he exclaimed. "Oh, the Gods, but that feels so fucking good!"

Lucian merely grunted his response, too caught up now in his frenzy of wild fucking. His nut sac slapped loudly up against Marcus' lower butt crack, banged against his lover's ball sac there. Waves of electric pleasure coursed through his body, emanating from his nuts.

"Cum again!" he grunted out to Marcus. "Cum again as I shoot my load up your virgin ass. Squeeze those cheeks for me. Tighten that hole! Milk my cock for all your worth!"

Marcus, his lean, hard body straining, did his best to comply. He raised his firmly muscled buttocks even higher. He worked his asshole repeatedly, squeezing the girth of Lucian's cock with his sphincter muscle, and then releasing it. He clenched his ass cheeks together, tightly, and then released them, repeatedly.

"Ohhhh... that's it," Lucian moaned. He was very close to cumming now. "Fuck me, you whore of Rome. Fuck my cock! Make me cum!" He was going full out now, plunging, plundering away, rutting inside Marcus like a man possessed.

"I...I...I think I'm about to cum again," Marcus moaned aloud. Gods above, I'm cumming again!"

Lucian could wait no longer. He reared back, pulled even the head of his cock free, and then jammed his prick into Marcus' butt once more, slamming it home all the way, to the very root of his shaft, down to his tightened ball sac.

"Fuck you!" he shouted, and again he pulled out his dick, only to slam it in again, feeling Marcus' sphincter muscle attempt to resist, only to have to give way once more. He forced open that virgin hole again and again. Marcus grunted and groaned the whole while.

What a glorious, tight, wonderful feeling it was having that asshole repeatedly resist and then grip the head of his cock, only to surrender each time to it, his ass impaled by Lucian's prick, as he shoved it deep inside, past that raped sphincter muscle.

"AAHHHH!" he groaned loudly. Slamming his cock all the way in, he shot his first jet of hot sticky cum. He felt it burst up the length of his cock, enter the head, and then spurt out, up and into Marcus' gut, erupting deep into his lover's belly.

"Fuck!" he groaned, as he kept pulling his cock back, only to plunge it again, spraying a stream of cum each time. "Fuck you!" he said again, as fucked like a rabbit in heat, screwing fast and furious, plumbing the depths of his lover's gut. "Take it, Marcus," he growled. "Take it all. Take my seed up your ass."

"Unhhh," Marcus groaned, as he endured the ass ripping of his life. "Fuck me, slave," he commanded in a harsh voice. "Fuck me hard. Oh Gods! I'm cumming now! I'm cumming! He raised his ass up even higher, letting Lucian have free sway over his buttock, to do with them as he liked."

Lucian was spent now. He slammed his cock home once more, balls deep one last time, and then collapsed on top of Marcus, forcing his ass down to the blankets with his weight. Even so, Lucian still had several spasms, as Marcus continued to milk his cock using his asshole muscle. He felt more sperm ooze from his cock into that gut, that tight, warm, wonderful cock-fitting glove of a gut.

They both lay quietly, panting for breath, Lucian bare-assed naked, still mounted atop of Marcus' lean body.

To fuck such a man, Lucian thought. This is as close to feeling like the Gods as one can get.

"Did you cum?" he whispered into Marcus' left ear. "Did

you cum again, my stallion?"

Marcus jerked his head in what Lucian thought to be a nod. "I did," he whispered. "I didn't think I could again so soon, and without any other kind of stimulation, but I did. I came all over the blanket."

"Perfect," Lucian said in a low voice. "The perfect fuck."

"I want more," Marcus whispered more loudly. "I want you to fuck me all night."

This comment surprised Lucian. "Doesn't your ass hurt from all of that fucking?" he asked.

Again, a jerk of the head, as a nod of sideways assent. "It hurt like all the demons of Hades have been up it," he acknowledged. "It burned and felt like you were punching me in the gut. I don't care. I feel like a bitch in heat. I want more. I want to feel you shoot in me over and over. Gods, but I wished I could have tasted your cum, felt it slide down my throat. I'm like a common whore," Marcus continued in that rough whisper. "I'd never thought I'd do any of this, nothing like this. But I loved it. Gods, how I loved it!"

"We're all whores when it comes to fucking," Lucian said in a low voice. "I sometimes think we men are worse than women when it comes to that."

"Where did you learn to do all this," Marcus asked, his voice filled with wonder. "How did you learn such?"

Lucian gave a little laugh. "I guess it comes naturally to me," he said. Then he kissed Marcus again. "Now," he added," what do you want to do next?"

Marcus gazed up at him, those penetrating dark eyes reflecting the glint of starlight in them. "I want to fuck you now," he said, "but I'm not up to it for a while yet. I've cum all I can for the moment."

"Then let's just sleep. Before dawn comes, we'll cum again,

and this time, you fuck me. And Marcus, I expect you to fuck me at least as hard as I fucked you, even more. We're both men and I like fucking like men, rough, fast, and hard! After all, with that fat monster," he reached down and grabbed Marcus' cock as he said this, "I expect, by the Gods, you can do a good job of reaming my hole."

"Oh, before I'm done with you, I'll fuck you so deep, you'll feel my cock coming up your throat from your belly," Marcus replied. Then giving a little growl, he added, "I want my revenge. I want to rape your ass, just as you've raped mine. I want to fill you with my sperm, breed you like a gladiator would a common whore, kiss you hard while I cum in you. You will know then who the master of Rome is!"

"You will always be my master in that regard, and I your willing slave." Lucian bent down and kissed his lover full on the mouth again. This time, it was a long, slow, languid kiss, and a deep one.

After a while, he raised his head. He said, "Like that?"

Marcus gave a little shake of his head. "Oh, no, Lucian," he said. "It's going to be a lot rougher than that when my time comes. When I'm done with you, you'll be walking with your legs apart, your ass dripping my cum out of it for hours, and your lips bruised from my kissing you, trust me!"

At this, Lucian laughed. Then he lay down next to his so masculine lover, his hard lean man, his Marcus. He was still his master in bed, as far as Lucian was concerned, for as wicked a pummeling as he'd given Marcus' ass, he had no doubt his arrogant Roman would be even better at it when he climbed atop Lucian, mounted him in turn. After all, he'd watched Marcus tear into Octavos' rear with a real vengeance.

They curled up together, wrapping a coarse woven blanket over their naked bodies as they did so. On their sides, Marcus cuddled close to Lucian. His flaccid cock pressed tight up against Lucian's supple ass, his muscled chest against Lucian's back. They waited for sleep to take them. In just a short time, Lucian heard the steady breathing of Marcus, indicating he'd slipped into a deep slumber.

Typical, Lucian thought. The man sleeps like the proverbial baby, as always!

Lucian just lay there quietly, so as not to disturb his lover, but still wide-awake, taking in the marvelous feeling of being so close to someone else, so in love with his man, Marcus, and feeling his naked body, his warm flesh pressed against him. How safe, how perfect, it all seemed this way. It was what he'd wanted for months.

And he knew tomorrow would bring not only a new day, but come that evening, it would be his turn to play the slave again when it came to fucking, as Marcus rode his ass for all he was worth. Lucian finally drifted softly off to sleep on this happy thought.

Above them, the stars twinkled on amidst stygian blackness of the night sky, as the Earth slowly rotated beneath them, as it had for millennia, as it would continue to do for millennia to come. And as always, the sun would come up tomorrow, no matter what.

About The Author:

Kem Austin is a rapacious writer, and averages about 4,000 words a day. He has several novels to his credit, two Regency romances, and a time-travel romance. Kem has written science fiction articles for such magazines as The Internet Review of Science Fiction, numerous articles for AlienSkin Magazine, Neometropolis, Midnight Street (UK), Doorways, and other publications.

Kem has had short stories published with Jim Baen's Universe, Aberrant Dreams, AlienSkin, Gateway SF, Fifth Dimension, Continuum SF, Sonar4, Uncial Press, Planetary Stories, Pulp Spirit Magazine, Sex & Murder, and many more. He has a novella coming out in early 2010 with Aberrant Dreams Magazine's first hardcover edition anthology, The Awakening. Kem's novella, Avenger Of The People, will appear there alongside the works of such sci-fi greats as Alastair Reynolds, Ian Watson, Jana Oliver, Robert Madle, and just so many others. There is even an introduction by Jack McDevitt. Kem has a short story, Green Waters, now out with Sonar4's Phase Shift anthology, and a paranormal story, Light On The Moor, coming out with Midnight Showcase.

Now, Kem Austin is not only a writer, but also a contributing editor for Currate.com travel articles, as well as being a reviewer for Novelspot. He is also a resident science fiction columnist for AlienSkin Magazine.

Although widely traveled and continuing to travel, Kem now lives in North Carolina. He enjoys contemplating ideas for new stories while watching the sunsets over the mountains and sipping a glass of red wine, preferably a decent Merlot.

Printed in Poland
by Amazon Fulfillment
Poland Sp. z o.o., Wrocław